LOSS OF THE DECADE

BRANDON ENNS

Copyright © 2016 Brandon Enns
Registered with Writer's Guild of Canada 2016
All rights reserved

Published by Brandon Enns 2018

No parts of this publication may be reproduced, stored in a retrieval system, or transmitted in any form or by any means, electronic, mechanical, photocopying, recording, or otherwise, without the prior written permission of the copyright owner.

This book is sold subject to the condition that it shall not, by way of trade or otherwise, be lent, resold, hired out, or otherwise circulated without the publisher's prior consent in any form of binding or cover other than that in which it is published and without a similar condition including this condition being imposed on the subsequent purchaser. Under no circumstances may any part of this book be photocopied for resale.

This is a work of fiction. Any similarity between the characters and situations within its pages and places or persons, living or dead, is unintentional and co-incidental.

Cover design and interior by www.ebooklaunch.com

To those still searching for what is right.

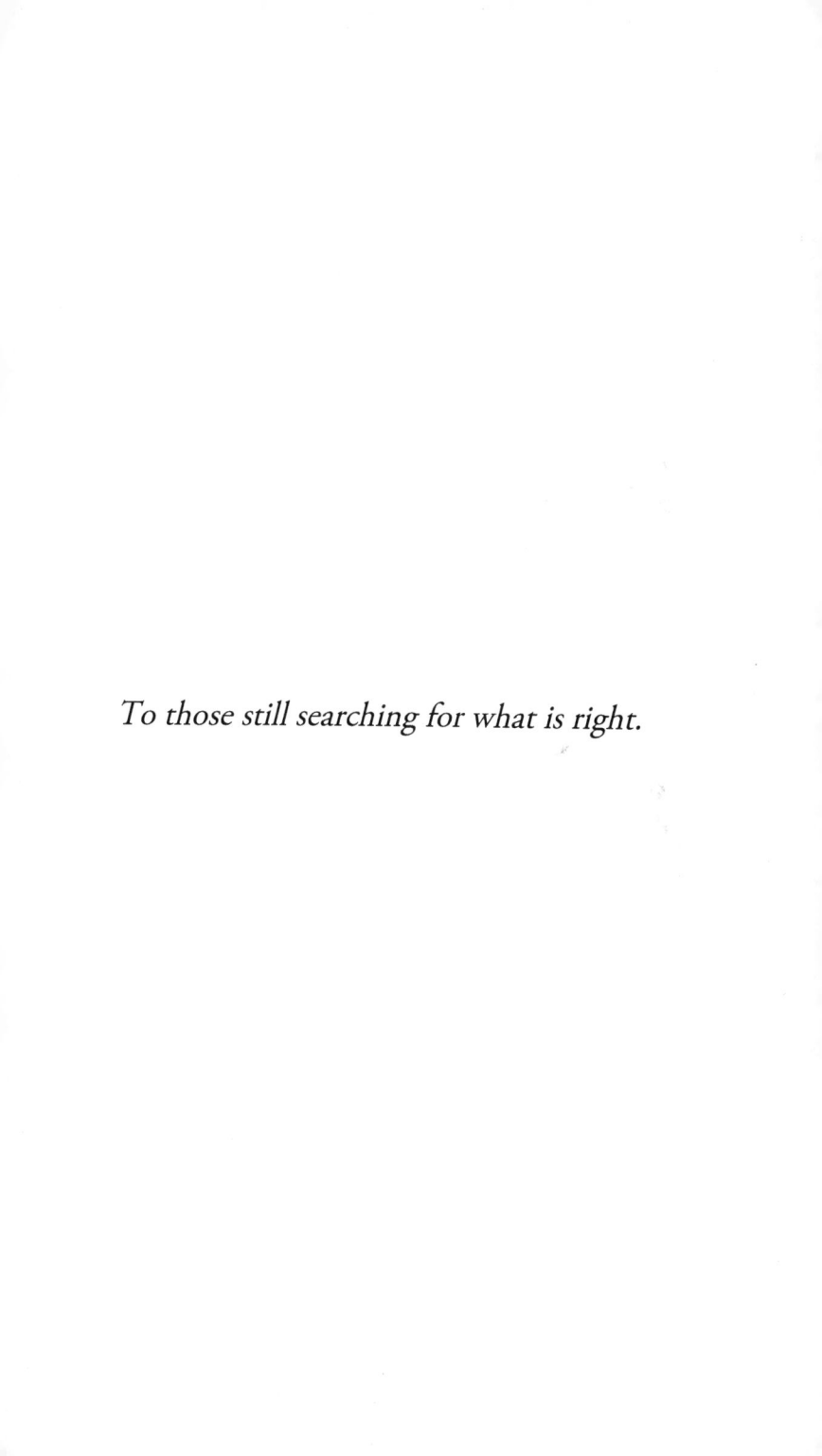

Prologue

Rocanville, Indiana. September 28th, 1979.

THEY SAT PARKED in a back alley behind their favorite ice cream stand on the edge of town. Deanna giggled in the passenger seat, listening to her favorite silly ad on the radio. A warm breeze rolled through his open window, smelling of autumn leaves. Her laugh was bordering on hysterical, her hand bumping up and down, risking her ice cream toppling over into her lap. Tom was going to tell her not to make a mess, but chuckled instead.

She was an absolute beauty, her blond hair in pigtails today, courtesy of a little help from Dad. She continued making a mess of her bubble gum ice cream, drawing a stain all the way around her mouth. His truck was still a little hot and musty, dust collected up on the dashboard. He turned the air conditioning on high and a cloud burst out at both of them, but she didn't notice, frivolously attacking her ice cream treat. He patted her head.

"Good stuff or what?"
She nodded yes but never broke stride from licking.
"Hey."
She continued licking. "What?"
"Who do you love the most?" he asked.

She squinted her left eye as she pretended to think. A familiar game they played. "Mmmmmm. Mom!" she teased.

"What?! Okay, but then who?"

Ice cream ran down her hand. "Rooster!"

"Rooster?! Really?" She'd named their cat Rooster. "Okay fine...but then who?"

She wiped the blue and purple off her face and then onto her brand new dress. Her mother was going to be a big fan of that. Deanna's face fell somewhat serious. "You," she said, looking away bashfully. He did the same with a subtle grin.

"Well, third place isn't the worst. You know Rooster doesn't take you for ice cream."

She kicked her feet back and forth over the edge of her seat and smiled at the mention of Rooster's name. "I saw Rooster poop in the sand castle box."

"He better have pooped there... Wait, you don't play with Rooster's sand, do you?"

She laughed and didn't answer. He couldn't tell if she was pulling his leg or not.

Deanna had worked the ice cream down to the cone. "Let Dad finish the cone."

She handed it over, no longer interested in it.

"Here, wipe your face on this napkin instead of your fifty-dollar dress," he said. "Okay, time to head back. Climb into the back."

"Nooooo."

"Hey, you're too small. These are the rules."

Tom unbuckled her, but then he felt something and heard something all at once. A hand grabbing his mouth, stuffing a cloth material into his throat before he could bite down. He heard a scream. It belonged to Deanna. Her pitch was piercing, the last thing he heard before a forced sleep.

• • •

The corn field he awoke in was half harvested. An amber sunset blended with browns and oranges. He was only confused at first, nothing else. But then realization struck, and with it, panic. Twisting and turning, he screamed his daughter's name over and over again until his voice lost strength. She was gone. There was not another soul in sight. Only him, alone in a field.

PART I

Chapter 1

Lost

Rocanville, Indiana. September, 1989.

TOM BENNETT STARED into the eyes of a sharply dressed woman. His psychiatrist, Anna, had dark hair falling halfway to her shoulders. Her eyes were a touch close together, her facial features pointed, but complimented by her oval face.

Tom's glassy gaze suggested a certain level of drunk, but the distinct sadness laying beneath suggested he had been hit by a freight train, one that ran him over time and time again. A lull hung in the air until a crease in the corner of her mouth formed. He turned to examine her psychiatry credentials on the wall. There were four, two of them Stanford. A prescription was all that he needed. But it wouldn't be that easy, already seeing that look in her eyes that said, *let's dive in.* It was irritating to say the least. Talking about his so-called feelings was going to result in about diddly squat.

It had been a few months of semi-consistent visits for Tom. His wife, now ex-wife, had begged and pleaded for him to go for years, until he finally caved once the insomnia became an issue, among others. His eyes fell in line with Anna's and for a moment, he could've sworn there was a sense of lust.

Nope, it was definitely not lust, it was her lack of patience.

"Tom."

"Yeah."

Anna leaned forward, hands cupped as she waited for a response. Looking over her shoulder through the window, he zoned out on two boys chasing and spraying each other with water guns. It was a nice September day, but still a little cool outside for that. She waited patiently until his eyes met hers again and she smiled, not overdrawn, lips tightened.

"Your dreams. Have they changed at all?" she asked.

Tom adjusted in his chair. He wasn't fond of how the room was put together, metallic decorations hung on the walls, even her pen holder looking like fake stainless steel. She was trying too hard to seem sophisticated.

"Not particularly," he answered.

"None at all?"

His mind went to a place that he hated going. In that field. Harvest had recently commenced. The ground was moist, as was the air. More rain was coming. He stood on corn stalk that lay flat. To his left, the corn stood tall.

Instinctively, Tom crossed his arms and narrowed his brow. "I'm fine. I just need a refill and my prescription expired. So if you got that pad of yours handy."

"They aren't Tic Tacs, you know." She scribbled something in her notepad. "As we had discussed last week, our plan was to pull back. Were you getting your refills on time?" She waited. "Or a little earlier for each refill?"

"I'm a big guy. A horse tranquilizer would be more fitting, but here we are."

"Yes, I could give you a higher dose-"

"Yes, let's do that," Tom interjected.

"This won't solve your problems, Tom."

He leaned back in his chair. Verbalizing the horrors of his past felt like he had been back in elementary school, about to take the stage to play Scrooge in *A Christmas Carol*. His chest tightened at the thought of taking the excruciatingly long walk onto the stage. Hundreds of people looking, waiting. Where were the words?

"Sometimes what's broken can't be fixed." The truth slipped from his tongue.

Anna countered with a common shrink response, no thanks to him. "You feel broken?"

He wasn't going to dignify that with a response.

"Walk me through the dream," she said.

Tom rubbed his pointer finger and thumb together, rotating in circles. The carpet under his feet was a mixed circular pattern of various charcoals. The smoky colors played with his eyes, somehow making him feel ill.

"I'm sorry, Tom. Losing a child-"

"Kidnappings are my specialty. I don't need a lecture."

She nodded and looked down at her notepad, tapping her pen against it.

"I know it can be difficult to discuss these matters with me. After all who would know better than you?"

"Then maybe we shouldn't do this," Tom replied.

"That would be a mistake."

Tom exhaled. "Why's that?" he asked.

"I don't think you need me to tell you why. You need to start seeing things from a different perspective."

"So you can cure me?"

She ignored the sarcasm and took his question head on. "Nothing will cure you, Tom. I want to help you, but you need to let me. Or else we're just spinning our wheels. Like anything, this needs to be a process. A process that requires your commitment, and that's not just you being here. I need you to actually *be here*."

"Here. Body mind and soul?"

"Correct."

Tom had nothing against Anna. Sure, he could put himself on auto-pilot and go through the motions, but that wouldn't have been doing either one of them any favors.

The thought of whiskey charged to the forefront of his mind. The feeling of that first sip, sliding down and warming the heart, calming the mind. It filled him with great comfort. It was beautiful every time. "What's the plan then?"

"What's going on at work? Any significant events as of late?"

"I can't talk about work."

Anna's warmth faded as Tom dismissed any chance of the meeting heading into a progressive region.

"You know you can. Physician-patient privilege."

"Yup. I got something just like that myself."

Tom checked his pager, pretending that something came through. "I gotta go, duty calls."

"I have you for another thirty-five minutes, Tom. You knew this coming in."

He rose to his feet, his massive frame leaning over on one leg from an old knee injury that had been flaring up as of late.

"Sorry, Doc."

Tom exited the office, leaving Anna alone in her chair.

• • •

Tom climbed into his old truck. Without hesitation, he reached into the glove box and grabbed hold of a mickey of Jim Beam. His eyes shimmered at the sight of the bottle, his holy grail. He paused for a moment, savoring the anticipation of the drink he was about to enjoy vigorously. He removed the lid and set it neatly on the passenger seat before tipping back the bottle. The burn settled in his chest with wonderful satisfaction and he was now ready for his day to truly start.

• • •

A man wearing a Boston Red Sox hat, pulled down low, watched Tom pull away from the curb and down the street. The satisfaction of witnessing Tom's misery was powerful. He despised this town almost as much as he did Tom. He disliked everything about it, down to the main street drug store playing the local radio station through the outdoor speakers. He had escaped this place many years ago, but couldn't keep himself from coming back to it. To see Tom breaking more and more each day was a sweet pleasure that could not be put into words.

Chapter 2

Jessica's Case

TOM DROVE SLOWLY THROUGH Main Street, Rocanville, Indiana, population five thousand. With the window rolled down, he could hear the faint sound of country music. On the street corner he spotted three young teenagers with skateboards, talking to a small boy with a backwards ball cap. The mother followed close behind and seemed to be sharing a pleasant conversation with the boys. A small town of ordinary folks, all unified as one. If only they all knew what was out there, what was really going on. Their ignorance kept them in the light for the time being.

He turned off into a residential area. All of the homes were dated but still charming. Some were white-picketed, some were cute and homey, some picturesque, some in desperate need of re-siding and paint. After taking a right and then a left, he finally pulled into the driveway of his home. The home that was filled with so many troubling memories, upstairs at one time was his heaven, down below his hell.

He got out of the truck and walked to the side of the house, down three steps, and entered the basement, which was his office space. Tom was greeted by his trusted partner, Reggie Fabro. Reggie was a stocky sixty-seven-year-old man that could easily be compared to a more rugged, less jolly, St. Nick. Although he appeared to have a rather tough exterior, his kind eyes told a gentler story.

"Jenny Hill keeps calling."

Tom was not at all surprised as he set his coat down on his crowded desk. Jennifer Hill was their most recent client. Tom and Reg had started their private investigations firm back in '74 when Reg had decided it was time to step away from the Indianapolis Police Department. He had plenty of fire in the tank still, but was tired of the protocol, tired of taking orders from people that had kissed just enough ass to be giving those orders. So he decided to go his own way, expecting to take on a smaller work-load. Wishful thinking in hindsight.

Tom had made detective by the age of twenty-five. He worked Gang and Narcotics Division for five years and, before leaving IPD, he worked two years under Missing Persons. He had learned more in one year working with Reg than other officers would learn in ten. It wasn't even a question when Reg left. Tom joined him and ended up taking full ownership of their firm. It was okay though, Reg was glad not to have his money tied up.

Like a lot of PI outfits, they had to offer a variety of services in the beginning, before they continued on with what was most important to them, which was finding children that had gone missing. In their first year, they had snapped photographs of cheating husbands and wives, provided security detail for nervous politicians and crooked money-men, and they even dabbled in cases of insurance fraud. Partway through year two, they had already earned themselves a strong reputation in missing persons and were able to specialize in the field. Sometimes the IPD would outsource and collaborate with them, and sometimes the two were left to conduct their business how they saw fit. Tom preferred it that way. No one to mess with his routines, no one at his side constantly, within an alcohol-filled breath's distance.

How on earth could he keep working in that field after his daughter was taken? How could he continue to involve himself in such a horrible world where he had been tortured the most? Because it was what he did. And if he could keep himself sharp, there was always that chance of cracking her case. She was still out there. He could feel it in his bones.

"Yes. I could have figured she would."

"Might be time to let her know where we stand," said Reg.

Tom entered another room in the basement office to examine four empty walls of cork board. A lot of time had been spent in that room. Many hours spent piecing together theories that had either dried up or led him to more questions that didn't have answers, the emotional ups and downs, all of it sticking to him.

• • •

Reg was busy on his computer after being ignored by Tom.

The framed picture of his wife, Dorothy, caught his eye. He was a little on edge today as she was going in for a check-up. It was routine, but he still worried. Reg had been married for forty years. He and his wife chose not to have children. It wasn't due to a biological roadblock, but more of a choice. As their thirties were filled with police work and his wife's fashion company, it slowly became a topic that came up less and less. Without ever having any finalized conversations, they both had silently agreed to lead a life without children.

The absence of kids was perhaps what drew Reg toward Tom. He had seen the potential in Tom when he first joined the force. A hard-nosed, gutsy cop that would do what was right no matter what the stipulations were. He had great respect for his gumptions and had no choice but to take him under his wing.

Reg opened up a game of minesweeper as Tom remained in the empty room.

"You want me to call Ms. Hill?" he called out.

"Call Dean. See if our status has changed at all," answered Tom.

"We're all a go."

"Check again to make sure."

"You got it boss."

He double-checked with Dean and gave Tom the thumbs up. Tom nodded and threw on his coat.

"What are you doing?" asked Reg.

"Heading over there."

"Well hang on, I'm coming with."

"That's okay, I can handle this one."

"It's a simple check in, I don't need a babysitter," Tom said.

He wanted to contest him, give him shit. A cooler approach prevailed. "I have no interest in holding your hand. I just wanna get out of this damn basement. Give me a break."

"Okay. I'm driving."

• • •

Tom noticed Jenny Hill standing by her window and watching as they pulled into her driveway. He walked up her front steps and before he could knock, her door came swinging open. She fit the image of a woman that was crumbling apart, with no appearance of having taken a shower in the last few days, her hair tangled and ratty, and no make-up to cover up the puffy bags under her eyes.

Tom's shoulders sunk when he saw her frantic wide eyes.

"Why haven't you been answering your phone?" she asked.

"I apologize Ms. Hill. I've been busy."

Jenny was unable to rein in her panic, clearly hanging on the cusp of a breakdown.

"I haven't heard from you all day. You said it yourself: the early stages are the most important. We're gonna be too late."

Tom motioned for her to take a seat, but she didn't follow his subtle orders.

"What do you know?" she asked quietly. There was that desperate look on her face, looking to him for answers he didn't have, and partly expecting bad news.

Reg had been standing just inside the door. He stepped forward and guided Jennifer to a chair.

"Nothing yet, I'm afraid. But we're working many angles," he said.

Her daughter, Jessica, had been gone for almost a week now, which was not a great sign. At least she was sixteen though. Meaning there was a good chance this was a "leave home early" scenario, likely involving a less than reputable young man. If she had been a young child, the percentages would've been earth shattering for any parent. But thankfully, there were some odds and ends that needed checking into yet. Unfortunately IPD had been sticking their noses in this one, taking the lead on questioning all of her friends from school. All Tom had gotten to see thus far were written reports. So, he had been looking into the father, still trying to find his whereabouts: old bosses, drinking buddies, etc. He had sure picked a convenient time to turn into a ghost. Odds were she was with him.

But according to some of the friends, Jessica Hill had discovered her sexuality in a fast and furious sort of way. There were more boys to find, he figured. So that pulled his focus away from scarce Daddy, for the time being.

"Do you think she's been eating okay? She hadn't been eating as much before she left. I know this because I always dished up her plate. We always sat down at six for dinner every night."

Jennifer's white cat jumped up on the kitchen counter behind them. He could hear it purring, closing it's eyes as the sunlight peaked through the window and rested on it's fur.

Jennifer carried on, "She had convinced herself she needed to lose weight, which is ridiculous if you ask me.

She looked great before, and I'm not just saying that because I'm her mother. Really, you need a little layer on you. Skin and bones just ain't sexy. Those models on the television and magazines." She shook her head with a scowl.

Tom wasn't listening to a word she said. His mind was with Deanna. He had been thinking about her none stop as of late.

Reg took a seat on the couch, and sunk in low, looking uncomfortable. Tom followed suit. "Ms. Hill," said Reg, "it's important to remain calm as best you can. Anything you can think of could help us locate her. We are still very positive about the situation. Her being sixteen is a good thing. Teenagers do this. Even when their parents think they wouldn't."

"But" She stopped herself from protesting. She proceeded to bite her nails as she looked out the window over Tom's shoulder, as if her daughter was going to walk up the front step at any moment.

"We are doing everything we can to find your daughter. Using all of our resources," Tom re-iterated.

"Do you have kids, Mr. Bennett?"

"No ma'am. You said the father lives in Kansas, correct? We haven't been able to get a hold of him yet. Apparently he's been relocated from his last position at the steel mill."

"I don't know nothing about that. He's a dead beat bastard. He ain't got nothing to do with this. He never even put in the effort to send a birthday card to my Jessica. Not one."

Jenny shook her head as she tried to fight off tears. Crying was another horrible by-product of their work.

Tears were even worse than hugs. When people cried in front of Tom, it made him feel some kind of uncomfortable.

"It's just hard, you know?" she said.

"Reg and I still have more of your daughter's connections to question yet. She'll turn up."

"Where is she?" Tears flowed down her cheeks and she clutched her own thighs, the whites of her knuckles showing.

"I'm not sure, ma'am. Not yet."

She collected herself, allowing Tom to relax a little.

"I know it's difficult to understand the toll it takes. Not having a child n' all."

"I have to remain neutral so I can do my job."

"Yes, of course."

Jenny handed a picture of Jessica to Tom. He looked at a school photograph of Jessica, she was cute, had a small smile, dimpled cheeks.

Jenny squeezed Tom's hand quickly and released when he looked down.

"I know you have some pictures already. But I want you to keep this with you at all times. A reminder," she said. "She's always been such a smart girl. Not sure where she gets it from. And she sings too. She's a really good singer. Bring her home to me please."

Tom accepted the photograph and stood up from his chair. His natural desire was to leave, but he needed to be certain nothing had been left out. Just the odd detail could lead to a break in the case, which he had experienced many times before. He had been looking for that odd detail for the last ten years.

"Was there anything else that you could think of that might help? Anything irregular?"

"No...no, I was hoping you had maybe figured something out, not answering your phone and all."

"Right, well we better get back to it. I'll be in touch."

Tom turned and left before Jenny could get another word in.

Reg rose and placed both hands on her shoulders. "Hang in there Jennifer. We'll get her."

"Thank-you."

• • •

They returned to the dim basement when the phone rang and Reg picked up.

After hanging up he walked back toward the door with a promising look.

"One of the friends came forward on Jessica Hill. Mystery boyfriend."

Tom wasn't overly enthused by the good news. They would have to go and retrieve her.

Back in '77, Tom took a bullet on the job and it changed the way he was in the field. He was nervous, hesitant. He had been able to manage it over the last twelve years, but something changed in the past year and he couldn't seem to shake it. Just the thought of a scenario involving gunfire made him terribly anxious.

"You need me?" Tom asked rather casually, as if suggesting, *you don't, right?*

"Yeah, I could use you. If you don't mind."

"Where to?"

"Indy. They had plans of running off to New York."

"How romantic."

Reg smiled and moved toward the door.

"Kid's probably in a band."

He handed over a thermos of coffee to Tom. "You look tired. Drink up."

"You look about thirty years more tired."

Reg stared at Tom with a straight face. "Why you gotta be a prick?"

Reg grabbed an umbrella from the corner and Tom smiled nervously before responding. "Must be love, Reggie."

• • •

Reg drove as Tom peered out the window. The country was bare and flat, nothing significant to examine but the odd tree line, yellow and orange leaves tumbling with gusts. In a split second, it appeared that they drove by a little blond girl. She disappeared as they whizzed by. Tom showed no surprise as he blinked his eyes in exhausting fashion. Just another friendly reminder. He was used to those. He faced forward and watched the yellow lines on the road, counting them as they passed, hoping to distract himself from the upcoming extraction of Jessica Hill. He then closed his eyes and drifted, sleep tugging at the corners of his eyes as he let go. He felt himself travel to where he was human again.

He was years younger, holding Deanna up in the air as he lay on the living room floor. The red shag carpet scrunched up in his toes as he held her up high. Tom could smell oranges; she was obsessed with different kinds of soap, all smelling like various fruits. As his little girl looked down at him, she was laughing her ass off, her face reddened and sweet. A small string of saliva sneaked out of her mouth landing square on his cheek, which set her giggles off even more, now gasping between cackles, like music to his ears. Tom couldn't think of a happier time than this, and if there was one, it would be with her. He launched her up in the air, then caught her, and she settled into his chest. He tickled her for a few seconds until she could hardly stand it anymore.

"Don't Daddy, I'll pee!"

Tom laughed and kissed her, then rubbed his scruffy facial hair on her cheeks.

He remained in a haze as Reg pulled up to the address of the boy's uncle. The neighborhood was lower class and all of the homes looked shoddy, aged, and wearing thin.

Reggie gave him a soft elbow.

"You ready?"

Reg grabbed a pistol from the glove box and handed it to him. As soon as Reg stepped out of the truck, Tom could feel himself shrinking. He assessed the house and its perimeter from the truck. There were no pedestrians in sight, front window curtains were closed, and there were steps up to the front door. They looked old, and would probably make a loud enough sound to alert someone on the inside. His mind raced with questions as he walked across the street slowly, nearing the front lawn: *What if she's dead? Will I have to wait beside the body? What if the guy pulls a gun?* His head was just about ready to explode. Or maybe implode.

They approached the house and he tried to release a quiet exhale of nerves without Reg seeing. None of this was supposed to encapsulate who Tom Bennett really was. He wasn't supposed to be fragile, paranoid, shaken, nervous; he was supposed to be the opposite of all that bull-shit.

As they neared the house, a loud *BANG* sounded off, followed by another. The shots echoed, almost piercing through him as he stopped dead in his tracks. Reg instinctively drew his gun and lowered into a crouch position as he approached the house. He turned back to Tom.

"I got around back, you got the front?"

Tom was frozen. What used to be routine adrenaline had now formed a new monster. He was overcome with the desire for inaction, fearing what was on the other side of the door. His pulse pounded so hard his ears ached. What began as an accelerated heartbeat had now escalated to an aggressive panic attack, constricting any type of movement or rational thought pattern. It felt like someone was standing on his chest.

"Tom! You good?"

"Yeah, yeah. Go!" He choked out.

Reg ran around the back of the house, remnants of his past mobility still on display. Tom remained in the same spot for a moment and then as he took a couple steps toward the house, his breathing worsened, his negative thoughts compounding matters. He clutched his chest and cowered in an empty garden right in front of the house, trying to fight it off. He thought of the girl on the highway, her face turning toward them as they passed on by, her golden hair blowing back in the wind.

Tom's breathing began to regulate and he took three sharp breaths before making his move. He came bursting through the front door and glided to the kitchen-living area. The lighting was dim, and the air was unclean.

Copper smells.

He held his gun up ready for action and the intensity on his face faded. Tom stood in the middle of the room, looking at one dead male, and a young female with a gun-shot wound. After a stunned moment, Tom rushed over to the girl. He applied pressure to the wound, blood gushing out of her midsection. He looked into her eyes, realizing it was indeed, Jessica Hill.

"You're okay. You're gonna be fine."

He removed his jacket and attempted to use it to stop the bleeding, but she was fading fast. Tom was lost in her eyes for a moment as she resembled a young girl that used to belong to him. His cop instincts kicked in as he called for Reg, while trying to stop the bleeding.

He grabbed the phone and dialed 9-1-1.

"This is private investigator Tom Bennett. I need an ambulance to 429 Widelyn Street. One male is dead, one female with a gun-shot to the stomach. Please hurry, she's bleeding fast." He hung up.

"Hey, hang in there, all right? Your name is Jessica, right?"

She was horribly white.

"Help me," she whispered.

"Help's already on the way. I just need you to talk to me for a bit. Can you do that?"

"Okay," she replied weakly.

"Jessica, my name is Tom. I'm gonna stay here with you if that's okay. You look like a singer to me. Do you like music?"

He could see she knew what he was doing. Distraction. She glanced at her stomach, then back up to Tom with horrified eyes. "Yeah." She nodded emphatically.

"I've been told I have shit taste. What do you like?"

"I don't know I-" she coughed, and fought through it. "Michael Jackson."

Tom's smile was all wrong and it disappeared quickly.

"Oh yeah? MJ? I can't say I'm a huge fan, but I get it.

Maybe he just reminds me that I'm a lousy dancer."

Her grip loosened and her crying face relaxed.

"Jessica, squeeze my hand, okay. It's important that you do that for me."

"I-I'm gonna die, right?" Her lip quivered.

Tom's hands were submerged in blood. He refused to look down, only focusing on her eyes. She was going to die.

"Nah, not a chance. You are way to tough. My God, you are gorgeous, you know that? You look like your mother."

Jessica smiled at the mention of her mother. And then she whimpered, the morbid reality settling back in.

"Take me to my mom, please."

The request cut hard. "We're gonna take you right away. I just need you to hang tight…Reg!"

Reg came bursting through the door and stopped as he got a look at the horrible scene. He was distracted by action outside in the alley. "You good?" asked Tom.

"Yeah, they got away." Reg glanced at Jessica, his face fell flat, and he moved to the front window.

Tom turned back to find emptiness. She was gone. Tom's head fell forward, his neck loose, jaw clenched tight gritting teeth. His hand was still gripped tightly around Jessica's. Already, her wet hands felt cooler to him. Blood was everywhere.

• • •

Reg drove out of city limits and into the flatlands.

He was far from oblivious. He was well aware of Tom's inconsistencies with his fieldwork, and worried that he was regressing, still stuck in his steel trap of a mind.

"You all right?" Reg asked.

"Fine."

"Been a long day. Best we get home and get some rest."

"I gotta stop at Jenny Hill's first."

Reg looked at his face, eyes blood shot, cheeks rosy. Drunk probably.

Reg had caught it around the office all the time. Didn't help that the office was the man's basement. What was he supposed to say? It wouldn't have made a difference what he said.

"I think that's something the police were going to handle," said Reg.

"She hired me, it's my job."

"I'll come with you then."

"No that's okay, I-"

"Too fuckin' bad, I'm coming."

Reg had been wanting to request a break for quite some time now. Not just for himself but for Tom as well. But that was foolish thinking.

Chapter 3

Goth Girl

SHE MOVED SWIFTLY to her locker with her head down. Her skinny and awkward frame was draped by her black Pearl Jam T-shirt and baggy jeans. She lifted her eyes to her surroundings expecting to see what she was indeed feeling: judgmental stares. The hallway parted around her like she was walking the Red Sea. It would be easy for her to wish she was like everyone else. To be the head cheerleader or the captain of the debate club, math club, even the marching band. But the Goth Girl, Ella, truly had no desire for any of that. She just wanted to be left the hell alone.

Her music was all she really cared about. Beautiful real words and stories that helped her escape whenever she needed, which was the majority of her days. She was impartial to the genre. As long as it told a story and painted a picture in her mind that helped her with that escape, she was as happy as she'd ever be. Metallica blared in her headphones as she opened her locker.

Out of the corner of her eye she could feel another stare her way. A jock wearing a leather football jacket stood with two buddies eying her up, joking with his friends. The one was tall and lanky, his hair blond with natural curls, unlike some of the boys who had perms. The other was stocky, athletic and powerful, his smile unkind like the others, his hair high and tight as a military-style crew cut. She imagined he got into his fair share of fights, winning all of them.

The jock advanced toward her and she pretended to fumble with her books, looking busy, but wishing she could climb into her locker and hide. She tried to grab hold of her books to get the hell out of there, but it was too late. There stood the jock as she tried to pretend he wasn't there. Listening to her music still, she ran the scenarios over in her head and each one ended with the handsome boy destroying her in front of everyone in the hallway. As he stripped her apart word by word, the entire student body would listen with great anticipation, giddy with the possibility of her destruction. They couldn't wait to get their dose of laughter for the day, while giving them something to talk about for the rest of the week. Even the teachers would leave their prepared curriculum at their desks and join the students in the hall, listening, waiting. After their moment of patience, they would get what they deserved. A much needed laugh.

Her nervous energy was obvious and she could tell the jock knew she was intentionally ignoring him. The music would no longer work as her defense. She turned to him, removing the headphones from her head. His hand was already extended. His smile was handsome and obnoxious.

"Hey," the jock started.

"Hey." *Okay that's enough. I know what your doing, please go away.*

"How's it goin'?"

"Good." She couldn't hide the tentativeness in her voice.

He paused. She breathed in and prepared herself.

"I've seen you in class, but I never got your name."

"That's weird," she said.

"What is?"

"That you don't know my name." She knew his name was Brian. But "jock" worked just fine.

His intent was unclear to her, his face confused by her last jab.

"Yeah, big school I guess. Anyway I was just wondering if you would like to come to a party with me on Saturday. It's at Jake Sherback's place. Should be decent." The jock waited for a response but didn't get one as she tried to locate words that would protect her. She could sense the stares from the outside again igniting her peripheral vision.

"I don't know if parties are your thing, but I just thought maybe you'd like to come with me. I dunno, I'm sorry for being so forward."

Was he actually interested in her or was this all part of his elaborate plan to humiliate her for sport? Like he didn't get enough sport screwing the girls in his own grade, when he wasn't busy throwing touchdown passes for the home crowd. Ella had never been desired by anyone, and it wasn't about to start now. She had always been good at bringing herself down to planet earth the moment she started to feel something fanatical in any sort of way.

"You want to take me to a party?"

"Well, yeah. It's gonna be the biggest party of the year. Everyone is gonna be there. You should definitely come."

"You've never talked to me once and now you want to take me to a party?" The sass felt wrong coming out of her mouth.

"What's wrong with that?" he answered smugly.

"Looking to slum it then?"

He looked lost, treading in unfamiliar water, legs kicking wildly.

"What? No. That's not what I-"

She cut him off mid sentence.

"The games exhaust me, Bri-dog."

"Bri-dog?" he laughed.

"B-cat, whatever."

Flabbergasted, he was unable to come up with a clever response.

She looked over the jock's shoulder to find his friends watching, snickering like the pieces of shit that they were.

"Let's maybe avoid the public appearances, champ. But maybe like a blow job on the football field or behind the bleachers. I just think it's best that I leave you with some good material, you know? No sense making a huge spectacle of it. Or is that what you need? An audience?"

She realized that her work here was done, as the boy's jaw was lying neatly on the floor, his mouth unable to form words. She placed her headphones back on with a heavy dose of Zen, and locked up her locker before leaving down the hallway. She felt him watch her move down the hall swiftly.

Loss of the Decade

• • •

Ella sat at her favorite old table, in her old, dated diner. She sipped her cup of tea and opened up Stephen King's *Misery*. Her cassette headphones blared a Pearl Jam tune, but she remained focused on her book for only a short moment. She lifted her head to look out the window at a pay phone. It called out to her as if she were expecting an urgent call from someone that mattered. But there weren't many people in her life that really mattered, only one in fact. The man that saved her years ago. Saved her from a treacherous, abusive father that she wouldn't have otherwise escaped. She owed everything to that man, although some days she didn't appreciate many of the aspects of her dim life.

She tried to read her book but was far too distracted, the words no longer painting a mental image as her mind wondered. The jock, Brian. She pictured him running his hand through her hair, daring brown eyes piercing through her, the longing to be touched, to be needed. He leaned in slowly, the anticipation melting her down to nothing, and she could hardly wait for their lips to meet, terrified and aroused. Their lips finally touched. She didn't want the daydream to end. Their kiss deepened, any nerves now turned purely to lust. His hand grazed her cheek and ever so gently he pulled her hair, the feeling raw and sexually charged. Her Pearl Jam song came to an end, closing out her fantasy.

The sweet old waiter came by with another tea bag and some hot water. He filled her empty cup and set the bag in. His hands were leathery and he stood with an awkward hunch, but never seemed to be in discomfort, a smile permanently painted on his wrinkled face.

"Here you go, dear."

She blushed from being caught in her daydream, as if he could read her thoughts.

"Thanks."

"Would you like a slice of apple pie? It's fresh."

"No, thanks…actually yeah, sure. Pie would be nice." She hadn't eaten a bite all day. Some days she couldn't fathom the thought of putting any food in her system; others she could eat like a savage.

"I know you probably don't want to hear this, but we've gotta beef you up my dear. It'll be damn cold out there soon."

She took no offense to the comment. He was right. "Better make it a big slice then."

The old man seemed very satisfied with her response.

"On the house." He winked.

It had been a full year now that she had been coming to that diner. Something about the simplicity of it made her feel safe and comfortable. It smelled of burnt roast on the outside, but was delightful on the inside, a mix of fresh coffee and fried bacon. It was old school. The classic red leather booths, slightly dim lighting, stools up at the main counter looking into the messy kitchen. She loved nothing more than the opportunity to be alone to read her books and listen to music. It helped that the place was almost always empty. It had it's regulars for morning coffee and then the brunch crowd but she didn't go during those times very often unless she had slipped out of school. This was more her home than any other place had ever been and she was thankful for it. Thankful for the old man running the joint, whose name she hadn't learned yet. She wondered if he had been here long, if he had family, or maybe a dog. She figured he had a nice golden retriever, loyal and loving. He would always make efforts to engage her in conversation, but she never gave him much to go on. Regardless, his presence was still enjoyed.

The man returned with her slice of apple pie, a scoop of vanilla ice cream tucked on the side. The slice consumed the plate and she couldn't help but laugh at the absurdity of the portion.

"You can't leave till it's gone, you hear?"

"Yes, sir."

The man nodded politely and started to leave when she blurted out. "Do you have a dog?"

He laughed. "As a matter of fact I do. His name is Paul."

"Paul?" she asked, implying that it was silly.

"You don't like it?"

"No, no. I do actually. I like that he has a human name. What kind is he?"

"Oh, he's a whole mix of mutt. Likes them damn milk bones to death. Every night before bed, like clockwork. He's a good pooch though, amazing how dogs can sense how a person is feeling. Had him for five whole years before my Debbie passed. Not one time did he set foot in our bedroom, not once. The moment she was gone to the next life, there he was without hesitation, in my bed with me. Yeah, I typically woulda fussed about it, but I didn't mind him there, and he knew that I think. Sorry. I'm a cliché old broken down peasant. You got more important things to discuss, with important people, I'm sure."

There was something so comforting about him. Obviously he had old man charm, but it was more than that. An acceptance.

"I'm here almost every night and I don't know your name, I'm sorry." Her voice was quiet.

"Franklin, my dear."

She extended her skinny hand.

"Ella."

"It's an absolute pleasure, Ella. You're an excellent customer."

She could feel her cheeks blush again and this frustrated her, being such a small compliment.

"I like it here."

"Well, maybe if you keep coming I can keep the lights on. How does that sound?"

"Really good. You own this place?"

"Sure do. Twelve years now." He looked down at her book. "Good read?"

"Oh, yeah. I'm not too far along, but it's good so far."

"I never cared for books. Music though…music can do marvelous things to a person. Amazing what a melody can do at the worst of times."

"What do you listen to?"

"Jazz, my girl. Hawkins, Goodman, Davis, Parker, The Duke. Yeah, they all got a place in my heart, that's for certain. Had to fill the space with something. You probably don't know any of 'em."

Ella was quick to respond, "I love Ellington. I listen to him every morning when I wake up, give or take."

"Morning? I found that jazz was almost meant for the nights."

"I need to feel grounded when I start my day."

"You should be on cloud nine to start each day. A little rock 'n roll might just do you some good tomorrow morning."

"What, like Elvis?"

He tilted his head in consideration. "Sure, ain't nothing wrong with the King. Other than doing enough cocaine to kill a small horse." His eyebrows lifted along with a grin.

Ella laughed naturally, happily.

"A laugh. I think we better lock up and end the day on a positive note. What do you think?"

Her smile faded. That damn trailer. Over half of her homes had been trailer park living. Some small apartments. She hated the trailers more though. She couldn't say exactly why, just did. Maybe it was the idea that they were in a 'park' surrounded by other trailers. And the people there... She didn't like the sadness in their eyes. It reminded her of what she was. Well on her way to nowhere fast. Always moving yet always stuck.

"I think you're right. Can I finish my pie first?"

"Of course! Takes me an hour to clean the damn kitchen. I got slow hands. They cause me a great deal of pain under cold water. You believe that? Just another ridiculous thing." He sighed. "Don't get old."

He smiled and staggered back over behind the counter, picking up a rag on his way. She took a massive forkful of pie and gobbled it up quickly, closing her eyes and embracing the satisfaction of the hunger pains she didn't realize she had.

•••

Ella walked through the rain toward a trailer park with her headphones in. She shivered hard from both the cold and the thought of spending another night in the mobile home. She made it up the steps to the door to find a notice tacked to it. It stated that they had thirty days to make three months worth of rental payments or they would be evicted. It would have been good news, if they had any money to relocate.

She entered the trailer and kept her hood up and head down as she attempted to pass Simon, who was cooking in the kitchen. His twitchy demeanor had always made her feel uncomfortable when she was younger, but now it simply annoyed her.

He shouted as she passed, "I'm making you favorite."

"I ate already."

She rushed to her room, closing the door behind her. Ella crashed on her bed and exhaled the stress from her body. She reached over to an old oak-furnished record player and set the lift arm down on the vinyl as it had already begun spinning. Reo Speedwagon took over the room as she closed her eyes and wished for a specific destination.

She pictured herself walking down a winding trail, surrounded by lush plant life. She was able to see a red sandy beach that went on for miles and hear the ocean water wash up on shore. As the lovely garden-like scenery fell behind her scope, only the swirling reddish hue of the tide surging up onto the unique sand remained.

Ella's day-dream was interrupted by a knock on her door. Simon waited for her reply patiently. She called out to him begrudgingly, and he opened the door.

Simon was a very short man. He had a distinct part in his hair, slicking the other side tightly to the left in a traditional comb over fashion, and his nose slanted to the left, perhaps from a fracture, although there were no bumps. Though he came across creepy at first glance, he could actually be quite sweet at times.

Throughout her young life they had been on the move due to Simon's occupation. His past involved pool halls and underground poker games. It didn't seem to match his personality or image in any way. He looked like he belonged behind a computer screen surrounded by three cubicle walls. She figured he'd grown tired of the anxiousness of being caught cheating or called out for hustling. This wasn't a difficult conclusion to come to, considering some of the ass kickings he had received on occasion, stumbling home black-eyed and bloodied. So that scene ended when they moved to Indianapolis. Before Indy, they had moved around lots within the state, never leaving the borders.

Now that they were in Indy, Simon had a grand plan that would net them a huge score, setting them up for their next move, one which they hoped would be more permanent.

Simon cracked the door open ever so slightly, head turned away.

"Are you decent?" he asked.

"No, I'm naked already."

"Can you please dress; it's dinner time."

She rolled her eyes and jumped off the bed, swinging the door open.

At the kitchen table, Ella poked at her food with zero ambition to eat, still full from the pie.

"How was school today?"

"Fine."

Simon looked down at her plate and she could already feel his concerning gaze for her scrawny frame. He then broke down into a sequence of nervous blinks, gearing up to make the meal more uncomfortable than silence.

"How's your friend? Cynthia."

"Doesn't much matter." She replied more hotly than she had intended.

"Why do you say that?"

Why did she say that? It was somewhat of a loaded question.

"Ella?"

"She's not really my friend," she replied. "We're moving soon aren't we?"

"You don't like it here?"

"A real fucking picnic."

In a knee jerk reaction, Simon slapped his fist on the counter, startling Ella. He hated it when she cursed.

"I just figured with the notice…it might be time. I think it's time."

"It hasn't been long enough," Simon replied.

"What is long enough?"

His voice came off cold and harsh. "When I say it is."

She breathed out through her nose, mouth tightly sealed for a moment. "You got another job lined up then? We need something to stay in this lovely castle."

She watched Simon as he ignored her question and proceeded to eat his salty, overcooked stir fry.

"We're gonna be out on our asses soon," she pressed.

Simon cringed at the second curse word delivered from Ella. She watched as his nervous blinks and red face both settled and disappeared.

"Please eat your meal."

She stabbed a piece of broccoli with her fork.

Chapter 4

Making Rounds

THERE WAS NO POINT in attempting sleep. After delivering the devastating news to Jessica's mother, he did the thing he hadn't done in quite a while. He retraced the day Deanna was taken. He went to the park where he taught her to throw and catch the baseball. It would usually only last about five or ten minutes before she'd be on the swing-set.

He parked along the fenced off playground and tried to remember a specific moment. If he could only watch the two of them tossing the ball back and forth. But there was nothing. Just quiet.

He stopped at the ice cream shop and walked around to the back alley where they had parked that day. There hadn't been one eye witness. The girl that had served them ice cream had left to pick up supplies and was gone for only fifteen minutes. The time was 7:35 p.m. There had been some daylight left. Surely someone would have seen the captor's vehicle. But it was on the edge of town, only one home with a clear vantage point from their backyard looking into the back alley. The home owners had been gone to the lake that day. Tom had met with them more than once, along with several other homes in the vicinity. Nobody had heard Deanna's scream. She must have been put to sleep immediately after Tom had went down.

Tom stumbled in a pothole, soaking his pant leg. He cursed and walked up to the back of the ice cream parlor and lit a cigarette. He hadn't smoked in a while, but figured his wonderful day was cause for celebration.

When he made it back to his abandoned truck that night, there hadn't been a trace of evidence left behind. No prints, no tire tracks, no residue of any kind, other than the chloroform that had been used on him. At first, he figured it could have been any number of degenerates in his town. But something as heinous as taking a child? If that had been the case, there would have been demands immediately after the kidnapping, or cold feet, having her dropped off back into his arms.

He looked across the highway and spotted a train with grain cars pulling in. One of the cars was dressed up to the nines in graffiti, bold letters and colors. He liked the way it looked. His cigarette went down smoothly, so he lit another and began his walk to the bar. He left his truck where it was. There was no sense having the entire town see his old rig parked out front of Leonord's Tavern.

• • •

The bar was no different than any small town joint. Darts and shuffleboard in the back, each table still sticky from old wing sauce, beer, and tequila. It smelled of deep fried snacks, moth balls, and dirt. He walked in, examining it all. There was a bar to his immediate left that was only used when the place was full, which was never; other than December 23rd when all of the college kids came back to town. Behind the bar was a jar of Slim Jims and potato chips tacked to the wall.

In the middle of the room was an island bar with chairs all around. He took the side that was less full and ordered an Old Milwaukee. The bartender was new and he didn't recognize him from anywhere. He was still freshly pimple-faced and looked like he arrived to work via his skateboard.

Tom noticed a couple familiar faces in the far corner, but didn't bother to say hi. It was Stan Miller, the local butcher, and his nephew. Patrick maybe? He worked at the auto shop in town.

Tom was already feeling a good amount of drunk, but the two cigarettes had dried out his throat. He drank the first bottle in a few big gulps and ordered another with a shot of Canadian Club on the side. To him, CC was 'the good stuff'. He'd always start with that or Crown Royal before switching to Jim or Jack.

Across the bar sat three idiots. Lowlifes that he had busted before on possession charges and another incident involving a minor. He was sure there were many other 'incidents' that went unaccounted for. All three of them should have been behind bars, but the system seemed to forgive those that lived dirty but not quite dirty enough. The Stooges were giving him eyeballs and slanted smirks. Another shot of whiskey, Jim this time. His hands felt nice and heavy. Beer would now be off the menu as he ordered a double rye and coke with a Jack chaser.

Two other young men entered, dressed in collared shirts, hair shining. They sat at the rounded end of the bar. Tom wasn't sure how much time had passed, but it didn't take long for the newbies to be provoked by the local legends. Words were exchanged and all men were on their feet.

Tom stood, a little waver as he found the center of his balance. He strode over, big lumbering steps, his boots clunking. All eyes were on him as he rounded the bar. He passed the city slickers and stopped in front of Owen Wilks, leader of The Three Stooges. He had a sad excuse of a goatee lightly colored with orange Dorito dust.

"Why do you even bother anymore, Bennett? You should drink at home. We like to be around positive-minded people." He smiled wide and laughed, a black hole among his row of uncleaned teeth.

Tom was so God damn drunk he couldn't come up with a single comeback. He couldn't even force out a laugh, as it came out more of a grunt like he was gonna puke instead. "One second," Tom said, then burped.

He turned around and faced city boy number one. He was curious as to why they were hanging out in Rocanville; probably someones nephews. Instead of conversing, he swung. He didn't just hit the guy, he punched *through* him. The young man was cold before he hit the floor. His friend, a smaller version, backed off immediately and tended to his woozy friend.

Tom turned back to Wilks and his pals. They were baffled. "Well shit, Bennett. Don't tell me you've crossed over to the good side?"

Tom laughed, and good old Owen laughed too. Tom hit him square between the eyes harder than the last guy. The other two were down his throat as he landed one more good shot on a different Stooge. Before long, he was being trampled by all three. The skinny bartender was not exactly quick to jump in, nor were the boys from the city as they fled out the door.

He received the beating of all beatings. Eventually, the butcher and his mechanic son helped to break it up.

Tom walked back to the edge of town where his truck was parked and hopped in. He drove home, and dialed his Motorolla along the way. Sissy answered and by his own luck, she was in town.

• • •

The top of his head was filled with goose eggs. His right eye was almost closed shut and his nose was most certainly broken. He set the nose back in place and growled. He then grabbed a hand towel and ran it under the tap. Just as he got most of the blood off his face there was a knock at his door.

Sissy stood in the hall. She wore white washed jeans and a baggy sweater. Her hair was a bit of a matted mess, but she didn't seem too worried about her appearance. Just one of the many things he liked about her. "Looks like you've already had some fun," she said.

"Just a bit. Should I have called sooner?"

"No, no. Looks like you didn't need me. I fancy a bump. You want?"

"No."

"Brush your teeth. You look drunk as a skunk."

She walked by, straight to the bedroom. "You smell like a skunk too!" she said.

He peeled off his shirt and applied some deodorant, gurgled some mouthwash, then followed her to his room.

"Cuffs or no?" she asked jokingly.

"No."

Tom flopped on the bed making it squeak. She hovered over him, running her hand along his battered face. "Jesus, what'd you do to yourself this time... You gotta look after yourself."

"Yeah. Well."

"Is there something you'd like to add to that thought?"

"Nope. That is all."

Sissy left and came back with a Ziploc bag of ice for his nose and eye. She grabbed his hand and placed it over top, on his busted nose to start. He winced. "Cold."

"I put some Tylenol on your nightstand."

"You are a dear."

"I know that," she said. "What am I gonna do with you?"

"What I pay you to do." Cold ice-water ran down Tom's chin.

"Pay quite handsomely, I might add," she said with a hint of sarcasm.

"Hey. It's a fair deal. I signed the twelve month membership, didn't I?"

She laughed and coughed. "I don't think that's how it works."

"Volume order. Discount."

"Who says I want the volume from you?"

"You do."

"Yes what a treat you are. I can't wait until those pants are off. Put your dragon breath all over me, baby."

Tom's eyes were growing heavy. "You're better than sarcasm."

"You're sweet." She shook her head and ran her fingers through his bloodied hair. "I need to be back in the city soon and you need some sleep."

"No, no, no." He groaned. "I'm ready." But he didn't sit up. He continued laying on his back, thoroughly enjoying her fingers through his hair.

"I'll be back in a week if you need. I'd like a sober round for a change. A nice ten minute bang for my buck."

"Ha, ha," he mumbled.

Tom opened his eyes as she continued to play with his hair. He noticed her wrist, a strategically placed wrist band covering up dark bruising. He tilted his head to get a glance at her other arm and saw that it was also bruised. Her face was normally clear, but her body was sometimes roughed up. One night, when they had both had too much to drink, she had confessed that she had a client who was giving her trouble. He was a semi-dangerous character of sorts, probably a low end gang-banger that thought he had some kind of power. It had been a while since he'd seen any markings so he figured she had dropped the piece of shit.

Tom held her wrist gently. "Is bondage often on the menu?"

Her cheeks reddened. "If it pays." She pulled her hand away and rested it on his head.

"Looks like you need a better safe word. One easier to remember." Tom sat up and examined her face for scratches or bruising. There was a small mark along her hairline.

"It's nothing I can't handle."

"I've heard that one before."

"Really, just leave it. I'm fine."

"Up my fee and cut him out. Seriously."

"No. I'm a big girl, Tom. Not my first rodeo." She was right on that one. Sissy was thirty years old, been in the game for almost a decade.

"Why do I get the feeling this guy is more than a regular?"

"He's just a client."

"Right." Tom wanted to ask if he should pay a friendly visit, but knew what her answer would be. Instead, he pulled out his wallet and handed her a paw full of cash. She snagged a twenty and left the rest. "What are you doing? Take it."

She planted a kiss on the dried blood on his cheek. "Get your shit together, Bennett."

She left and he slept like a heavy rock for a couple hours. His sore face and bruised ribs kept him up most of the night.

• • •

Tom looked out over the city from a high vantage point. There were bright lights everywhere, vast and far. Laughter rang out sporadically down below on ground level. *Where am I?*

He was on a ferris wheel, rounding through the peak height of its rotation. He looked to his left and found his daughter, Deanna. Tom ran his hand over her bright blond hair.

"Do you like it here?"

"It's pretty."

"Not as pretty as you, kiddo."

"What should we do when we reach the bottom?" Tom asked.

"Can I have some cotton candy?"

"Sure, just don't tell your mom."

He knew he was dreaming. It was almost always the same one. Tom enjoyed it like it was brand new, absorbing every facial expression, every word that came out of his daughter's mouth.

Deanna beamed with excitement. "I like it here."

Something as simple as that, he was in awe of.

"Well let's come here more often then."

"You mean it?"

"I mean it."

As they neared the bottom, he pulled his eyes off of his daughter for a quick glance at his surroundings. The faces of the people were all blurred, even all the booths and rides in the distance, blending and fading like abstract brush strokes on a canvas. The vividness retreated. He focused purely on her face, her bright blond hair as powerful as the sun on a cloudless summer day. The wind gusted through her hair, carrying along with it, the scent of fried mini-donuts.

An abrupt shift in time left Tom standing at a shooting gallery. He looked to his left, terrified that Deanna was gone, but their she stood, shooting plastic

BB's at the cans. After missing the majority of her shots, she looked at her father with disappointment-not disappointed from missing out on a prize, rather disappointed she had let him down. His hand rested on her back. Tom grabbed hold of the plastic gun and took aim. With laser-like precision, he fired off shots in a consistent rhythm, pegging each can off its stand one by one. On the final can, he missed, quickly adjusting to finish it off, but he was too late. The young man working the booth handed him a teddy bear, but all Tom could see was the sterling heart shaped necklace on display. It reminded him of his mother's necklace.

His mother had fallen ill and died when Tom was only six years old. He had few memories of his mother, but one that stood out was looking down at her in a casket. He noticed the beautiful necklace she wore and hoped that they would let her take it with her into heaven.

He handed over the teddy bear.

"Thanks daddy!"

"Sorry, Dee."

"That's okay, I like the bear. He's so soft!"

"Hey, you wanna go get that cotton candy?"

Tom handed her some cash and she scurried off. He turned back to the young man working the booth and handed him some cash in exchange for the necklace. Tom rushed back over to Deanna, scooped her up in his arms, and kissed her face as she devoured the cotton candy. He pulled away to look at her sweet, joyous face.

• • •

Tom's eyes opened to the sun peeking through the shades of his bedroom window. He awakened in bed with all of his clothing still on. Sweat ran down his face as he had his own steam room occurring under his clothing. He jumped off his bed and ran toward the toilet in his bathroom. It had been a while since Tom had been that hungover. He hurled his insides into the porcelain bowl, over and over again, unable to stop ridding himself of the demons. Just as he caught his breath, thinking it may be over, a re-enactment began, razor blades slicing and dicing in his guts, the burn in this throat intense. He tasted sour bile. It was strange that he felt so sick, considering he was well beyond seasoned.

He collapsed to the side of the toilet, a string of saliva hanging from his mouth. Though the purging had finished for now, the old familiar pain of losing his daughter all over again, set in. He tried to picture her in his mind, but she was gone.

Chapter 5

Girl in the '50s

THE MAN WHISTLED A tune while he scrubbed a plate that was already clean. The tune was an eerie one, belonging to a horror film, used as it's main score.

He was a doctor. A GP. He was always interested in rare cases that fell outside the scope of the common colds and flu's he always dealt with on a daily basis. He had other interests too. He wanted to travel, but unfortunately it would likely remain just an interest and not something he practiced. His situation just didn't allow for it. He had never traveled outside of the State of Indiana, but longed to tour other countries, especially Europe, Iceland specifically. He was fascinated by the Silfra Fissure, whereby the water was so clear that its depths appeared to go on forever.

He walked down a winding set of stairs and into an open basement. At the far end there was a bar with three crystal bottles of whiskey and scotch. He opted for the scotch today. It was light and smoky, reminding him of campfires. He sipped a small taste, letting the liquid roll around his tongue once before swallowing. He held up the classy glassware with its rough edges, admiring it. He ran his finger over the design as he walked over to a stereo system and turned it on. Classical music poured out through the surround sound, deep and soothing. His day of work had made him wonderfully gleeful. He was delighted to diagnose a patient that day, a young boy who had come in with a rather nasty rash. It was most prominent around his neck and had an odd blueish-hue faded into the red. It was familiar to him, having studied it in the past. After taking blood and a swab and sending the boy home, he could hardly hold his excitement as he raced to the archives. The anticipation did not disappoint. He was over the moon to discover it was indeed Merkel-Cell Carcinoma, a rare form of skin cancer. He had spent two extra hours doing research after work, but could no longer ignore his rigid schedule. He had to get home; his breaking of pattern was already ludicrous enough.

He moved toward the wall by the bar and slid open a hidden entrance, revealing a steel door.

• • •

Two thousand seven hundred and eighty-six, eighty-seven, eighty-eight...

A young girl in a flowered dress sat on the edge of her bed. He was late.

Time wasn't something she had been able to track as she was not granted access to a clock, but her daily regime had instilled a sense for estimates of time.

She was alerted by a noise coming from the other side of her bedroom door and exhaled with relief. She looked down at her bright dress that matched with the 1950s theme of her room. The duvet was a flowered print, while the walls were shades of pink and violet. The night stand by her bed was beautiful and rustic.

She was a nervous wreck, her nails chewed. He was *always* on time. Each day was always the same as the last. If he were to adjust the schedule, he would discuss the desired changes and make sure she would be able to handle it. Her day typically went something like this:

Wake up.

Brush hair.

Apply deodorant.

Man enters, leaves bottle of water, tooth brush with toothpaste, fruit, protein bar, multivitamin.

Short discussion, he leaves for work.

Brush teeth, spit in provided bowl.

Make bed.

Select dress. Put on dress.

Read book.

Eat protein bar. Take vitamin. Drink from water bottle.

Read book.

Stand by enclosed window.

Read book.

Push ups.

Read book.

Sit ups.

Read book.

Lunges.

Read book.

Jumping jacks.

Read book.

Attention span begins to dwindle.

Thoughts of the outside world.

Touch self. Stop touching self.

Read book.

Hand sanitizer. Eat apple. Drink from water bottle.

Do or DO NOT apply make-up. Dependant on man's mood in the morning. If he was happy, apply. If not, do not apply. He will say it was done all wrong.

Make sure bed is wrinkle free.

Count the seconds, close eyes if it helps to relax. Five to fifteen minutes. He should arrive within that time frame.

Special note - Shower takes place every Sunday. Blind fold, walk hand in hand through steel door, take immediate left. The bathroom door closes and blindfold is removed. He watches but makes no sexual advances. Time to look at her own reflection in the mirror after shower.

After his arrival, her schedule was not quite as rigid. There were variances. One example was whether he wanted sex or not. Supper often varied as well. She liked pizza the best. His visit was sometimes very brief, while other times it would go on well into the night. But he always made sure to leave when she was getting tired. Her internal clock, as he called it, was spot on and had to be respected.

The heavy handle slid and made a clunking noise. She clenched the edge of the bed, a habit she couldn't help.

It had been years since she had been taken. That bedroom had become all she'd known, her memories of her past continuing to drift away from her. Were her parents still looking for her? She could no longer remember what they looked like, what their voices sounded like, how they used to interact with one another. What were they like? She believed that her mother was a firm woman, never slow to scold if it was needed. Her father, a sensitive man that would always do anything for her, spoiling her on many occasions. Or was it the other way around?

The steel door swung open. As always, he looked quite nice. He was distinguished, handsome. It all started with his gaze, which varied from visit to visit. His looks were complex. Buggy eyes, full lush lips, nicely flowing black hair, large ear-lobs, strong jawline, short, but fit body. He appeared to be somewhat giddy, which was a good sign usually. Too much happiness was dangerous though. One false step and he'd change in an instant.

A large grin crossed the man's face. "There she is."

He took off his jacket and set it on the bed. He studied her for a moment, analyzing every fraction of her face, not her body at first.

"That dress. You are stunning."

It was wrong for her to enjoy his compliments, but it was difficult not to.

She knew her complexion was pale and spotted with pimples.

"I see someone forgot to complete the process."

His smile and kind eyes remained and she released her clenched fists.

"That's okay, honest. I was thinking we could just stay in tonight anyway. What do you think sweety?" he asked.

Staying in was a fine idea, given it was her only option.

"I'm sorry. You are gorgeous without all that makeup. I prefer it. I had only thought we were maybe going out to the ballet tonight. I should have called and told you."

Ballet sounds lovely, my sweet captor.

"It's okay."

He tucked her hair behind her ear and proceeded to lean in and kiss her neck. His lips were so soft. She turned her face away. She was weaker today, an oncoming sickness lingering within. She looked toward the window at ground level. Sunlight peered around a wooden block that was caged and locked in. Her greatest frustration that she felt each day was her concealment from sunlight. Oh, how she loved and cherished the sun.

His touch trickled down from her ear, down the nape of her neck, and settled in circular motions around her nipple. She was conflicted by two extremes. She moistened between her thighs as he touched her breast softly. The horrific pleasure took over. If only she could stop this act with an excuse he would deem worthy. But she couldn't think of one, she didn't want to think of one, only wanting his hand to slide down her abdomen. Let the pleasure take over, and the mind fade outside these walls. She realized that her internal debate had triggered tears. *Stop it. Stop crying.* The man moved back up to kiss her and noticed her damp face. For the slightest moment he looked beyond hurt, the insult forcing his rage up to the surface, but it quickly washed away.

"I'm sorry. I am no gentleman at all. You probably didn't get out today."

He walked over to the window and put in a combination for the padlock and opened up the metal casing holding in the wooden frame. Sunlight flooded in and she closed her eyes, taking in the warm rays as therapy. She wanted to drink in the light and keep it inside.

"Thank-you," he said.

"For what?"

"For everything you do. Taking care of things when I'm gone."

"It's nothing."

"No, no. It's everything," he replied.

She tried to think of something else. Maybe what the smell of trees would be like. But it was no use, she was stuck in the moment. Stuck in that room.

"We gotta get away one of these days. When I can get a couple weeks off work. How does that sound?"

She regained her composure, despite hearing the familiar tune. "That sounds wonderful. I can't wait."

The man was greatly satisfied. He started to kiss her neck again and then he unzipped the back of her dress.

Chapter 6

Anniversary

Tom spent the morning upstairs watching re-runs of a highlight package on ESPN. He fixed himself a turkey sandwich with mustard and mayo and chased it with a tall glass of milk to aid his hangover. He felt utterly lifeless still. Today marked the ten year anniversary of his daughter's disappearance and he was paralyzed by the weight of it. Ten years.

After he grew sick of being a blob on the couch, he got his act together and vacuumed the floors, wiped down the kitchen, and put away the dishes that he'd left drying in the sink. In the midst of his chores, his stomach had settled. He drank two glasses of water and made his way into his bedroom. He changed the bedding and ran a load of laundry. It all took less than a couple hours and he was left with nothing to do but work.

Tom sat on the edge of his bed, admiring Deanna's stainless steel necklace. He flipped it open and stared at a picture of them in a photo booth at the fair. She was draped over his shoulders laughing and so was he. As soon as he let himself enjoy the memory, he imagined Jessica Hill submerged in blood, his hands covered in it.

He didn't want to go down into that fucking basement.

Tom shot up off his bed and charged down into the basement.

Ten minutes later, he was sorting boxes and hoisting a desk into Deanna's old case room. He populated it with every applicable file (three boxes worth), a computer, telephone, and desk supplies. Then came the cork board work. He had a full room of it to operate with so he started with his entire list of suspects and all research materials he had on each of them. He kept them well separated and organized so it wasn't a mishmash of information.

He was ready to siphon through old files and drink Jack and Coke from his coffee mug well into the early morning, but he couldn't ignore what was going on with Sissy. Tom riled himself up, picturing that scumbag throwing her around. He snatched up his coat and went outside to his truck.

• • •

This wasn't the first time Tom had followed Sissy. He had always worried for her. Tom knew most of her daily routes from previously monitoring her. He spent the next twenty-four hours tracking Sissy. Her apartment, Sparky's bar, Thien, a Vietnamese to-go joint (she loved the noodles there), an ugly little gym, a couple house calls, back to her apartment, then off to Sparky's bar again. Outside the bar, Tom noticed a man that had been sitting in his car. As soon as Sissy walked in, he followed behind. It was his guy. Tom had seen her with him on more than one occasion and had conducted a little follow-up surveillance on him a few months prior. Tom noticed, as the man walked into the bar, that he was strapped.

Tom went inside and took a seat at the bar. He ordered a Jim and coke and watched Sissy with peripherals. The man walked straight up to her and Tom saw only fear in her eyes. He clenched his jaw and downed his drink. Tom was losing control of his pulse, a milder form in comparison to the Jessica Hill case. He locked eyes with Sissy and her face sunk, then she turned back to the loser who now had his hands on her arm. She pulled away and he snatched her arm more tightly the second time, leaning in and whispering something nasty in her ear. Tom shot out of his chair and strode over. He had forgotten the fact that his one eye was closed shut from the brawl two nights earlier.

Tom just stood there and stared back and forth between the loser and Sissy. The guy had tattoos up his neck, and stood just as tall as Tom. "Can I help you?" he asked.

"Sorry to interrupt, but are you Cecilia?"

She nodded yes, her eyes begging him to leave.

"Okay, I thought so. I'm Rick, we spoke on the phone."

"Right."

"What is this?"

"I uh, have an appointment here with Cecilia."

"Well, now you don't. Take a hike."

Sissy lifted her head. "Sorry, I double booked. Take a rain check?"

"That's okay." Tom's hand slid into his pocket, his fingers fitting neatly inside the grooves of his brass knuckles.

"You can go now," the loser said, flashing the gun on his hip.

Tom smiled, removed his hand, and struck him to the right of his nose, crushing his cheekbone, sending him to the floor. Tom grabbed him by the collar and hit him even harder in the ribs. The loser moaned, blood trickling down his face. "You're a dead man," he muttered.

Tom brought him in close and whispered. "You don't know me, but I know all about you. I think it'd be best if this was a one-time incident. Sissy is letting you go as a client. You are to never bother her again."

"Or you'll kill me?"

"No…maybe I'll have a visit with your sister. She's been home lots lately. She not nursing at the hospital?" The loser's tough guy exterior faded. Tom jerked his collar. "Then I'll break your arms and legs and fold you up like a pretzel. But I won't kill you. There's no fun in that." Tom was nose to nose with him. "Stay. Away." He pulled out the loser's gun and kept the clip for himself and tossed the gun. The message had clearly sunk in as he staggered to his feet, holding his stomach, and scampered out the back of the bar.

Sissy looked furious.

"I had to say that stuff. I'd never… You know that."

"How'd you know about him?"

"How do you think?"

"You've been following me? Following him?"

"It's what I do for a living."

"You don't know a thing about him, and you don't know a thing about me. What gives you the right to do that?"

"You'd rather him keep beating on you?"

"It's more complicated than that."

"Seems pretty clear-cut to me."

"Everything is clear-cut to you, Tom. Stay out of my life."

"I'll take you home."

"No, Tom. You're not hearing me. This needs to be finished."

"What-why?"

"Because I don't need some ex-cop trying to save me all the time. And because you're dangerous. I can see it sometimes, in your eyes. I see love and I see tenderness, but I also see something toxic. And I don't need either of those things in my life."

She slung her purse over her shoulder, her eyes apologetic. "And I don't think you need me."

"Well. There you have it."

"I'm sorry." She touched his arm. "Take care of yourself, Bennett."

He watched her walk out the door. His heart had been ripped to shreds before, but this was a different flavor. Tom perched up at the bar and crushed five more drinks before jumping into his truck for a dicey ride back home to Rocanville.

• • •

Tom sipped his Jack and Coke from his coffee cup as he had planned. He had spent the last two hours going over files. His head was swimming and he could no longer focus on his paper-riddled walls. He dropped his head to the desk with a thud and picked up the phone off the receiver. He hesitated, then dialed.

Tom's ex-wife, Allison, was awoken by her phone ringing on her night-stand. Groggily, she spun out of bed with a heavy sigh, having a strong inclination as to who would be calling her in the middle of the night. It wasn't the first time and it wasn't going to be the last. Before taking the call, she glanced over at a handsome younger man who began to stir, confused by the call. Her new husband, Derek Richter, groaned from being woken up. The red light from the alarm clock glowed on his skin, his abs flexing as he sat up. She shared a glance with him, a sense of understanding before he even asked, "Who is it?"

She shook her head in frustration to which he replied, "Tell him I say hi." Derek was a sensitive, caring man. He made efforts to include Tom, who out of habit and principle made sure he kept himself at a distance. She knew Derek had great sympathy for Tom and held no hostility toward him. It was no ordinary situation of the replacement and the ex hating each other. It was just, complicated.

Allison picked up the phone and stretched the cord as far as it could go, out into the hall away from Derek.

Almost whispering, she said, "Hello."

Without any urgency to his tone, Tom replied with a simple, "Hey."

"It's late, Tom. What's wrong?"

He lowered his head, looking down at his luke warm drink.

"Nothing is wrong. Sorry, I guess I lost track of time."

Tom stared up at a missing flier of his daughter on the cork board wall. He didn't like that the photo looked so similar to all of the other missing children photos, usually the annual school picture. This one was her pre-school picture, with a generic blue back-drop, unable to match the depth of her blue eyes.

Allison changed her tone from scolding to concern, "You aren't sleeping."

"No, no. I've been busy that's all. Just a long week. How are your boys doing?"

Allison had two boys one year apart after remarrying. They were high energy kids, busy with sports, similar to a past version of Tom even though they weren't his sons. Sometimes he thought how they would most likely get along well, but that was moot. They were not his to get along with. They deserved to live a normal family-of-four-lifestyle, without another man lurking around in the shadows.

"Clark has the flu, been a tough couple days for him. Johnny went three for four last game. Boy swings at anything and everything. I don't blame him, kids can't throw strikes yet. Derek says hi."

Tom could feel a sickening quiver lump up in his throat, frustrated with himself for seeking comfort, for bothering Allison. She deserved to be free of it all.

"Are you sure you're okay, Tom?"

The genuine concern in her voice only made him feel worse.

"I'm fine Al, really."

"You can't just call us when you're drunk. It doesn't work like that."

Tom stiffened up in his chair, "No I'm not-yeah, no. I've had too much to drink. Sorry for calling so late, tell your boys I said hi."

"Tom-"

He quickly hung up to avoid any further discussion. Tom finished the last of his whiskey and slid the bottle away. He tried to picture Deanna's face, but she was a blur.

Chapter 7

Clear Slate

ANOTHER HEADACHE, ANOTHER DAY. Starting now he'd mix in more water with his whiskey. The roar in his head was horrid, but at least he didn't feel the need to hug the toilet. Tom groaned, willing himself to get out of bed, when he was surprised by Reg standing in the entrance with two coffees.

"Daylight in the swamp," he announced loudly.

"I hate it when you do that."

At least there was no specific case on the docket. Today he would sift through some news reports, conduct some half-assed prospecting, and more importantly, bury himself in his daughter's suspect list.

"Get up. Day ain't gonna wait, let's go, let's go!" Reg shouted.

Tom sat up and accepted the cup of coffee from Reg. He took a cautious sip and turned his brow up in disgust.

"Christ, I thought I told you to dial it back?"

Reg got a rise out of his response. "Put lead in your pencil."

"Put vomit in the toilet."

"You look like the shit I took this morning. If shit was ghost white. Which is interesting because I watched a documentary on alcoholism and they said that's often one of the signs of liver failure. Something to think about."

"What, no Mash re-runs on last night?"

"Listen, you let me know if you ever need to step away for a while-"

"We aren't doing this," Tom interjected.

"Well, quit screwing around then and we won't have to. I'm heading downstairs. Talked to Dean this morning and he figured he might have something new for us. Gonna let us know."

"Okay, I'll be down in a bit."

Reg left and Tom stared out his window. Out on the street a few kids were playing on their bikes, two parents chatting behind them. The one girl had a little pink bike with tassels on the handles and training wheels in the back. She turned around, her hair curling away from her face. It was Deanna. He wasn't fazed at all by the hallucination.

He never described them as hallucinations, simply his mind doing what it needed to do, which was remind him that she was still out there waiting for him. They helped keep him focused on the task at hand, bringing him back to the center of his own world, erasing outside concerns. But he had a business to run still. The work helped keep him sharp, especially when the cases he worked were so recent, the missing person having just disappeared. It was a good feeling to have to have clear leads, rather than looking for a needle in a haystack stacked on another haystack.

Tom headed downstairs and dumped the pot that Reg had on the burner and started from scratch. He scowled at him with a low grumble and Tom blew a kiss.

"Pussy."

"Yes, Reginald. We all know the measure of a man is based on his roast preference."

He watched every drip until the coffee pot reached about four cups and he pulled out the pot prematurely and filled his thermos before sliding it back in. The drip continued.

"You ruin the balance doing that. Your cup will be just as strong as the batch I made. Foolish child."

"That's not how it works, you grumbling old bastard. You know what? You're right. My head hurts too much to deal with you. Any arguments today will end with a simple Archie search on the interwebs."

"If your body can't function the next day-"

Tom cut in and finished the commonly heard sentence. "Then it was too much. Yeah, you're not kidding old timer."

"I'd appreciate you cutting the old talk. A person is as old as they feel. Got it, you *old* miserable prick?"

A laugh burst out from Tom's chest. The goodness that came from laughing was nice, but brief. Tom tasted mint, bile, and strong coffee. He'd have to brush again after a proper cup. "You win again, you young stallion."

"Let me get back to work. God knows you won't accomplish a damn thing today."

"Hey, I work best under these conditions. I feel guilty about the prospect of letting you down due to my hungover state. Therefore I work harder."

"Sure."

"Don't kid yourself. You're playing minesweeper half the time," said Tom.

"Am not!" Reg barked all child-like.

"Sure."

They both gave each other the finger and Tom forgot how poorly he felt for a moment. He stepped into his daughter's case room, feeling Reg's stare of concern.

For years, Tom had been focused on three main suspects. He had explored other options in the past, most specifically, upset parents and relatives to victims that were never found, or found dead. Fathers and mothers that thought they knew the best approach, so blinded by trust in their children's honesty that they couldn't see the correct direction of the investigation. The direction that Tom and Reg knew was best. "My kid would never do that." "No, not my baby. She wouldn't touch drugs." "He'd never go there. He'd never do that." "That other kid is a liar. They don't know my son/daughter." "Her father has nothing to do with us." Yes, Tom had heard them all. He would always remind them that they were paying him for his expertise, for results. And the results, although far from perfect in a world of the improbable, were better than much of the alternative options. Regardless, many still felt the need to butt heads, perhaps giving a sense of "fight" for their child's return, but whatever it was, it seldom helped.

Tom referred to the those angry parents as his "B" list. Within his "A" list, he had Connor and Leanne Harrison. Their child was Ivy League material in the making. A handsome boy, structured and privileged lifestyle, but more importantly, intelligence complimented by a stubborn drive and focus at the age of twelve. He was going to be someone important, but then he was gone. They interviewed countless PI firms and other specialists within a relentless twenty-four-hour period, while IPD worked their investigation. They chose Tom.

The ransom request came via email to Connor. The drop site was organized, but nobody showed. No further contact. Nothing. Ghost.

Their personal driver would drop off the boy, Jared, at his private school everyday and also pick him up at 3:30 p.m sharp. His schedule was like clockwork, the family having his entire month-to-month charted out to the hour. They claimed the boy liked it as such, but Tom figured there was probably some resentment there. That day, the driver had picked him up and about halfway to their house the driver passed out, and the car steered gently off the road into a light post on a sidewalk. That was where the kid was nabbed. There was an eye witness, but the van's plates weren't registered. The cops were delayed getting to the scene and the van was found ditched outside the city. That was where the trail ended.

Tom had looked into the driver, but toxicology came back and he had indeed been drugged roughly thirty minutes before his arrival at the school. He said it hit him all at once like a ton of bricks. But had it all been part of his plan? Was he working with someone else? Why let the ransom go? Why stay living in the same area, even to this day? He had zero history with the Harrison family before taking the job. He was security detail, decorated career, winding down to a quiet retirement with private work. He'd even been on a detail for President Reagen for a few months-a fill-in for an injury-but still. It couldn't have been him. They pulled up surveillance from a coffee shop he had went to every day before picking up Jared. There was nothing there either.

It wasn't like Tom to get stuck for more than twenty-four hours, but he was in this case. He had nowhere to turn, and after a week he was replaced by a different PI firm based out of Louisville. Later, Connor and Leanne had tried to file a lawsuit against Tom, but there was no sufficient evidence for negligence or malpractice. One day he had failed to conceal the liquor on his breath and Leanne was absolutely furious. Later, she confronted him about working other cases during the same time, which would have been a breach of their contract. He didn't know how she knew, but it was the truth. He thought he could handle the work load, he needed to. But there was no proof that he was drunk on the job during his investigations, nor was there that he was actively working other cases they'd kept on the DL.

Deanna had been taken September 28th, 1979. Jared Harrison in August of '76. With the resources the Harrison's had, it was entirely possible they hired someone to take Deanna, though he didn't think they could be that heinous, granted you never think anyone would be capable of such a thing. But, their boy remained missing to this day, and the parallel unknowns with his daughter could have been a fit punishment in their damaged eyes. It was possible still. What a discouraging word. Possible. Never probable.

He sifted through other client files with similarities to Connor and Leanne Harrison. Lots of the victims younger, before their adolescence, some missing spouse's files, then he stopped on Jerry Lehman. A highlighted suspect on Tom's "B" list that had been dismissed as he was deceased. He hadn't been able to shake that one.

Jerry had some disagreements with Tom in the beginning and it affected their search. Jerry thought (unlike most parents would) that his daughter had indeed fled, only to a familiar spot in the country that she cherished. The notion was highly unlikely. The distance was much too far for her to walk it and there was no way she would have caught a ride from anyone. She was only five. But, Jerry was insistent that she would have taken her bike. With her small stature, it would have taken her at least two hours to bike to her destination. Tom was of the mind-set that she had been taken from somewhere near the church. There was, however, another angle with the country spot. If they had made regular visits out there, it was possible they were being watched by someone that lived in country between Rocanville and Indianapolis.

Jerry's daughter was taken in May of '78.
He was a minister in Indianapolis making the commute almost every day from Rocanville. He still had faith with he hired Tom. God would provide answers, Jerry believed. It was all happening for a reason. All that fun stuff. He had faith in Tom, faith in God, faith that life would work out the way it should. But that faith yielded nothing. It didn't help Tom find his girl.

Jerry was devastated. A year later, his own personal search efforts stopped when he decided to take his own life.

Tom could still picture Jerry's face, bones shattered so badly, his face unrecognizable. The fall from the bridge was not overly far, but he had launched himself head-first into the rocks. They needed dental to properly ID him. Tom shook his head emphatically, ridding himself of the gruesome memory. The blood-splattered pattern on the rocks…

The last swallow of coffee was ice cold. He had little on Connor and Leanne Harrison. Connor was a complicated man in his world of business. Imports and exports. Exquisite furniture, various styles of steel art, among other metals. He accrued half his wealth through work, half through foreign investments, but Tom never had access to his financial records. He had no idea what exactly his portfolio was comprised of. The Harrison's were difficult to research. But shady business didn't necessarily mean any evidence of kidnapping to be found, even if they were his culprit. Regardless, Tom needed more information, without it, looking into them would be a waste of time again. He'd have to trip them up on something first. Get access, discovery, and follow. He needed more coffee.

Tom exited Deanna's case-room into the main office. He started another pot of coffee, ignoring Reg as he yammered about Tom getting some rest for once.

He needed some air.

Chapter 8

Normal

ELLA SAT ALONE AND WATCHED the various cliques socialize in the cafeteria. Her gaze fell on the table of popular girls with their colorful skirts and tight tank tops shaping their small breasts, exaggerating the size. The one girl, Amanda Benson, laughed at a joke told from across the table. Her smile beautiful. Ella imagined that her laugh sounded lovely, sophisticated. She had a nice body, too.

Ella had always connected to the boys much easier, they were simpler, easy to play with. Now that she had reached the heart of her teen years, boys weren't an option. With sexual attraction playing such a pivotal role, she didn't have the looks to be involved with any of the boys. Some mornings she would catch herself doing what she despised other girls for doing, analyzing herself in the bathroom mirror. She had no ass and her collarbones jutted out. When she pushed her arms forward, her shoulder blades stuck out, making her look like a gargoyle.

As Ella picked at her inedible meatloaf dish, a girl two years younger took a seat across from her. The girl had short red hair and glasses. She was a petite little thing, shyness clearly her primary personality trait. She looked at Ella with a timid glance. Ella soon realized that her own face was resting in an unpleasant, uninviting form.

"Can I sit here?" she asked.

Her freckles were dark, dotting most of her face, most prominent around her nose. Her eyes were bright green, reminding Ella of a cat.

"I think there's room." Ella gestured toward the empty table.

The red-head flashed a nervous smile and looked down at her plate with the same displeasure as Ella.

"Based on the way it jiggles, I'm guessing this wasn't made from scratch. It's bad enough going with meatloaf, but would it kill them to have a cook make it in house." She poked at it with her fork.

The red-head laughed with nervous excitement. "My mom's is disgusting too," she said.

Ella didn't give her a reply.

"I like your bracelet," said the red-head.

Ella looked down at her black band with subtle pink lining on the inside.

"Thanks."

Another awkward pause required another compliment.

"You have pretty eyes."

Ella found the compliment off-putting, knowing that the girl simply needed a friend and was making false statements about her appearance to gain her affections. "Why are you sitting here?"

The girl's face reddened. "I have no where else to sit."

"Listen, sitting with me isn't gonna do you any favors with anyone. You're what? Grade eight?"

The girl nodded as she began rubbing the top of her right hand. It was difficult not to feel sorry for her.

Ella continued, "You'll lose that layer of chub and you'll be very pretty. You have a sweet look. Some of the boys will show interest soon enough. And it'll be the nice ones, not the jerks. Trust me. You're not doing yourself any favors sitting across from me. There's no need to be so pathetic and needy. Just be patient."

The girl processed everything, the insults, the compliments. Finally the smoke cleared from in front of her eyes and she answered simply, "If what I look like is so important, maybe I could hang out with you for a year, until I'm better looking."

Ella studied the girl's face. It was like looking in a mirror, vulnerability staring back.

"I'm moving. Sorry." She got up from her meal to leave, not wanting to stick around for the formation of tears.

"You can at least finish your lunch."

Ella looked down at it then smiled at the girl. "You can have mine."

Ella wandered down the hall to her locker and exchanged her binder for another. As she locked up, she noticed the jock and his two friends exiting the school. She contemplated talking to the boy for a second time. If he was being sincere, should she really be denying herself the chance to be normal for a change? Maybe she could go to the stupid party and stay for just a little bit. Toe the water and if it was too cold she could always just leave, no pressure. And if it was all one big joke, they should be moving sooner than later anyway.

Ella approached the three guys as they were getting into their car. Two of them shared a smile before they got in, while Brian waited for Ella to speak.

"So, where was that party you'd mentioned?" she asked.

She could see before he answered, he held up a hurtful guard from their last encounter. His eyes narrowed. "Why would you care?"

"Yeah, I'm sorry about that earlier."

"Yeah, okay-"

"Listen. I'm a bitch sometimes. Comes with the image right?" She stood tall, trying to earn his interest back.

"It's all right, really."

"I'm not used to cute football guys coming up and talking to me. Usually AV club and skids, you know?"

She couldn't believe she had called him cute. She didn't know where to look. The ground seemed safest.

He laughed and waited until her eyes lifted back up to meet his. "So…" he led her.

"Yeah, um. Are you still going to the party? At Jake's is it?"

"Yeah, I think I'll still go."

"All right well…maybe I'll see you there then?"

"Yeah, of course. I'd like that." His response left her euphoric. It was unchartered territory for her, new and exciting.

She displayed her best smile, turned and walked away.

He called out, "Hey." Ella turned to face him.

"I'll pick you up if that's okay?" he asked. "Nine works?"

She nodded yes, trying not to look too happy about it. Remembering she couldn't be seen at her trailer, she made a suggestion, "You know that old diner on 8th? I'll be there."

Before turning to walk away she blurted out, "It's not gonna happen...what I said earlier." Referring to the blow job. She continued to walk away when he yelled out, "Hey! I didn't get your name! It's Ella, right?" She didn't turn back, instead extending her arm with a wave, enjoying the suave moment. It was her first.

• • •

Ella sat in her usual spot in the diner sipping her cup of tea. As she watched the rain pelt the pavement outside, her foot tapped a mile a minute. The music playing in her ears was ineffective, unable to deliver any sort of escape. There was no downplaying or avoiding what she was feeling. She had let herself get up, avoiding the fact that she would most likely crash back down. She checked her watch to find the time was 9:45 p.m. There was no knight in shining armor that would arrive to save her, no escaping who she was, and what she was a product of. There was only her, and that was not going to be enough. As a dark, classical tune took hold of her headphones, her mood was guided to where it belonged. Ella jolted out of her chair and exited the diner into the pouring rain.

She soldiered through the night. Cold, wet air touched her skin.

She arrived at the party. The blaring music and drunks out on the front balcony did not intimidate her whatsoever. She sneaked in through the back door and tripped over a bunch of sneakers. The music was blaring, laughter and loud conversations were blending to form a dull roar. Once she walked up the short steps and into the active kitchen, she felt eyes on her immediately, but didn't care, not as much anyway. She made her way through the crowd of drunken teens in search of Mr. Football. She wasn't exactly sure what she'd do or say, but for once she didn't fret over the details.

Ella made her way into a clearing in the living room and in the far corner she spotted the jock leaned up against the wall, making out with an attractive brunette. It wasn't Amanda Benson. It was Stacey Perkins. She was beautiful too. His hand caressed her face, running into her hair. Suddenly a brutal confrontation was no longer an option. She crumbled. Her eyes welled up. She rushed quickly through the crowded room with her head down, hoping no one would acknowledge her or check to make sure she was okay. Thankfully, as she made her way out of the house and down the street in the rain, no one had rushed to her aid.

• • •

Ella entered the trailer with her hood up, trying to avoid Simon on her way to her room. He was sitting in his recliner watching something on their small tube. He scared her with a shout, "Stop!"

Simon approached her and slowly removed the hood of her coat, revealing her tear-stained face. He gently placed his finger on her chin and raised her head. His dark eyes searched hers, his face tense. He hugged her. She hugged him back.

"Can we please go ahead with it?" she whispered, her lips wet with salty tears.

"We need more time. Are you okay? What happened?"

"What difference does it make? If we don't do it now...what if we don't ever-"

He shushed her and she wiped her runny nose on his chest.

"Will you tell me what's going on?"

"It wouldn't change anything."

"How do you know that?"

"I'm ready now."

His sigh was heavy as he patted her back. "I know. I know."

Chapter 9

Take Me to Church

SOUTH INDY, FOUNTAIN SQUARE. Offbeat, quirky, art scene, indie music, hole in the wall restaurants, youthful. It was a place to live for young artists, not so much for a decorated and retired security detail specialist (who more than likely had tucked away a respectable amount of money-only an assumption). Joseph Walsh lived just off of Fountain Square in an old bungalow home that had been kept in good shape. It reminded Tom of the house he grew up in, plain white siding, bedroom windows up top overlooking the street.

He knocked twice before hearing him yell, "Yeah! Coming!" Joseph opened the door, squinting at Tom. He was a great big man with long limbs, and massive hands, surely a tough customer. His hair was silver and silky smooth, tossed to the side. He was very tanned, skin slightly leathered.

"Mr. Walsh. You remember me?"

"Of course." He didn't smile, his face positioned in a scowl.

"I must say I'm surprised at your choice of locale."

"Good restaurants. You ever have peanut butter on a burger?"

"Can't say I have."

"You should."

Tom nodded and an awkward pause followed. "I have a few questions for you. Can I come in?"

"Yes, of course."

Tom followed him inside. Kitchen was to the left, living room to the right.

"Coffee?"

"Had my fill this morning."

"Beer?"

Tom hesitated. "Sure."

Joseph took his recliner, Tom the couch. "Before you dive in, I'll let you know like I did last time, I'm censored on a lot of your questions. I hold confidentiality with all my past and existing clients."

"Existing? You're still working?"

"Semi-part time. I'm sure you know how it is. Can never stop completely." His mouth opened again, as if he was trying to take back the words. "Sorry."

"It's fine. You're right. Even if…she was with me, I'd still probably be doing this," Tom said.

"Because there's no one else to do it."

"Exactly."

He chuckled, a lighter side revealed on his face. "We are fools. There is always someone next in line."

"Maybe they're not good enough."

"Maybe not," Joseph agreed and sipped his cold beer. Tom did the same.

"So, lay it out for me."

Tom appreciated how direct he was. "Last time we spoke-"

"I was an asshole that didn't help you."

"No I-"

He held up his hand. "I might be again. No promises."

"Maybe I'll have to ask the right questions." Tom peeled the label of his beer. "We first met regarding the Harrison's child disappearing obviously. We jogged your memory as best we could and nothing of significance came up. Has that changed?"

"It hasn't. Chloroform was what came up in screening. Took anywhere from fifteen to thirty minutes of exposure to knock me out."

"Any idea how they got it into your system?"

"Sure don't. Don't think I ever will. Maybe through the vents. But I remember seeing Jared in the back seat. He didn't conk out. Obviously I'm a lot bigger."

"But you're in the front, taking the brunt of it."

"It should have been visible."

"Maybe you didn't notice?" Tom suggested.

"I notice everything."

"Chloroform was used on me as well."

"Yes, I remember you saying that last time. Diazepam mix?"

"Yeah. It was pretty much instant."

"Anything Connor or Leanne say to you regarding the incident that you can share with me?"

"They shared a lot of things, I guess."

"Connor works in Imports and Exports. Any other specialty items he deals with other than art and furniture?"

"His business isn't any of mine."

"What was your relationship like with the boy? Jared."

"He was a good kid. We spoke some during our travels."

"What about?"

"School, sports, teased him about girls. Nothing about his father being a major cocaine runner, using his business as a front."

"Is he?"

He smirked with a subtle shake of his head. "You better finish your beer."

Tom waited.

"No." Joseph confirmed his exaggerated joke.

"He spent a lot of time with his parents, not much of a life outside of school and his house," said Tom.

"Your question?"

"How did he feel about all that? Did he confide in you? Involving any frustrations with Mom and Dad."

"Is this line of questioning being utilized for your daughter or for their son?" he asked. "They're wealthy folk. They always got what they wanted. And when they didn't get their son back they had to blame someone. You didn't get them what they needed. You were shit to them because of it." His stare was unapologetic. "They didn't kidnap your girl. And they didn't hire someone either. I know them well enough. You can trust me on that."

He hadn't given Tom an ounce of that last time they spoke about his daughter's case.

"Now, is it possible that Jared's case is linked to your daughter's in some way? Sure. It is possible," he said.

That was a road Tom didn't want to go down. He'd need the Harrisons' cooperation and that wasn't going to happen. And he couldn't trust them, despite

Joseph suggesting otherwise. "So they watched him like a hawk. His schedule planned out meticulously, every day, every week, every month."

"Yeah, they were strict. Disciplined. So was the kid."

"What'd he do for fun?"

"Fun? His academics were his 'fun'. He was a good little lacrosse player too, I suppose."

"You ever take him to his games or practice?"

"No. That was his parents."

"What'd Connor and Leanne do for fun around their work schedules?"

"Hard to say."

"Okay…"

"Confidentiality."

"So you drove the kid to and from school. That was it."

"That was my duty, yes."

"And that'd be the only time you'd see him?" Tom asked.

He saw a quick flicker of his eyes, questioning how he should answer. "Sometimes I'd step foot in the entrance of their home. That was it."

"They never once had you drive their son elsewhere?"

He adjusted in his seat and sipped his beer.

"Give me something. Please," said Tom. The label was now hanging from his beer bottle. He set it down on the coffee table and leaned forward. "Everything was so unclear. I never got answers from the Harrison's. I wasn't able to. Any information that can help me move on to a different suspect."

"On occasion I'd guard the house while his parents were at church."

There it was. Something new. "Why wasn't he at church?"

"Sundays were time for him to get ahead on his academics. They worked with the teachers, had him on a time line to graduate two years early at sixteen. They'd catch him up on the sermon with a summary."

"Intense, to say the least."

"Crazy comes in various forms," said Joseph. "Stern parenting is far from the worst."

"Which church?"

"Holy Angels. North."

It rang a bell. Jerry Lehman? He thought it was possible that was his church. When his daughter went missing, he had resigned shortly after, he remembered. Maybe he was the minister there? If Connor and Leanne had no hand in Deanna's disappearance, maybe someone within the church took exception to Lehman's death. Someone close enough that knew Tom was working the case with IPD.

Tom finished his beer with a big gulp. "You're positive they had nothing to do with my daughter?" His gaze was intense, he felt alive again from asking about her.

"As positive as I can get."

Tom rose to his feet and shook his hand then walked to the door. "It was a difficult case. Unusual."

"I understand. Parents of the child wouldn't."

"Thanks for your time, Mr. Walsh."

Before he stepped out the door, Joseph said, "Hey... Sorry."

Tom nodded and left.

• • •

He got out of his truck and walked over to the front steps of Holy Angels Anglican. He had called in advance and the kind woman had informed him that the minister would be having his 5:00 p.m coffee outside as he does everyday. The front of the church was brand new. It was white like ivory with massive windows taking up most of the space, the sun reflecting off of them, giving it an extra holy look. Around the back side, the building was made of brick, much older. The front had been an add-on, probably within the last couple of years.

Jim Doherty was around the age of sixty, give or take a few years. His face was rather wrinkle-free for a man his age, but consisted of faded pocketed scars from previous acne perhaps. His shoulders were narrow, bright blond hair wavered in the breeze, a noticeable strand out of place. When Tom approached, Jim smiled and took another sip of coffee.

"I just love these new steps. I'm a bit of a people watcher. Is that strange?" His voice was soft, not quiet though.

"Not at all. I'm the same. Nice face lift you guys got."

"We were due. How can I help you, son?"

"I'm a private investigator. Used to be with IPD, but I have my own private practice now." He didn't seem to register any surprise from the introduction. "I was wondering if you would be so kind as to tell me a little bit about Jerry Lehman."

His mouth tightened, a sadness registered. "I thought you were here for confession. I've punched the clock out already." He smiled. "Of course we could do a more unofficial confession here if you got something bothering you?"

"Maybe another time."

He closed his eyes and nodded. "Can I get you some decaf?"

"I'm fine thanks."

He took a second look at Tom and something clicked. "You worked Jerry's girl's case."

"I did." Tom shook his hand. "Tom Bennett."

"Jim."

Tom sat down next to him and looked out at the street. The sidewalks were busy with pedestrians checking out some smaller clothing stores, the streets just as busy with cars moving through traffic hour.

"Everyone's always in a hurry."

"Yeah, unfortunately I seem to be trapped in it," said Tom.

"It's all right. Most are. Just important to take a breather once in a while. Sit on a step or a porch. No thinking, just looking."

"What do I call you? Father Jim?"

"Oh, Father, Minister, whichever is comfortable. Just Jim works fine too."

Tom nodded. "You took over for Jerry as soon as his daughter went missing?"

"I did. Terrible thing that happened."

"Were you already a clergy member here or were you hired from the outside?"

"I was here. I was fortunate they wanted to provide an opportunity from within. Keep it in-house, so to speak. Wish it had been under different circumstances. Mind you, a position like this, at a church like this, a guy only gets a shot if the minister moves or passes on. So it could have been poor circumstances any way you slice it, I suppose. But that girl. She was so sweet. No father should have to go through that."

Tom flinched and looked away, distracting himself from self-pity. "Did you talk to him after her body was found? Before he…passed."

"Yes, many of us tried reaching out to him, but he had blocked us out. He had blocked everything out, Tom. Once the hope was gone, he just didn't want to find his way back to life."

"Was he a good at his job?"

"He was excellent. He…how shall I say this? Stuck to the rules a little more than I do. His sermons were long, by the good book, very structured. But he was wonderful around the clock, helpful with any community event he could get his hands on. The older folk especially adored him. Those same folk maybe aren't as fond of my, let's say, more youthful practices." He laughed under his breath as he squinted at the busy street.

"Was there anyone he was particularly close with inside the congregation? Perhaps within the clergy?"

"Honestly from what I had seen, no. He kept to himself. I never noticed him showing any favoritism or mixing in any personal life with specific people. Just a good man to everyone. An excellent leader in the church and in the community."

"Did Jerry have any half-siblings?" Past records had told him no, but it was worth asking.

"No, I don't believe so."

"And you're sure nobody in particular he was close with? A relative maybe?"

"No, sorry. What's this about?"

"A missing child. Could be linked to the church."

"Oh my." He shook his head and set his coffee down on the step. "I can assure you there is nothing going on in our church. Not under our roof. I would never hide such atrocities."

"It's not like that, Jim. It would be more of a vendetta."

"And you think Jerry would be involved in such a thing?"

"No, but someone close to him perhaps, or connected in some way. Someone that would be angry from his death."

"He lived such a private life, kept his attention on his daughter when he wasn't in the church. I'm sorry, I wish I had more for you."

Tom took a quiet breath and debated not asking. But he had to. "Would you be able to provide me a list of names? Your entire congregation."

"I can't do that. There are matters of confidentiality here. The police department would have to come forward with a warrant."

"I'm aware. I'm private though. No IPD involved. They aren't a partner on this."

"Can I ask who's missing?"

Tom looked out at the street. "My daughter." His voice was hard, forced as such.

The silence was crippling. Jim blinked a couple of times as he searched for appropriate words. "What possesses a person to take a child? To hurt a child. It makes my job difficult. Difficult to not be angry sometimes. I'd tell you I'm sorry and to trust in God's plan, but something tells me that wouldn't do much good for you right now."

"No. It certainly wouldn't."

"Well, I am sorry, Tom." He sighed. "But he does care deeply for you. God feels your pain."

"I'll be the only eyes on your list. Not even my partner will see. You have my word on that."

Jim paused, then turned and glanced up at their new front entrance. "And you think someone within the church that's connected to Jerry had something to do with this?"

"I do."

"I spoke with Jerry after IPD and your outfit had moved on with their search. He was angry. But a man of faith is still a man of faith. He knew of the pain that you are feeling now."

"I know. But what if there was someone else not so pure?"

Tom waited in silence for about thirty seconds as Jim stared at the busy street. "I'll give you the list. Just what are you hoping to find?"

"Relatives, past crimes, really anything we can search, proof of relationship inside or outside of these holy walls."

There was a look of concern on his face.

"Don't worry, I won't be approaching people. Not without coming to you first. It just gives me something to work with. Tell me, what do you know about Connor and Leanne Harrison?"

"I know of them. They used to make it most Sundays, I think. But I haven't seen them around. Big congregation, it is difficult to keep it all straight."

"They went to this church?" He just had to make sure it was solid.

Jim nodded.

"Did you ever see them conversing with Jerry?"

"I don't know, maybe. I have no idea if they were associated outside the church. A minister is always there for his or her people. Whenever they need."

"But they weren't friends?"

"I don't think so. I can't be sure though. From what I knew, Jerry was a private man."

Two suspects that had been under the same roof. It was something to go on. "I understand. Thank-you, Jim. This means everything."

He nodded sadly. "You take care of yourself."

• • •

First thing the next morning, Tom went down to his office and sat at his computer. One pot of coffee later, he called Dean, his old partner from his days in the IPD. "Old" wasn't the right word though. Dean came onto the scene as a rookie while Tom had already entered the prime of his career.

"You know, Dean," he said. "I'm looking at a bottle of Johnnie Blue, not entirely sure how it got here."

"Sounds about right. You looking at the bottle at seven in the morning."

Dean had no idea how bad his drinking had gotten, deeming the joke, no joke. "What do you need?"

"I'm gonna be sending you a list of people. I need you to run them through the database, see if any charges come up on any of them."

"Sure. Anything else?"

Tom was hesitant. He knew he'd catch grief from Dean if he brought up anything to do with Dee's case. "Yeah. Look into Jerry Lehman for me. Anything on his past, including family members. I can't find his file, must be with IPD."

"Why do I know that name?"

"Worked his missing daughter's case."

"Suicide after?"

"That's the one."

"Why?"

"Just digging at something. Could be linked to another case."

He sensed Dean was about to ask more questions, but he stopped himself. "Okay."

"Thanks Dean. Bottle will be hand delivered. I'll email you that list right away."

"Sure thing."

Just as he hung up, he received a new email. He browsed through it to find a list of the congregation dating back through the years before and after Jerry's daughter was taken. Sure enough, the Harrisons' had come and gone. They were in the registry for five years and were off the list in '79. Their son had been taken in '76. Tom found it rather coincidental that they left the church the same year Deanna was taken. If they didn't have anything to do with his daughter's disappearance, perhaps they knew someone on the list that did. And maybe they had information on that someone.

Chapter 10

The Stand

HER BOOK COLLECTION was extensive, her closet stocked full, along with the book shelf in the corner. Not only was she treated to any fiction she desired, her captor had strongly urged her to focus on any and all types of non-fiction books. On Sunday, after her weekly shower was completed, they would discuss whatever she was currently reading. Education was at the center of her existence since she had been in that basement and she owed all knowledge she had obtained to him. He had explained to her the traditional setting in which educational procedures took place, and stressed the improved styles in which their learning process would function under. In short, it was conversational. Questions that spawned more questions, peeling the onion, as he would say. Though he was a doctor that had navigated through a rather rigid and traditional education, he believed there were more effective ways of teaching.

She used to love their evenings spent together. There was so much to learn and she absorbed everything he taught her like a sponge. He was a fine teacher and he had always told her how she was an even better pupil. He had helped her see things from all angles. Truth and fact were not always so definite. When she was younger, they covered everything. Art, American History, all forms of science, maths, literature. She could read for hours on end.

She knew many things, and yet knew only those four walls. The more information she obtained, the more she desired escape.

Never once did he share his name. He said he didn't believe in names. She remembered having a name. But it was gone now. It may have been gone for a long time.

The days had grown terribly lonely while he was away at work. Thankfully, she had recently come across *The Alchemist*. The pages hadn't stopped. She read another book after, only to return back to it for a second read. She was inspired and she was crushed. The power of dreams and the ability to seek and fulfill her life's meaning tore at her soul. Dreaming was a dangerous concept in that basement.

She lifted her head to find her friend in the corner looking at her bright-eyed. The little girl wore pig tails and was missing two teeth. She had a mischievous grin and dimpled cheeks she wanted to pinch. "Are you thinking about outside again?" asked the little girl. She called herself Sam.

"Trying not to."

"Have you picked a name yet? You promised you would."

"I don't think I can do that, Sammy."

"But you need to pick one like I did. Please."

She stood up and glanced over at her book on the bed. She smiled again and turned to Sammy, her name found from within the novel. "Santiago."

"I like that." Her toothless smile was so cute.

"What brings you to my humble abode today?"

"I was hoping you could play a game with me."

"Which game?"

The little girl walked into the closet and pulled Monopoly off the shelf.

They had played this out far too many times. Santiago wasn't crazy. Not yet at least. She understood that the little girl was only a part of her imagination. Sam was possibly a past version of herself, but she couldn't be sure. Perhaps she was a younger sister that she didn't remember having.

Santiago watched intently as Sammy set up the board. There was no reason for it, no profound discovery, no eureka. She felt something just click or shift. It had happened once before. A simple innate realization. "I can't play Monopoly."

"Scrabble?"

"No."

"Kerplunk?"

"No."

"Can we please, please, please play Monopoly?"

"I can't."

Sammy furrowed her brow and crossed her arms. "But I want to!"

"No, you don't. Because I don't. I need to…face the music." She had just recently discovered that phrase in one of her novels. "Now you go on and get out of here. This is no place for a girl your age. And I'm not

Santiago. Go on, the next game won't be any fun. Trust me."

Her eyes were clouded, her lip in a permanent position of pout. "Will I still see you?"

She wanted to hold Sam's hand, but refrained from extending her fantasy. "I don't know, Sammy. I don't think so."

Sam's shoulders bobbed as she hugged herself, unprotected and scared. Snot ran down from her nose and settled above her lip, sticky and thick. "Where do I go?"

"Back where you came from. Where you're supposed to be."

"But I wanna be with you." She was a betrayed and delicate little creature. But she wouldn't go. She was stubborn.

"Leave!" Santiago screamed.

"Stop it!" Sammy's eyes were wide, her face red, her own startled voice scaring her.

"Leave!" Santiago's voice boomed. "Please! Leave!"

"Stop it, stop it, stop it, stop it!" Sammy's screams were as desperate as a child being ripped out of the arms of her loving mother. Santiago sat there, in the corner of her room, knees to her chest, eyes closed, head tucked, as she whispered over and over again. "Stop it."

Noise emerged from outside the steel door. Sam was gone, maybe forever. She sat on the edge of the bed, ready for her master. He entered with hard eyes. She had seen that look enough times to understand what would follow.

She popped to her feet and walked assertively up to the man. He stepped backward, his hands rising up to his chest as a barrier. She forced herself in and ran her hand through his hair and looked deep into his eyes. She noticed a whiskey glass in his hand. *Did he always bring a glass in with him?* She hoped that wasn't the case as there would have been many missed opportunities in the past.

"You shouldn't leave me so long. I have needs too, you know." She nibbled his ear-lobe and whispered, "Figured you would have known this by now." She kissed him aggressively and he pulled away for a moment. Her lustful eyes proved too much for him to bear and they kissed again. He grabbed hold of her arms, his grip tight.

It had all started not long after her first period. That was when the dynamic changed from father and teacher to "lover". It had destroyed her. Any love she had had for the man was stripped away the moment his hand rested on her inner thigh and his eyes changed into something awful. He was a different man. And so commenced the last couple years of a relationship that ruined her one day at a time.

Santiago pulled away and held his hand down to his side gently. She grabbed the whiskey glass that was still in his other hand and placed it on the top of the headboard. She could feel he was hard against her leg and she looked down, trying her best not to break character. "You don't need your drink now, do you?"

He didn't smile. He looked at her the way she looked at the box of pizza when he'd bring it into her room once a week. She was just a meal. An object for his pleasurable gain. He pushed her to the bed and she lost control of her position, further away from the whiskey glass with his body pressing down on her. She was not built to put up much of a fight, so if she were to strike, it had to be placed and timed perfectly. There was only one shot here.

His breath tasted of mint and whiskey, and he smelled of fancy cologne that had been mixed with subtle body odor from a long day of work. She wished he was an unattractive beast, but he was handsome, and part of her always wanted it.

He ripped her dress off, then her panties. His first smile took shape when looking down at his own belt as he removed it. Santiago shuddered at the sight of his evil grin.

With his pants now dropped to the floor, she pulled him toward her. She bit down on her lip and thought about the blue sky and white clouds circling around the bright sun. She tasted her own blood from the teeth imprints left in her lip. She took the pleasurable abuse, his face buried in the sheets next to her. When he was violent, he never looked her in the eyes.

She couldn't move. She wanted to be aggressive and make her stance, but she didn't know how, paralyzed by the moment, by the aftermath that would come if she failed. And if she succeeded.

Santiago flipped on top of him and he seemed to oblige. She pleasured him until finally, he closed his eyes. Santiago was very much aware of her racing heart. She reached over to the top of the bed frame, grabbed hold of the whiskey glass, and smashed it as hard as she could into his head. She sat still, her body failing to move.

He was unconscious.

She looked down at the black curly hair on his chest. Had he always had chest hair of that magnitude? Was she just noticing this now?

She climbed off the bed, still entranced by his motionless body. There was blood around his head, staining the white sheets. Hands shaking at her sides, she finally built up enough courage to turn toward the door. She pulled the heavy handle upward and pushed the steel door open. There in front of her, sat a telephone next to the couch. It was the first time she'd been immersed into the basement without a blindfold on.

Chapter 11

The Call

HIS TRUCK SMELLED like burning oil. Maybe a leak. Tom pulled up to the sidewalk next to the playground by Rocanville Elementary. He sipped his black coffee, the dark and stale flavors pasting to his tongue. He stared at the playground where he had spent many hours with Deanna. He looked at his dashboard clock and decided to give himself twenty minutes before he got back to work.

Tom jumped to the sound of his Motorola 8500X ringing. He ignored the call and reached for a mickey of whiskey from the glove box, but it rang again a second time. He was reluctant, but finally picked up on the fifth ring.

"Tom here."

He could only hear muffled static on the other end as he screwed off the cap of his drink. Just as he was ready to give up on the call, a voice broke through.

"Dad?"

"Who is this?" he spat out, urgency consuming his voice.

He leaned forward with his other finger in his left ear, blocking any potential outside sound. She was trying to reach out to him after all these years. But how would she have tracked down his cell number? They had ads in various papers and were in the yellow pages. She could have found it that way.

A couple words were said, but the static was way to thick for him to make them out.

"Who is this? Hello? Hello?!"

After some more muffled noises, they hung up.

There was hardly enough time for him to comprehend what he had heard. It couldn't have been, could it?

His excitement evaporated and doubt filled the void. He thought of his time spent in a mental institution, St. Vincent.

There were no multiple personalities, no severe hallucinations, no alter ego, no dissociative identity disorder, only a need for alcohol and the obsession to solve his daughter's case. His Doc agreed that he was not experiencing hallucinations in the "traditional" sense, meaning they were not elaborate or widely spread, only seeing her face here and there. That was all. But that didn't mean he wasn't prone to exaggeration, nor did it mean that his alcohol consumption was standard in any way. He drank every day, all day, until it had become his crutch, and without it, he couldn't do his job efficiently. It was a reliance that eventually required him to be hospitalized full time and to be shut out from his world of finding Deanna. His stay there had brought an abrupt halt to his search, and he was dragged in kicking and screaming as one would imagine.

Tom closed his eyes to try and think in a clear linear path, recalling the phone call as objectively as possible. Did he actually hear the word dad?

He checked the number, but it was listed as unknown. He pressed redial and his heart elevated again. After eight rings the call was disconnected without any opportunity to leave a message. *Burner cell phone in a place with poor service? A land-line? The call was so unclear though. Underground with poor connectivity? Maybe a pay phone? Maybe her captor had some way of distorting the line. Why provide the opportunity of access?* Tom felt so helpless in this moment, wanting desperately for it to ring again, but he knew it wouldn't come.

He put his truck in drive and took off down the road before turning onto Main Street.

Tom entered the office looking as though he had seen a ghost. Reggie, usually astute, recognized his friend's distressed face. He ran his hand through his bushy white beard as he examined Tom's disheveled state.

"What's wrong?"

Tom had reservations about going down this road as he knew how Reg would react. It would begin with a definitive doubt about what Tom claimed he had just experienced, along with a non-judgmental concern for his current health status. With no energy for a debate, Tom tip-toed around his partner and friend.

"Nothing is wrong."

Reg didn't press. "They found the new one."

IPD had been on a case and were looking for assistance from Reg. Apparently they didn't need him anymore. "Runaway?"

"Yup."

Tom looked around at the office, his eyes being drawn to Deanna's case room. Tonight he would spend his whole evening there, working an angle on Connor and Leanne, and drinking.

"Go home to your wife," Tom said with a fake smile.

"Nah, I got some things I can still be doing. You know, business development and what not. Someone's gotta push the paperwork around here. God knows it ain't gonna be you."

"No, no. I'm gonna call it too. 'Bout time we had a weekend. You leave the paperwork to me this time."

Reg was skeptical and hesitant to leave, probably realizing that Tom was just getting rid of him to drink.

"You good?" he asked.

"I'm great. Gonna try and catch up on sleep."

"Okay, well, I will get out of your hair then. Leave you to make a mess of this place," said Reg as he grabbed his coat to leave.

Tom's shoulders relaxed slightly. Encouraging Reg on his way out, he added, "Maybe Dorothy will have sex with you tonight."

"Better stop at the pharmacy first."

"Double dose."

"We're the same age as far as I'm concerned," said Reg.

"Whatever you need to tell yourself."

Reg put on his fedora and exited the basement office into the rainy evening. Tom went over to a desk in the far corner that appeared to be unused. He slid open one of the drawers exposing a thirty-year-old bottle of Crown Royal. As he ran his fingers along the ridged outlines of the glass bottle, he thought of his trip to British Columbia with his wife, Allison.

He had proposed there in the mountains, the snow deep and powdered. They hadn't the faintest clue how to ski properly so they just rode the gondola the whole day as she marveled at her engagement ring. They were so happy then. She was so beautiful, her dark eyes, freckled nose, how smart she looked in her glasses. She *was* smart. And the way she used to look at him, it was powerful. Even after they were married, there were still times earlier on when she'd make him feel weak in the knees. And they had made this wondrous and beautiful girl together.

He grabbed a glass out of his other desk and flipped it upside down for a moment, hesitating, his classic tradition. He flipped the glass back over and filled it up. He took a large sip and coughed. There was an old bottle of diet Coke in their mini-fridge that would work. He was breaking rules by mixing a drink that should have been served neat, but Tom didn't feel like sipping tonight. The Coke bottle made no noise when he twisted the cap open, but he used it anyway. After the first hit of rye and Coke, he knew the satisfaction would not end until the bottle was near gone.

He ended up on his ass in the corner of the room with a heap of files on his lap. He lay his eyes to rest and could feel himself slipping into what he hoped would be a vivid dream, when his clunky cell phone rang.

"Who is this?"

Muffled static surged into his ear, much like before. Through the static he heard a very unclear voice that cut through. "Dad?"

She sounded distressed. Clearly she was calling from a place she was not supposed to. Tom's voice was timid and fragile with his response. "Is that you?"

After he heard more static, he pulled out the antenna and rushed over to a computer in the main area of his office. He logged into the Indianapolis Police Department platform-he was a limited access user-and opened a call tracing software within the network.

"Can you hear me?" he asked.

"Yeah, I can hear you."

"Can you tell me where you are?"

The static surged and then settled. "I don't know."

"Do you have time to call another number? I want you to call my land line, okay?"

"Okay."

"It's 317-635-9888. Do you have it? Can you write it down?"

"I've got it." More static.

"Okay, just-" She hung up.

His heart was drowning in stomach acid as he waited.

After typing in three more passwords, a map of the United States appeared, waiting to conduct it's search. Tom placed his hands on the desk in front of his telephone. His entire body was vibrating. The ring made him jump. He picked up.

"Dee?"

"Can you hear me?" "Yeah, yes, I can hear you. Is that you, Deanna?" "I-" Static consumed her voice again.

"I'm having troubles hearing you but please stay on the line. Do you hear me? Whatever you do, do not hang up the phone okay? Stay on the line for me, Dee. It'll tell me where you are. I'm gonna find you. I will come get you."

The static increased. "Are you there?"

The line went dead. He hadn't kept her on long enough to get an exact pinpoint, but his search had narrowed down to the state of Indiana. She wasn't far.

His computer then beeped at him, and he checked his email. A new message from Dean Patterson. He opened it up to find a detailed report with a long list of names, almost all of which were marked NC, non-conviction. He scrolled through all the names to Harrison. There were no records on either of them which he expected. He continued on to the second report that included Jerry Lehman's birth and family records. Both of Jerry's parents were deceased. His father had died first, his mother when he was twenty-two. He found his way into Holy Angels and then went to the University of Indianapolis, earning his major in Religious Studies, his minor in Communications. In his final year of college he had a child with a woman by the name of Paulette Graves, who left shortly after the birth of his daughter. Afterward, Holy Angels still accepted him back and he assumed his position at the church and was later appointed as Minister there. No criminal record on him, of course.

During the search for Jerry's daughter, Tom had spoken briefly with Paulette on the phone, as did Jerry. He had informed Tom that there was zero concern that Paulette would have had anything to do with her disappearance and they paid her no further attention.

Tom fired off another email to Dean asking for any information on Paulette Graves. They had too many theories back then, but she was worth looking into now.

He closed his eyes. He remembered the way the Harrisons looked at him when he came to them with no news, only dead ends. They didn't believe such negative results were possible. Tom was supposed to find their child.

He paced around the room trying to rack his brain for any kind of leads, but there was just nothing there. He could only think about Leanne. The thought of staying in his basement was eating him alive. He had to go see her. He didn't know what he'd say or how he could possibly get through to her for answers, but he had to try.

He waited by the phone all night, but no more calls came in.

• • •

The next morning, Tom drove to Indianapolis. Meridian Street was segregated from the other neighborhoods, wrapped up in their world of luxury. Tom drove by mansion after mansion, passing a security officer who was watching him and his truck with hawk eyes. He pulled up to the Harrison's address, the front steps leading up to a miniature version of the White House. Perhaps an exaggeration, but it was elegantly designed after the Colonial period with modern tweaks. It stood out as old fashioned compared to the other, more contemporary homes.

He could remember the last time he was there. He didn't make it to the long stone steps leading up to the door. He was escorted from the front lawn. Maybe by the same security guy?

He stared out at the house for a while until there was a tap on his window. The neighborhood officer. Tom stepped out of his truck and revealed his PI badge. "Former detective with IPD. I'm here to see Leanne." Former IPD sounded better than private investigator, which could easily be confused for Nancy Drew.

The officer was skeptical. "She's expecting you?"

"Of course. You can escort me to her door if you'd like," he said as sincerely as he could.

"What's this about?"

"Honestly, Officer, the matters are confidential, no outside parties. No disrespect, I must be discreet at this point in time."

He looked at the badge one more time. "Bennett... I've heard of you. You've handled some big cases, haven't you? Collins! That's the one. That was a huge bust. Why'd you go private?"

"Needed a change," he said. "May I carry on officer? Punctuality is a must."

He eyed him up one more time for safe measure. "Yes." He handed him his badge back. "Carry on."

"Thank you."

He headed the opposite direction, but kept a peripheral head tilt, most likely still unsure of Tom's true intentions. So was Tom. He walked over to the door, his nerves hitting him all at once. *Do they have her stowed away somewhere? Were they that vindictive?*

He knocked. Leanne opened. "Bennett." Her eyes were wide, her mouth sunken into a terribly bitter frown. "You kidding me?"

"Leanne, five minutes of your time. Please."

"And why the hell would I grant you five minutes?"

"It's important. A child's life is at stake."

Her eyes narrowed. "Like when my Jared's life was at stake?"

"Please. Leanne. It's-"

"Important? You said that." She looked out at his parked truck then back to him. "I think I'll move forward with that restraining order this time."

"I can't tell you I'm sorry anymore. I'm all out of sorries. I just need your help."

"How could I possibly help you? You're the best." She practically choked on the end of her sentence. "You did nothing. The police. Nothing. While my son lay down his head only God knows where at night. His stomach grumbling. While I was stuck in this damn house." She probably hadn't had a trip down memory lane in some time. "We told you to leave us be."

"It's my daughter."

She looked away at first. "I know. It was your daughter the last time you tried to claw your way into my home." Her eyes softened slightly.

"I did what I could." He barely whispered the words.

"I don't know if that's true. My boy's disappearance didn't keep you from drinking on the job. Your arrogance...we told you. This took everything. All your resources, all your energy. You didn't even give us half your energy. Working other cases at the same time. That wasn't our agreement. Don't try and deny it." She scrunched up her nose in disgust. "Just you and your liquid courage. Well screw you, Bennett. You didn't give a shit about my boy." No doubt her rant had been recycled and revised many times in her mind over the years. The live version probably wasn't as good as she'd wished it'd be, but it still found a sad place within Tom.

She continued, "I'm sorry about your daughter. I really am. You know what it feels like. The horrors of it." Her face was cold and harsh, eye contact moving in and out. After a pause, she slammed the door and Tom threw his arm in the way, blocking it.

"You were friends with Jerry Lehman. Weren't you?"

She turned back and opened the door.

"You went to his church. You stopped. The day he resigned, after his daughter went missing, you left the congregation, didn't you? You were close?" He didn't hide the emotion in his voice, accusation in his question. "Were you close with his daughter?"

She laughed hysterically as it mixed with a strange cry. She exhaled, as if she were about to take ten more deep breaths to calm down. "We had hardly spoken one on one until our boy went missing." Her face cringed in pain. "We needed something," she raised her voice, "It was faith or nothing. He was there for us when the authorities failed us."

"Was there anyone in the congregation troubled enough to take a child? That was connected strongly to Father Lehman. That loved him possibly?"

She shook her head no. "When I heard about his daughter, I tried to tell him not to use you. I told him all about you. And he still trusted you. Now he's dead."

"You spoke about each other's cases?"

She looked just about ready to take a swing at him. "We offered each other sympathies. You know, like people do. Sometimes we send flowers, food, cards."

"I don't think flowers would have made you think any better of me."

"You're right on that one."

Tom had been on the receiving end of blame more than enough, but her words still hit home pretty hard.

"You understand the statistics of these cases. Do you?" Tom asked.

"Yeah. Yeah, I get it." But she didn't. Could he really blame her?

Her watery eyes were ready to spill. A painful silence followed, the memory of their children looming in the front yard behind him. "I don't think there is anyone inside that church that will give you the answers you're looking for. Our children, they're just gone." She vacuumed back her tears. She was most likely well-practiced at this.

"You didn't take my daughter." It was supposed to be a question but came out as a statement, clear as day.

Her head lowered and her body shook. She wept on her front steps.

What was he doing? Accusing this woman of such an unspeakable act, a woman who knew first-hand exactly what he had been going through.

He watched her cry. He could feel the same sobs building in his chest, but forced them down, and stepped in close and held her awkwardly. She was startled at first, but then accepted him, wrapping her arms around. She cried quietly into his chest and then straightened up. His neck was wet with her tears. She started punching at his back, her groans painful and raw. As soon as she started to slow her cries, she pushed him off of her, his back foot tripping up on the top step. He shuffled to his right leg, straining his bad knee.

He was about to leave when she spoke instead of slamming the door like he had expected. "When did she go missing?"

"September 28th, 1979."

She narrowed her eyes, thinking of the day, now over a decade ago. "Hang on."

She went back inside. Last time he was there, Tom got off with a warning from the courts as Leanne tried to push a restraining order on him. He stood on the front step for about five minutes when she returned with an old letter. She handed it over to Tom. It was an old flight itinerary; they flew US Airways to Paris. Round trip September 21st to October 21st.

"Just another thing that we tried. It of course didn't work," referring to her and her husband Connor. "We didn't take your daughter, Bennett. We'd need energy to do something like that. We were dead then. And we're dead now...I can provide you with a list of alibis if that will make you feel better. Both here at home and in Paris."

"Maybe you hired someone," he said with zero conviction.

She closed her eyes. "Just stop. Stop looking. Trust me." She crossed her arms, adjusting her gray cardigan in the process. "Check anything you want. You have my full cooperation. Bank records, call logs, anything. I don't give a shit." She looked up at the ceiling like she was going to sneeze. "Whatever you want, Bennett." Her voice was monotone. "Whatever you need."

"Where is Connor?"

She shook her head at the ground. "Living out of a hotel, but not for long. If you want a look at any of our financial records it'd be best to do it now, before the company dissolves. I can provide you with our personal banking anytime."

"What?"

"We sold. Larger outfit made an offer we couldn't ignore. A perfect divorce gift."

"Oh, I, uh...when?"

"We've been apart for ages. Connor's leaving the country. He thinks it will help. It won't, but I hope it does."

She was about to cry again, but refused it. "So yeah, you let me know what you need. I'm half ownership so, like I said, full cooperation." Her eyes glazed over.

He couldn't look at her. There was nothing left to say. "I'll, uh. I'll let you know. It might not be necessary. Are you in the book?"

She nodded yes. He turned and left for his truck, fighting off his quivering lip.

The officer had walked back around, seeing the commotion on her front step. He looked like an owl, eyes wide, glancing back and forth between Tom getting into his truck and Leanne still watching from her front step. When he drove away, her door was closed.

• • •

When he got home, Tom flopped onto his bed and stared at the ceiling fan as it went round and round. Just like his never-ending search. Only dead ends and others he'd let down.

But this time there was hope. She was alive. *She* had called him. Perhaps Deanna would call again, this time with some answers. His emotional conversation with Leanne had drained everything out of him. Without any aid of sleeping pills, he could feel his heavy eyes close and his mind drift to a place that didn't exist.

PART II

Chapter 12

Resolution

TOM STOOD OUTSIDE of Anna's office, holding two coffees, his hands scalding hot. He had fallen asleep when his head hit the pillow, only to be awakened repeatedly throughout the night. He was exhausted. Working with a clear head was going to require assistance from Anna.

His daughter was still alive and the feeling was so surreal. She was calling him from a phone that her captor was clearly not aware of. The timing of the calls was random, which seemed strange to Tom. Most captors' schedules were consistent, their opportunity to be exposed around the same time of the day or week. He wasn't about to get hung up on that detail though. She was in Indiana somewhere. Alive.

Anna approached and she looked surprised to see him. That surprise was quickly foiled with the probable assumption of him using her for Ativan or Zolpidem.

Anna looked at his coffee cup and smiled, "Six a.m. I'm guessing you are *still* awake."

"Actually got a few hours."

"Good. Just because work doesn't officially start at seven, doesn't mean I'm not billing you for the first hour."

"But I got you coffee." Tom handed her a cup.

She stepped in closer and her brow narrowed from his stench. "Jesus, you smell like a whiskey barrel."

"There's some in your coffee too."

"Better not be."

Tom followed Anna in through the reception area and into her office. Anna stepped around her desk and rolled her slender shoulders back as her pea coat fell off. She was attractive, but he had never looked at her body that way before. Her arms and legs were creamy white with a shine. She took a seat and crossed her legs, her calf muscles long and flexed for a moment.

He followed suit and he could tell she was already examining his blood-shot eyes. She pointed her chin up to assert the beginning of their formal meeting.

"Tom, I want you back on our regular schedule, twice a week."

"Yeah, I agree."

Cat had her tongue for a brief moment. "Thank-you. What brings you by this morning?"

Tom gave her a "you know" look.

"You're seeing her," she said.

"Yes and no."

"What are you seeing?" She leaned forward ready to engage, pen in her grip.

He simply wanted some answers void of fluff pieces. How could he block out the hallucinations and daydreams, reduce the drinking (and manage the cravings that went with it), and get the rest he needed to effectively dive back into the case? Looking at the same information that he had pored over time and time again was hard enough. There was no time for psycho-babble bull-shit, getting him to realize some deeper meaning. He needed the ability to look at old information from a different angle. A fresh mind. A fresh perspective. Sleeping pills would be a good start.

Her tongue touched the corner of her mouth, perhaps a paranoia of some morning peanut butter hanging about. Then a big smile, she almost laughed. Anna's demeanor was normally very rigid. Professional. She spoke with a hint of jubilation. "I'm really glad you're here, taking the initiative, despite your failure to book an appointment." She pursed her lips. "I know this more than likely involves your work and that's okay. I can help you, but you need to share. And I'm gonna keep using clichées until you meet me at least a little closer to the middle."

"The drinking. I need to quit. Or at least dial it back."

"That's good to hear. Can I ask why now?"

She just couldn't accept the good. Of course she needed an explanation. She was the gatekeeper, blocking him from a clear head.

Tom hesitated and she carried on with, "Don't feel like you have to spill everything at once, let's just start with one thing." She held up two fingers indicating not peace, but the second cliché question dropped with a sly grin on her face.

"Well, I wouldn't say I'm hallucinating. It's just."

"You're seeing Deanna?"

"Yeah. Whenever I see a young girl I see her. Like literally, her face. But without looking at a photograph, my mind's eye view of her is, I dunno, different sometimes. Like any blond child could be mixed up as her."

She nodded, understanding. "It's far from uncommon, Tom. More frequently this time?"

"Yeah, but that's not even it. Something just feels different this time."

"Why are you holding back from saying what you need to say?"

Tom laughed through his nose at her third cliché. "Because it sounds crazy. I'm aware of it. But it's just–"

"Crazy. I'll decide that."

"Oh, but it is."

"I've been told I'm a good listener."

"A hundred bucks an hour, you better be."

"One twenty now, actually." Anna leaned back.

Tom noticed her pen and note pad that she usually fiddled with throughout their meetings was placed on her desk out of arms reach.

He looked down at the ground as Anna waited patiently.

"She's been calling me."

"What does she say?"

"Nothing really."

"Then how do you know it's her?"

She had Tom cornered and the thought of saying the word brought forth emotion he'd rather see buried. "Dad. She says Dad. Asking if I'm there."

"And this happened more than once?"

Tom nodded.

Anna continued, "And this feels different because you've never experienced it before or because it feels too real to be a hallucination?"

"Of course it feels real. It *is* real." Tom could feel his voice cracking a little, but his stubbornness was able to override it. He soldiered on. "Trail has been cold for over five years."

"You've put so much on yourself. And what you've done is stacked even more on with your work. Drawing on those same emotions. All the guilt and pressure your feeling is just being magnified by cases at work." Before Tom could object or deflect, she continued. "Do you think you've been effective with your work? Like you're the best version of yourself today, better than your past self?"

Tom paused.

"Not physically of course," she added.

"What does that mean?"

"No offense, Tom. It's an age thing. Physical peak is twenty-eight. Didn't you know that?"

"I'm not as good in the field. But I'm... It's difficult to gauge. Statistically, we're a little behind but close to past years, I guess. The end results vary a lot. A sample space, of say one year, is not near enough. It'd only be worth while comparing decades, five years minimum. But, I would say I'm not far off from my so-called physical prime." Lies. He was a mess.

"Forget the stats. Just your gut instinct. An impulsive answer."

"No." Tom scrubbed his hands together. "Probably not."

"Why do you think that is?"

"Because I've been damaged by personal loss, and the build up of lost cases over the years has taken a toll."

Anna reached for a pen and lobbed it over to Tom. "That was you being an ass, right?" Tom rolled his head to the side and his neck cracked accidentally. Something released making his head feel lighter.

"Don't tell me what you think I'm going to tell you by the end of our session. I just want to have a conversation with you, Tom. I'm not looking to back you into a corner."

He actually felt bad.

"Do you still feel fulfilled by your work?" she asked.

"Someone's gotta do it."

"Does it have to be you?"

Tom replied with a firm, "Yes."

Treading lightly, Anna shifted the conversation. "Okay. Has anything happened on the job lately?"

Did she know about Jessica Hill's case? As much as he disliked her process, he was aware of her talent. She would have made a fine analyst, probably with the FBI. Therapy for the staff, stripping apart suspects, profiling; she would have been good.

The back of Tom's chair was too rigid. She should have more comfortable chairs for her patients.

"I'm sorry. Are you able to talk about it?" Anna asked softly. He hated it when she asked questions with kid gloves on, which was often enough.

"No point in that. These things happen, part of the job."

"It's okay to be upset. Feeling guilty is normal."

A jolt of anger grabbed hold of his words, making them sharp and snappy. "I don't feel guilty."

Anna backed off defensively. "Okay."

"I see what you're doing." Tom's eyes narrowed.

"And what am I doing?"

"Connecting my client's daughter to Dee. Christ, I expected more from you, Doc." He paid no attention to the hurt look on her face as he went off. "There's no hidden version of my past self, no boyhood experiences making me feel the way I feel, no other traumatic experience making me insane, no emotional connection issues from the divorce, no fruity poem, no song, no god damned painting that is gonna help me. So can we just cut to the fucking chase? I just need your help, okay? Is that too much to ask?"

Anna absorbed the outburst. "You find it strange that the phone calls happened right after your case with the young girl, Jessica?"

"How'd you even know about that?"

"You mentioned it briefly last session without saying it. That and I watch the news."

Great.

She followed up. "I know what you're looking for here Tom. A strategy session, not therapy. But in order for one to exist we have to acknowledge the other. We need to find a different way for you to deal with your guilt. If you can-"

He couldn't take it anymore. Like a spillway opening, it came pouring out. "I can't! I lost my girl! I did! I lost her. I don't deserve forgiveness from anyone.

I don't want it." He grabbed hold of his composure and the handles of his chair, lowering his voice now. "This is real. I know it is."

Anna rose from her chair and sat next to Tom. She had never done this before.

"You were a wonderful father. This wasn't your fault. Keep loving her for the nice memories. The drinking, the cases, it's all just noise right now. Noise that's keeping you in one spot. In this terrible place that you can't escape, leaving you so utterly exhausted every waking moment. Time only moves forward." She placed her hand on his wrist. He felt the hair on his wrists fall flat, ironed out by her warmth. "There's no answer. There's nothing I can say in one session that will make this all better. No solution. We make small changes, we discuss, we be human. I'm not looking for a resounding clarity where you break down completely in my office and we build you back up from scratch. That's not how it works. You're an intelligent man. You know that."

Her hand was so soft. He thought of Sissy.

"I don't know what to do," he mumbled.

"If you're able to trust me, and commit to me, we should start from the beginning."

"I trust you are gonna run be bankrupt."

"Quit bitching already. I'm the best shrink in all of Rocanville." Anna's charming smile found a way in. He trusted her and it was horribly annoying.

"You're the only shrink in Rocanville."

"True."

"What would you like me to say?" he asked.

"Tell me about your first incident with your job. The one you had mentioned to me briefly. It's important."

"But you already know what happened."

"Yes. I've read the reports. I want to hear it from you. I want *your* story."

Tom attempted to be as nonchalant as possible. "I was in Indy. Nothing in particular to the case. Just another sleazy older boyfriend taking advantage. We went in, Reg and I." The memory came flooding in for Tom as he told the story to Anna.

Tom had found himself in a residential area not all that different from where he found Jessica Hill. It was possible he had blended the two memories into one horrible blob. He'd walked around back and Reg had gone through the front entrance. As Tom approached the back, he saw a young girl playing with her dog in the neighbors back-yard. They locked eyes briefly and Tom mouthed the words "go inside".

"Reg took the front; I took the back. People we questioned around the neighborhood called him Pitsy. He had a record. Robbery a couple times. One was at gun-point. There was this little girl in the neighbor's backyard. I told her to go inside. She looked a lot like Dee."

After a pause, he said, "I turned back and approached the door, ready for just about the worst on the other side. And then…it happened."

"What happened?" asked Anna.

"I was shot."

Tom remembered the door flying open and Pitsy, early twenties, arm-sleeve tattoos, pointing a gun at him. Pitsy's eyes were filled with surprised fear, a guy with no options. Pitsy fired a shot into Tom's midsection. Even though it was a memory, the pain settled in, the smell of hot lead shifting up to his nose.

Tom had looked him in the eyes for a moment in disbelief. He sprinted passed Tom, leaving him standing in the same spot on the back porch. Tom looked down at his midsection and the blood started to soak through his shirt. The breath in his throat came out shook.

The next thing he'd seen was Reg running toward him, catching him.

"It's a surreal thing. Being shot. I had been in so many of those situations before. But taking a bullet is strange. The heart, it stops. It sinks."

He remembered looking over to his right as Reg tried to check the wound. He'd watched the little girl run back into her house and the dog followed.

"The girl. She saw it happen I'm sure. I watched her run back inside. I remember hoping she didn't see the blood."

Tom collapsed to his knees and Reg caught him.

Tom was still trapped in the memory as Anna's voice softly broke through. "What were you feeling in that moment?"

"I was feeling like I was going to die. Like I was trying to fight off this calmness." He wasn't scared saying it out loud.

"What else?" she persisted.

You know what else, Doc.

"Tom."

Tom's chest was tied in wretched knots and his throat tightened up. "Dee," he said.

"What about her?"

"I was worried about her getting home from school. I was supposed to pick her up. Allison was out of town then. How was she gonna get home?" He lowered his head. "I was supposed to pick her up."

Anna, still sitting next to him, inched a little closer and rubbed his back with soft strokes. He couldn't let himself crack. He sucked back the tears so hard his back ached.

"If it's possible, I'd like to take the first slot of your day. Do you still need me twice a week?" he asked, on the verge of babbling like a child.

"Of course. I was gonna kick you out anyway."

He laughed. "I feel so used, Doc."

"You go get more than three hours of sleep, please and thank-you. I read somewhere that some people get as much as eight hours in a night."

"No promises." He breathed in one more time before rising to his feet. In his breath he caught a scent from her hair. Coconut.

He forgot to ask about the sleeping the pills.

• • •

Tom walked into his basement office feeling uplifted, almost good? He expected the sensation to be short-lived.

Reg was in the middle of sorting some case files when he realized Tom was standing in the entrance.

"I was beginning to think I owned this well-established firm."

"Not my fault your old ass is up at four thirty every day."

"Early bird, rook."

"Since you got things under control, you mind covering for the morning?"

"Sure, kid. What you got going on?"

"Found some new energy. I'm gonna go for a run."

"You're gonna run? Like jog?"

"Yeah, jog."

Tom grabbed his cassette player and untangled the cord for the headphones.

"That's cheating you know. Listening to old Merle is a cheat. Aids the mind."

Tom laughed out loud. The feeling stacked onto his already freed state of mind was almost more than he could take. His body shivered with uplifting excitement.

"Merle Haggard?"

"Yup."

Tom glanced briefly at his old casing room and quickly averted his eyes, focusing back on Reg.

"Well, all right old timer. Don't light the place on fire while I'm gone."

"Thought we covered the whole old thing. Come over here and say it to my face."

Tom exited.

Each heavy stride increased the burning wheeze in his lungs, the sharp pain in his side, his heart hating him for doing such a cruel and foolish thing. Although he wasn't particularly fat or soft, his cardio had been ignored for far too long. As the whiskey sweat beaded down his face, he found himself running out of steam at

Allison's new place. An idea slapped him in the face and he turned around and ran back, halfway to his house, before having to stop and walk the rest of the way. He hopped into his truck and made a quick trip to the local sporting goods store and purchased an metal baseball bat for Allison's son, Johnny. It was an Easton, a -9 bat that Tom could hardly feel in his big hands.

Tom returned to Allison's, parked, and walked up to the front door. The truth of it all was he missed her, not purely in a romantic way, but just being around her, the way it used to be. He remembered her smile, the way her eyes lifted with delight. It was often more of a laughing smile, as the two went hand in hand.

He stood at the door, staring holes through it. A troubling memory hijacked his mind in the midst of his search for some form of redemptive happiness.

After Deanna had been taken, Allison had done some heavy convincing with Reg, urging him to sell their business. A horrible fight ensued afterward and he remembered seeing her in Deanna's old room. The door was cracked and he peered through. Allison curled in the fetal position holding on tight to her daughter's teddy bear as she sobbed. She had always pushed for him to grieve and find a way to move on, and he resented her for that. But in that moment, it had dawned on him, she would always be messed up, just as he was.

Tom knocked on Allison's door. She answered and her original reaction was that of nervousness, clearly not in the mood to deal with a suspected drunk Tom.

Tom started, "Hi. Sorry."

"What's up?" She looked down at the baseball bat.

"Just figured I'd stop in and say hi. Been a while," he answered casually. "Figured Johnny could use a twig if he doesn't already have one of his own."

"Wow. He will love this. They just have the team supplied bats right now." She smiled uncomfortably. "Yeah um, come in. Good to see you." And just in the nick of time, her new husband, Derek, walked out.

"Oh, Tom. Good to see you. How are you?"

"Good. Shit, I got you guys at lunch I bet."

"That's okay. You should join."

"No, no. Thanks though. I was just uh...I got something I wanted to talk to Al about."

"Say no more. I'll be in the kitchen." Derek left.

"He's such a nice guy. Always hated that."

"I know. Everything all right?"

"Yeah, yeah I think so. Anna has me working on some things and, uh..." Tom floundered.

"Oh." She was caught off guard. "I didn't know you had been seeing Anna. What is it?"

"I just wanted to say that I appreciate how you have been toward me since the divorce." Tom sighed, building up the courage to continue on.

Allison shuffled slightly toward the wall, shocked. "Of course, Tom-"

"I haven't been doing overly well. Things had been getting worse and I-"

Tom was hit with an odd faint feeling. This was not from nerves, but something else. Black spots began taking over his vision one by one. A wave of nausea grabbed hold, followed by a sharp pain, like a cork screw twisting in his side.

He tried to continue past it. "I just wanted to say-"

The pain increased, flaring in his back, hot like coals. His vision became completely compromised and he collapsed to the floor. He threw up violently, feeling the tenderness of his rib cage from his last purging session. Allison dropped to the floor with him. "Tom, are you okay? Shit."

The pain increased, his mind begging to power down.

"Derek!" she yelled. Tom felt her hands on his shoulders as everything went black.

• • •

Tom sat in the driver's seat of his truck. In the back seat sat little Deanna. He was confused by the vividness of the dream. *What just happened?* One look at her smile and he didn't care anymore. She reached out to grab his nose and he growled, "Hey" and fake snapped at her. She giggled.

Suddenly a man reached through his unrolled window and rammed a cloth forcefully to his mouth until he drifted off, his daughter screaming in the background.

In a disjointed continuation of his dream state, Tom was suddenly positioned in his old case office from the basement, plucked and placed there. Tom stood in the suspect room. The walls were completely covered with papers. A never ending collection of suspects, case files, time lines, connections, were plastered all over the walls.

Deanna appeared behind him and pointed at the wall of unorganized papers.

A dark figure then appeared beside her and held her hand. She was unafraid, accepting the strangers hand without any resistance. She pointed at the wall again. The room started to shake like an earthquake as papers flew off the walls. Finally, the shaking came to a stop and Deanna and the dark figure disappeared.

Tom turned back to the wall to find two names that were all too familiar: HANK COLLINS and his son ABE COLLINS.

• • •

Tom awoke in the hospital, feeling like he had just drunk an entire bottle. He shifted in his bed and felt a tug. He turned to find Derek staring back at him.

"There is a tube in my penis."

"Unpleasant I'm sure."

"Quite."

"You feeling okay?"

"I'll be fine."

Tom peered through the window and could see Allison speaking with the doctor. Anticipation of bad news would have been welcomed not long ago, but now it was different. There was reason to stay alive. *Find her.*

• • •

Allison listened intently to the doctor. She was short and stout, long black hair down to her butt. She looked like a beautiful Oompa Loompa.

The doctor spoke first. "His health is not good. He has pneumonia right now, which was the reason for his collapse and high fever. His immune system is in a poor state due to his drinking. His liver has significant scarring and will proceed to cirrhosis if he continues at this pace."

"Okay."

"We will get him on antibiotics and with lots of rest and fluids, he will be fine. For the short term. But he needs to cut out alcohol and improve his diet. You had said the drinking has gone on for about ten years?"

"Yes." You have no idea, she thought.

"I'm sorry. His liver is in a state that compares closer to fifteen to twenty years of alcoholism. A drastic change in your husbands lifestyle is required, without question. At this stage, he cannot give it up all at once. That would be incredibly dangerous. He needs to ween himself off slowly. I've prepared a one year plan for him. Just follow along the calendar, monitor his consumption. His daily intakes are all listed out." She handed over a little notebook. Her other hand had a stack of brochures that Allison had seen before.

Allison hadn't corrected the doctor, calling Tom her husband.

The doctor handed her the brochures. One was an AA brochure, the other one on liver disease. "He's gotta find a way. Through what channel, that's up to you two. Here are some options that would help if he's willing," she said. "There are also programs for him.

Facilities that will help wean him off. I recommend this strategy over doing it on his own. I just want to emphasize that he can't quit cold turkey. Quite literally it could kill him."

"Thank-you doctor." She took a moment before entering the room, willing herself to face stubborn Tom. The moment expired and she walked in.

"Thanks for bringing me in," he said.

"Well, we weren't gonna leave you laying in a pool of vomit."

A silence consumed the room as she stared daggers through Tom.

"What did the doctor say?"

"You have pneumonia. Antibiotics and rest and you'll be fine. But-"

"The drinking."

"It has to stop."

"I know."

"No Tom. It has to."

Chapter 13

Collins

THE SMELL OF FRESH AIR was much more inviting than the array of sanitizing odors he had inhaled in the hospital. The cool air revived him, taking off the edge of his headache that had formed upon his catheter removal. He climbed inside his truck and was immediately greeted by his cell phone ringing.

"Hello."

There was a familiar sound of crackling static on the other end.

He waited. "Deanna, is that you?"

"Dad?" The sound was so clear.

It was her, no question. He just wanted to be there with her. To carry her out of whatever dark hole she was trapped in.

She spoke again, sounding panicked. "It's-it's me. I need help. Please."

"It's going to be okay. I'll find you. Just say your name."

"I-" she cut out slightly. "need your help."

"Can you tell me where are you?"

"I don't know," she replied, sounding shaken.

"Are you hurt?" There was a noise-free pause. "Please tell me something."

He could hear crying through the distorted noises. It killed him.

"This isn't working-" Static. "I-you need to-" The distorted sounds blared through his phone like a snow storm.

"Are you okay? Are you hurt? Deanna!"

The line went dead. "Wait! Wait!"

He hit the gas and spun out of the hospital parking lot.

• • •

Tom entered Deanna's old case room and immediately started ripping papers off the walls. He stripped it all down until there was nothing left but Hank and Abe Collins. He wasn't much for superstition or destiny but…it had to be a sign, right?

He reeled himself in, only to remember how Leanne looked on her doorstep, the drained look in her eyes; he had to put Connor and Leanne Harrison aside as suspects, for now at least. She had said he could look into them for everything. Alibis, financial records, phone calls, everything. She had nothing to hide. Normally, he'd be more cautious, not at all dismissive. But this was different. There was just nothing there any more. Only a mother tired of hurting.

Tom had to re-focus on the Collins men. Both were criminals void of conscience.

Hank Collins was as ruthless as they came. Years back, while Tom was still with IPD, Hank took a step forward in the drug world. His gang was smaller than its rivals, yet they managed to solidify more jobs than the rest. They pushed more product and killed more people, were more discreet, organized, and feared by other drug syndicates. There was no myth like he was Keyser Soze, rather the truth that they were a well-oiled operation that you didn't cross. If you were lucky, you joined them, or partnered with them. And they had been growing in numbers, slowly but steady.

There was a chemist that went unnamed so they called him "Cook". Subtle enough. DEA had been pursuing for a couple years, but were unable to locate him. He had been circulating an enhanced form of heroin through a random string of questionable drug research facilities across five states that they knew about. The product was sparsely moved in small quantities and any leads only ever had enough weight to carry the DEA toward distributors, never to the source. That was where Tom got involved with IPD, as more of a foot soldier, but was still involved nonetheless.

The drug itself was able to administer a longer sensation or "rush" with reduced times of "nodding." It had properties that made it less addictive physically and registered fewer and less harsh symptoms in the aftermath. The IPD wondered why they would create a drug that was less addictive and pump such small quantities into the system. It soon became clear to Tom and the DEA that this was a long-term play. After all, just because it wasn't more physically addictive, didn't mean people wouldn't want more. The plan was for the drug to become mainstream and Collins and his troops would be at the top of the pyramid controlling the limited supply.

As crude as Hank Collins was, he was no fool. Every action made was for the sake of business, and if his murderous cravings were satisfied in the process, then so be it. He had been looking for a right hand man, hopefully taking over a large portion of day-to-day operations. There were a few respectable suitors for the position already within the crew, but they didn't have the business sense he required. His men were loyal and well trained, but there was nobody he trusted with running it the way he did. Dean, Tom's former partner in the IPD, had been working undercover with Collins when they realized he was connected to the new chemist. With no signs of getting any closer to the Cook, IPD wanted to take Collins's operation down. Yes, the Cook would find his or her way to the next bidder or vanish, but they couldn't miss the opportunity on Collins's operation. It was going to be a huge bust for the DEA and also the IPD.

Looking at a photo of Hank, Tom thought of that night.

• • •

1972.

Terravin Pharmaceuticals. Red cherries lit up the night outside the small facility. Tom moved down a long dimly lit hallway, gun cocked and ready. He could hear gunfire in the not-so-far distance, on the same floor. *Dean.* He picked up his pace, moving toward the sound of a gunshot, but was blindsided from a room to his left. A well dressed bearded thug fired a round just as Tom spotted him in his peripherals. The shot barely missed and Tom dropped to the floor, firing a shot into the thug's leg, then head, leaving a gaping hole and a Jackson Pollock on the wall behind.

He moved back down the hallway, eyes glued open, no blinking permitted. He turned the corner with his gun raised but found no one, the sound of footsteps no longer present. Tom changed directions and the smell of shit hit his nose. Preparing himself for a dead body, he turned into the room to his right and kicked the door open to find two more suited goons. The one had soiled himself upon death, the smell mixing with coppery blood. The other lay upright against a counter, his hands folded over his stomach, his eyes rolled to the side.

Tom continued down the hall and heard two more gunshots fire off. He picked up his pace again. He felt fluid and responsive, yet rigidly calculated, almost mechanical. He would never voice such a thing, but he lived for these situations. He felt like a soldier and at large, he was one. Tonight was the night he would take out the Collins clan.

Tom heard another gun-shot and then conversation between two men, followed by a laugh and a "shut the fuck up." One deep exhale and Tom turned the corner to find Dean leaning up against the far wall, and at the end of the hall, Abe and Hank discussing a plan to escape. "Put one in his head, we'll find a way out," said Abe.

Hank shook his head. "How we gonna get out, you dimwit? We need to use him. I'll take the roof, scope for any positioned snipers, you take this nigger out the front doors. See them make a move on us then. There's a parking lot east of the building, only a few steps over. Pick a car. When you're close I'll open fire on those pigs for distraction. You hightail it outta hear to our safe house. They won't open fire on you with the pig to your hip."

"What about you?" Abe replied.

"Don't worry about me."

"I'm not leaving you behind, pops. No way."

"Listen to me-" As Hank protested, the sound of gunfire opened up and didn't stop outside the building. Men shouted out orders as the gunfire continued to snap off into the night. Meanwhile, Tom had been inching closer down the open hall, each step lighter than the previous, the Collins men still with their backs turned as their ears perked up.

"Reinforcements pops." He slapped his dad in the shoulder. "I told you."

"How in the hell did they know? I didn't tell them about this."

"That's family."

They shared a glance without exchanging words, Hank clearly agreeing with murdering Dean who sat defenseless and bloodied. Abe raised his pistol and Tom broke into a sprint right at them, "No!" They both turned and Hank fired off two shots, the first one missing Tom, the second hitting him in the leg, but he hobbled through it, gun raised. The bone in his leg was hot with lead. Tom fired off a shot hitting Abe in the arm, his gun dropping to the floor. The hallway echoed with the shot, the walls amplifying its harsh volume, cracking ear-drums. Hank and Tom exchanged shots, both ducking as if to be quicker than the bullets. He could see Hank's gun was no longer responsive, out of ammunition. Tom caught him flush with a bullet in the shoulder, but it hardly knocked him back as he was now barreling down on Tom, knocking the gun from his hand. He hadn't realized at first, but Hank had a knife.

Dean had shuffled to the gun and, *POP*. He put one in Abe's leg and he howled in pain. They were going to prison, not a morgue. That was the plan anyway.

Tom dodged a knife jab and booted Hank in his right knee, folding him like a cheap tent. Hank swiped at his leg with the blade, catching him pretty good, giving him enough time to rise back to his feet. They exchanged punches back and forth until Hank made another attempt with the knife at Tom's throat, but he quickly grabbed hold of Hank's wrists.

The knife neared Tom's face and he grit his teeth, arms burning from holding off the brute force and determination of Collins. The blade neared his eye.

His arms were on fire, shaking as he felt the knife inch toward his eye. Clenching every muscle in his body, he altered the direction of the blade to his shoulder. Tom let go and the knife plunged into him. He grit his teeth and head butted Hank as hard as he could, sending him staggering back a full step. Ignoring the pain shooting through his body, Tom ripped out the knife and stabbed Hank in the midsection, dropping him to his knees. Then a punch to the jaw, a crack sounding off of Tom's thickly padded knuckles. It was over.

Both he and Dean were now armed, the other two disarmed. He rushed over to Dean and helped him up.

Hank's entry wound was off-centered, left of his belly button, blood still spilling like cold motor oil. He pulled out his phone and told the rest of the crew to send an ambulance inside. The gunfire had ceased outside and Tom prayed that they had numbers. Their SWAT team was limited and had taken the other side of the building while he and Dean took the other. If they hadn't won the battle outside they were sitting ducks. Tom and Dean were too banged up to meet a second wave of thugs coming in. He called another one of his contacts, who answered quickly. "It's clear now. We're sending paramedics in."

It looked like a war zone outside. There were officers being loaded into ambulances, some that were clearly dead. Tom's heart sunk at the scene of blood and red lights. He didn't let the paramedic work on him very long. The cut in his leg would have to wait for stitches, as would his shoulder. He walked toward his car in the midst of all the chaos and lights. Hank, his stomach all bandaged up, was being escorted to an ambulance by his car. Tom intercepted to get the last word.

They stood eye-to-eye and Hank spit in his face. "Already dead."

Tom wiped away the spit. "You killed an innocent kid." A young man the DEA had their hands on, getting them information that Dean wasn't able to. Once the Collins men were taken out, he would've gotten a fresh start under protective.

Hank scoffed. "That was no kid. He was a wasted resource that had to be put down." He shifted his hands in his cuffs and tried to stand tall, despite his terrible stomach wound. "Would you like me to lose sleep over that one?"

Tom wanted nothing more than to put a gun to his head and pull the trigger. "His mother was in the house."

"Bitch would be dead if I knew that. But I don't gotta tell you about dead. How's that daughter of yours doing?"

Hank flashed a crooked smile, his teeth a shade of yellow, the blue and red lights lighting up his bald head and bearded face. Tom clocked him with a right hook as hard as he could, wincing from the knife wound in his shoulder. Hank fell up against the car and Tom hit him twice more. Fighting free from two officers attempting to restrain him, he got in one last shot, splitting him above the eye. The officers pulled him away from Tom.

In the distance, Hank's son Abe, watched in cuffs.

Chapter 14

May, 1979

Five months before Deanna's kidnapping.

ALLISON WAS DRIVING, halfway home from Indianapolis. A quick day trip for shopping. She checked the rear view mirror to see if Deanna was asleep in her booster seat. Her eyes were growing heavy as she stared out the window, making a smacking sound with her lips, her chubby cheek protruding. Bored, Allison wanted to make conversation with her girl, but it was best if she fell asleep in the car first. Transporting her from the car to her bed was always an easy task; she'd never stir. Allison joined Deanna with a quick glance out at the fields to her right. Seeding was well under way. After a two day delay from rain, the farmers were back out with the drills. The smell of the soil mixed with diesel fuel reminded her of playing outside for hours on end during the summer days when she was a child, and eating hot dogs at the local summer festival. The only thing missing was the smell of manure.

She kept her eyes on the road for a while then back to Dee. She was out cold, looking so damn cute with those cheeks. Back to the fields, farmers sat on the tailgates of their trucks, enjoying a home cooked meal. They kissed their wives and mothers on the cheeks in the midst of mouthfuls of food. Her heart was full, but her stomach let her know that it was not, grumbling unimpressed.

• • •

She fumbled for her keys at the door with Deanna slung over her shoulder, limp arms draped around her neck. She placed Deanna in bed. Dee immediately rolled onto her belly and straddled the pillow, drawing a big smile from Allison. "Sleep tight, stinky."

She walked back out into the kitchen, all the lights still off as she opened the fridge to see if there were any leftovers. Shake and bake chicken, mashed potatoes, and cream corn. It would be devoured. *Too bad, Tom.* He was working late again, or was at the bar, which as of late he'd pass off as "work". The drinking had always been casual and seldom, but lately was becoming a little too frequent for her liking. A conversation needed to be had, but he'd just play it off as no big deal. Best put a pin in it before it *is* a big deal, if it wasn't already, she thought.

She closed the fridge and set the plate on the counter to flick the light on. She turned to grab a glass from the cupboard and saw something in the corner of her eye. There was a man in the entrance. She screamed, then told herself it was just Tom who had startled her, but it wasn't Tom. He wore a black ski mask.

Allison froze and he just stared at her with hands at his side, his beady dark eyes blending with the mask.

The phone next to her would be dispensed with quickly if she made a move for it. She wanted to protect her daughter in some way, but it was probably best to pretend there was no daughter to speak of. Maybe he didn't know. *Please God, I hope my scream didn't wake her.*

She backed up to the fridge. "What do you want?"

He didn't say a word, his face resting in the same position, his dark eyes locked in on her.

"My husband is a cop."

Again, not a word.

"What do you want?" Allison looked to her right at the knife block.

"Come with me, please." His voice was deep and rich.

"So you know my husband. Did he arrest someone you know or something?"

"Something."

She remained silent, ready to pounce on the knife.

"I need you to come with me. Transportation is out back."

Just go with him. Dee will be safe then. "Fine."

At the worst possible time, Deanna started to fuss from her room. "Mum, mum, mum!"

Allison thought she might pass out, but maternal instincts kicked into overdrive. He didn't flinch from the sound of her girl crying out for her. His eyes flicked over down the hall, then back.

Allison lunged for the knife block, but he was all over her, his strong hands gripped tightly around her wrists. She screamed, and he punched her in the face, sending her to the floor. Her nose felt broken, eyes clouded with tears, the taste of blood on her tongue.

She popped up quickly, guarding the hallway, and took a swing that he easily dodged. His hands then wrapped around her throat.

"I only need you."

Allison could hear Deanna crying from her room again. "Mum?" His grip was getting tighter. She was about to submit and agree to leave when she spotted another man enter with a gun. It was Reg. He placed the tip of the gun to the back of the man's head, and Allison crashed to the floor gasping for breath.

Reg spoke. "Move and you're dead before you hit the ground."

The intruder cowered down to his stomach, hands behind his head, his eyes glaring at Allison. She booted him as hard as she could between the eyes.

Chapter 15

Visitor

INDIANAPOLIS STATE PENITENTIARY didn't look much different, its old and crumbling facade, fence, and wire, all beaten down and ready to cave in on itself. A nervous energy stirred within Tom. He cursed himself for being weak.

A man cutting a small patch of grass outside the gate had stopped and looked Tom up and down. Tom nodded hi and so did the old man. Since being out of the hospital, Tom hadn't found consistent sleep. He was only able to muster an hour at a time, which even then he questioned how much of it was actually sleep. The dreams of his daughter hadn't ceased, if anything they'd escalated with greater torment. And the lessened drinking was making him feel sick.

After the arrest and demise of the Collins enterprise, there had been remaining foot soldiers outside prison walls, following commands from Hank. Tom and Dean each faced some dangerous moments, forcing both of them to distance themselves from their families. The attempt to kidnap Allison had been rather destructive to their family. What they would have wanted if they had succeeded in taking her, he didn't know for sure. A few possibilities were likely: his life, money, leverage to provide them assistance with their illegal activities. Probably one of the latter two before they'd circle back around to killing Tom. He would have gladly exchanged his life for Allison's if it had come down to it.

The man that tried to kidnap Allison went by Tyson Davies. Through interrogations he remained absolutely silent with his lawyer at his side. Not a word was spoken. He plead guilty for attempted kidnapping and served five years when in reality, with some cooperation, could have done much less time. After all, he had been unarmed. There was a getaway vehicle that Reg spotted, but it had taken off when he approached the house. After Davies release, he disappeared into thin air. It should have never happened, but it did. It seemed odd that Collins would have gone to such lengths and spent considerable resources to make a pawn in his arsenal disappear. Unless, they figured he talked and took care of him the way criminals do.

That harrowing night showed Tom that his family wasn't safe. Allison had done a tremendous job shielding Deanna from the intrusion, but it came at a price. Allison struggled with her day-to-day from then on, her paranoia making life difficult. Tom did his best to console her, but she was always scared, understandably, unable to shake the feeling.

Tom had joined Reg to help keep an eye on Dean's family as well. Allison and Deanna were sent to her sister's in St. Louis and kept under protective custody while Tom tried to sort out the mess of sloppy seconds that Collins sent after him. They ended up arresting four fairly large players that had been living underground since the bust.

Tom had looked at every old case that ever involved Collins and could not make any connection to what he might have done with his daughter and what he would be planning. He'd interrogated every imprisoned member of his organization and nobody had any information for him, nor would they tell him if they did, even when offered a reduced sentence and cozy set-ups.

Tom looked up at the crudely faded walls, following a stain that led into an air vent. He was feeling a strange dissonance, fear two-stepping with courage as he envisioned his daughter in peril.

He sat on one side of the glass, waiting to speak with Hank. Finally, he walked through the door in cuffs, being escorted by a guard, Tom's old friend Smitty. As soon as Hank lay eyes on Tom he turned around and exited. Smitty grabbed hold of him and Hank whispered something in his ear and left.

After escorting Hank back to his cell, Smitty came back through the door to chat with Tom.

"How you doing, Tom?"

"It's good to see you. It's been too long."

"Maybe answer one of my calls then." He eased the tension with a smirk.

"I know, it's been...busy."

"Didn't notice your name in the log book this morning. Why you mixing it up with Collins?"

"Something came up."

"Something came up, eh?"

"I have to talk to him."

Much like everyone else in his life, Smitty looked annoyingly concerned. "I don't know if that's such a good idea. You really think you should be giving this guy any reminders?"

"He's tried before. Didn't work out so good for him."

"And you wanna have to worry about that shit again?"

"I don't have a choice. Not like seeing me face-to-face will change whatever he has planned."

"What's this about?"

"It's important."

Smitty exhaled. "And you need a receptive two-way conversation?"

"I need information."

"Yeah, okay. It's good to see you, man."

"You too."

Ten minutes later, Smitty opened the door, and with his tail between his legs, Hank walked up and sat down across from Tom. He was favoring his right hand, perhaps an injury recently sustained. A scuff on his neck was surrounded by a deep red mark. If Tom looked close enough he could see boot marks, or so he assumed. Hank picked up the phone, his face stone-like.

Tom led with, "You and I have had this conversation once before."

"Your precious Deanna." His voice was smoky and hoarse. "She still away on vacation?"

Tom imagined cracking his face open with brass knuckles.

Hank's voice dropped into a deeper, gruffer form. "You took my boy from me."

"Did your men take my girl?"

"You're all the same, you pigs…pride. You wear it on your sleeve, you feel the need to show it off, but it doesn't mean anything."

"Just answer the question."

"You think I'm finished with you? I'm coming the fuck after you."

"Did you take my girl?" Tom said, feeling a storm coming. Hank laughed.

"Did you take my girl!?" Tom shouted, and he rose to his feet, his chair scooting behind him. Hank was quick to respond. "We don't take no girls! We got code, you scum fuck. Stealin' little girls ain't what we do. What's the matter with you? If you are digging at me as your number one, God help you, brother."

Tom's fury subsided as he searched for the truth on Hank's face.

"It's actually good seeing you. Seems to be sparking some creative thinking. You best be keeping your head up, Bennett."

"It's up."

"Hell's just starting to heat up again, haven't you heard?"

"Yeah. And they don't answer to you no more. Haven't *you* heard? Yeah, your boys. Chico, Harley, Ferny. All gone. Just bars for them. Keep my head up?" Tom looked to the left of Hank, another inmate on the phone, his eyes fixated on their boisterous conversation.

He refocused on Hank. "Looks like you've been treated to some meal privileges, Hank."

Hank flashed his teeth and scrunched his nose humorously. He was calm now. "There's more of us. There's always more. We don't die, Detective. All you did was force an evolution. A wake up call for a slightly complacent business. Success for too long pulls blinders over the eyes. I'll admit to my errors. I deserved what I had coming." He pointed the phone at Tom and waved it around, then pressed it back against his ear. "I just hope we get to you first. I'd hate to miss out on ripping your teeth out."

Tom narrowed his brow, intrigued by his last comment. "Who would get there before you?"

Hank adjusted in his seat and released a short chuckle from deep within his fat belly. Tom pressed on, "What'd you mean by that?"

"You really aren't on your game anymore, are you?" Hank was amused.

"Who's after me?"

For not agreeing to a discussion at first, old Hank was sure enjoying himself now. "Fun to see you squirm."

"Do I need to remind you what my friend can do for you inside?" Hank's grin turned bitter.

"You really wanna put that kind of pressure on a guard? You sure he's a friend? 'Cause I got a few of those in here."

"He's a big boy."

"Physical pain can always be tolerated," Hank replied with distaste. "All I know is you had a tail.

Someone's been watching you," he said. "You're a popular man."

"When?"

Hank's stare was still angered, his eyes attempting to pierce a hole through Tom's forehead. "Oh, I don't know, Detective. Maybe around the time you killed my brothers and got my kid locked up."

"What'd they look like?"

"I don't know. There was two of 'em. One skinny like a rat. I tell you what though. They finish you off before I do, I'm gonna do some bad things to them."

"That right?"

"You can count on it."

"These two guys. For how long?"

Hank lay his head back and exhaled. "Hard to say. Year maybe."

"And what are you watching me for now? You know you can always just call me if you're feeling lonely," said Tom.

"I would. But it's this damn glass between us. I want to feel your touch, Bennett."

"Oh, you can feel my touch anytime you like."

He chuckled and clapped his hands together. "I miss this."

"You don't have any action on me. Why even bother with the bull-shit at this point?" asked Tom. Hank belched into the phone and scratched his beard with a fist.

Tom looked around the room, the other inmates chatting to loved ones with slouched shoulders. He continued, "I didn't target your boy to dangle him out in front of you. You were both scooped up in the same sting. When you're ready to do business with me again, you just let me know. But right now, I just need to find my girl."

"So? You were looking for her the last time you sat in that chair."

"This tail. Just before you got in here?"

"As I said, 'bout a year. The skinny bitch and the muscle."

"Not before then?"

"Not them," said Hank.

"What does that mean?"

"It means, genius, that you've always had outside interest. And no, I don't know who it was or if they have your kid. Jesus, Bennett, I don't know why, but I just feel like being honest with you. It's your charm, I think. I feel like our romance is back. Can you feel it?" He licked his lips, a half-grunted laugh escaping, shaking the tips of his silvered beard.

"Yeah, I feel it." Tom rose and sat back down. "This code of yours. Prohibiting you from kidnapping little girls. Is that something Abe would follow?"

"Your head would have been on a spike if Abe had something to do with it…he's an honorable man though." Hank didn't hide his fatherly pride for his son.

"Honor…you must use an alternative to Webster's dictionary."

"You'll see. Soon enough."

"If I recall, your sentences were like father, like son. Got another dozen or so laps left."

He smirked. "You really aren't in any sort of pig-loop anymore, are you?"

Tom straightened in his chair, ready for unpleasant news. "There was no deal for him to make. There's no way he'd be getting out."

"You suck at this. Breaks my heart, actually."

"There's no way he'd give up the Cook. He'll be dead as soon as he steps outside that fence."

"You think I'd lie about having an army still? You insult me far too much. Patience is a valuable thing. You wouldn't know much about that." He sniffed in some phlegm and horked up and swallowed it down. "Whether you like it or not, there is a storm coming. This war is inevitable."

Tom got up from his chair, his legs shaky, knees desperate to buckle.

He walked away and Hank slammed the glass with his hands and yelled something that Tom couldn't make out. He didn't care. *Bring on a war if you want.*

But that was adrenaline talking. Tom didn't have his edge anymore. It was gone. And being hunted wouldn't exactly make things easier moving forward.

Tom walked back to the same position outside the gate and the old man was still cutting the grass out front. He stopped and turned off the machine this time and simply stared at Tom.

"Nice day," Tom said.

"Mmhm. Sure is, ain't it. You visiting?"

"Yeah."

"Haven't see you around before. Must not be no regular visits."

"No, sir. Not too fond of the place."

"People in it aren't so great either. I supposed that ain't entirely fair. Some are okay."

"Yeah, well. I don't plan on coming back anytime soon."

"Shame. Thought you'd offer to buy me a cold beer, maybe."

The creases around his eyes were deep.

"Maybe next time. I got something I need to do first."

"Looks as though you've been doing that something for quite sometime. Best finish it soon. Big rain coming, better have an umbrella with you while you working."

"Let's take a *rain* check on that beer, yeah?"

"I'll be here. Holding you to it."

Tom walked to his car and opened his glove box, a mickey of whiskey sitting there waiting. Just a nip. Doctor's orders.

• • •

The wall of suspects stared back at Tom. He took down the pictures of Hank and Abe Collins and crumpled them up in his fist, dropping them to the floor. In his other hand was a bottle of whiskey. Since the hospital he had felt, achy, shaky, and agitated from his withdrawal. Now, after getting a strong dose of his medicine, he could function properly again.

Could Abe have been involved? There were more men on the outside. Much more, according to Hank. I need confirmation on Abe's supposed release first. How long had this been in the making?

Though it was counter-productive, Tom wanted some coffee so he went into the main office and poured himself a cup from the old rusty pot. He walked back into his case room with his coffee, his mind adrift, and Reg approached stealthily from behind.

"Jesus." Tom jumped.

"Sorry. What're you doing in here?"

"Oh just…" Tom looked at the bottle of whiskey. "Working."

He saw Reg's eyes lock in on the bottle, unwavering.

"Care to join?" Tom asked.

"I would but my wife is waiting for me at home. Dorothy doesn't like it when I'm late, you know that. Just wanted to stop in and see how you were doing. I was hoping I'd find this basement empty." Reg put his fedora back on and continued, "Do me a favor and take it easy will ya?"

"Don't worry."

"You make that hard sometimes."

"Get your ass home."

"I'll see you tomorrow then."

"Yup."

Reg left, leaving Tom alone the way he liked it. He sipped his coffee frustratingly, trying to get a handle on who had been watching him. *Would Abe conduct such a move without letting his father know? And why have me followed before hand, playing the waiting game? Why not just pounce once he was out of prison?*

Holding his daughter for ten years without a word just didn't seem right for the Collins playbook.

Chapter 16

Escape

THE PHONE WAS SITTING right there, ready for Santiago to grab.

Trembling in shock, she looked around the basement, examining the brand new setting. There was a television, a record player, black leather couches. She ran her hand on the leather, it felt cold and smooth and she wanted to lay down on it.

The man was still on the bed unconscious, a small collection of blood formed around his head. Santiago could not keep her mind on one concentrated task. She had thought about this moment for years, and now when the moment called for action, she felt a strong sense of concern for her captor. Her instincts were pulling her back into the room to check on him, to help him. She stood there with her hand on the leather, thinking of outside.

That blue sky, the plant life, the smell of fresh air lifting her into the clouds. This was the plan, and if she didn't execute now, she would die down there. Maybe not today, but at some point, she would die if she stayed. A wispy, high-pitched cry vibrated out of her as she slammed her two fists together, over and over again, her sharp knuckles mashing together on impact, a thick thudding sound as her skin gave way and cracked open. She looked at her red hands shaking, her breath trapped in her throat. She was trapped in her own skin.

She stared at the phone and slowly inched her fingertips toward it. She could remember dialing the phone once as a small child. She knew its function from books she had read throughout the years, and from distorted childhood memory. The other option was to run. Get outside the house, and get as far away as possible. The problem was that she'd seen open land through her window and was uncertain how near the next house was. If people were close by, and she went to them, would she be protected? Would they help her? If he woke up and came looking for her, would he convince them that she was unstable? Or maybe they were working with him, ready to take her in. She turned in a full 360 degrees, hoping Sammy would appear and tell her what to do, but she had shunned poor Sammy.

There were two phone numbers that she was familiar with. She had learned both from her parents. 9-1-1 was the first. The second one she had practiced many times. Although she couldn't remember anything about her parents, that number was ingrained in her brain. Funny how her mind worked. She couldn't remember their faces, but she could remember those numbers.

Hands still shaking, she picked up the phone off the receiver and started to dial. It was a struggle just to press the buttons down. As she dialed, she could feel a presence behind her. *Was he still passed out?* The smell of cologne stung her nostrils and she began to dial quicker, closing her eyes, trying to remember. The cologne grew stronger as a dial tone was activated.

She could hear his breath, feel it down her neck. Finally, she turned to face her captor. His body was stiff, head off kilter with eyes wide and enraged. She couldn't move or cry. She couldn't feel disappointment or panic, love or hate. She was weak.

The man grabbed the phone from her hand and placed it back in the receiver gently. He then placed his hands around her throat with a soft touch as he stared deep into her eyes. He didn't understand. She could see him struggle with it, unable to understand the reality of the situation. In a way, he was trapped just as she was. Santiago had tried to manufacture her love for him during her tenure, but she couldn't ignore the truth.

His hands were cold and clammy around her thin neck. *Just kill me.* Feeling a new sense of defeat, a new low, she placed her hands gently around his. *It's okay. You can do it.*

His somber confusion formed a vengeful rage. He began to squeeze and she could feel the blood collecting in her head. The pressure was immense beneath her eyes, black spots taking over her vision. Now was the time. She deserved to be set free.

Her eyes drifted back, a light presence lifting her feet, she was floating. But then, she was struck in the face sending her head first into the cold leather couch. Pain sensors were firing, and yet she was still able to appreciate the cool, smooth feeling of the couch. Her odd satisfaction ended abruptly as her hair was tugged, pulling her up to her feet. Her scalp felt both a sharp burn and release as a fistful of hair was removed from her head. The man's voice was deep and cracked. "Never again." The words hit her like a trip hammer, reconfirming her entrapment.

He dragged her by the hair to her room, her feet barely touching the floor as he used all of his power to keep her upright. He launched her onto the bed and immediately pulled down his pants. She had hoped the abuse would simply involve fists, but that wasn't the case this time. She had hurt him deeply and he was going to get his pound of flesh. She planted herself upright on the bed, her hand sliding in the bloom of blood on the sheets. It felt warm and slick. As she prepped herself for the worst, she noticed a shiny metallic piece. It stuck out straight from underneath the mattress. A bedspring coil that had broken free and poked through the sheets.

Without wasting any time, he was on top of her. Her scream felt empty. She gripped the piece of bedspring tightly. She marveled at its presence for a moment and then let go.

• • •

Tom was already at his daily limit of alcohol, but he needed one more before he went back home to Rocanville. He had set up the meeting with Dean at one of their old watering holes, the Slippery Nipple. It was the oldest pub in Indianapolis that had local talent on a small stage during the weekends, the feature performance often consisting of the Blues. During the week it was a lot quieter as long as a person avoided the lunch and supper crowd. They had amazing chicken wings there, smoky and ultra crispy on the outside. The owner, Denise, had collected more beer label neon lights than any bar he had ever stepped foot in. The dingy place was lit like a damn Christmas tree. But carols weren't sung there; the regulars were lonely souls wanting only to stew in their thoughts and boozy fizz. Denise only had one hired man that Tom knew of. She was there almost 24/7, behind the counter. Denise always found a way to pick him up, which wasn't an easy task. She was built like a truck and had a subtle outline of a mustache, but had pretty dark eyes and lush flowing black hair. It was oddly confusing.

"Well, if it isn't my two-timing bastard of a man."

"Denise."

"You figure you can take off for months on end and then step foot back in this bar? Real cute, Detective."

"Oh, I think you'll take my money just the same."

She gave him a once-over, obviously happy to see him. "I was worried you had gone sober on me. God hates a coward."

"Sobriety can't seem to settle in. How about you?"

"Please. Gotta make the bums in here look somewhat attractive. Girl's got needs just as much as the rest."

"That's fair."

"Speaking of which, when are you gonna give me some? Been a single man for a while now, ain't ya?"

"I'll never be single, Denise. Plus, I don't think I could keep you satisfied."

"You're not wrong on that one." She poured each of them a generous double of Jameson whiskey and they exchanged cheers.

"Let's make the next one Crown."

"Canadian Club work?" she asked. Tom nodded in agreement.

Dean Patterson entered the bar looking overly sharp in a navy suit. He over did it with the three-piece. Dean had a scar over his right eye from a hand-to-hand battle with a petty thief. He was lucky his eye hadn't been fished out.

Even though Tom was trapped in a maze of shit and misery, and was supposed to be mad at Dean, seeing his face brought a smile to his own.

"Dean."

"What's up, Bennett?" He took a seat beside Tom up at the bar and slapped him on the back. "Good to see you. Things are good?"

"Oh, real swell."

"That good, hey? I feel you, world is crumbling, my friend. There never was a bottle of Johnnie, was there?"

"Oh shit! I forgot. And no, there wasn't." He flagged down Denise. "Two double Johnnie's. Blue."

"I'm gonna need to see some cash up front," she joked.

"Heard you're in line to make lieutenant soon," said Tom.

"Yeah, I dunno. We'll see. I don't wanna get too far ahead of myself. You know how this shit goes. Politics, my friend.

"Thanks for meeting me." Tom sipped his whiskey. It was so smooth.

"No problem, man."

Denise placed the drinks in front of them. They tapped glasses and each took a healthy sip, breathing out the fumes.

"You just looking for a drinking buddy then?"

Seeing his friend had almost made him feel happy. But then he remembered what Collins had told him about his son getting out, cutting a deal with the DEA. Surely Dean was aware of what was going on and it pissed him off that he wasn't informed.

"What you need, Tom?"

Right out with it then. "Abe Collins. What the hell, Dean?"

He shifted in his chair, his lips tightened. "Tom, you know we can't divulge information like that with you or Reg anymore."

"Deal's already done?"

Dean nodded with his eyes down at his drink.

"When?" Tom asked.

He was hesitant. Tom scowled and an answer came. "A few days."

"Wow. You guys sure work fast, don't ya?"

"Come on, Tom. Bigger fish. You know how this goes. Plus, it's all DEA. Only reason I'm in the loop is from my time under-cover. Don't be pissed with me."

"You should have told me."

"I couldn't."

"Don't matter."

"Listen. Paperwork is being pushed through. I was literally gonna tell you tomorrow, as soon as I got the okay."

"The past doesn't go away with these guys," Tom said.

"We've already been building a case back up against Collins's new crew. We take down the whale first, then back to cleaning up what we'd done already."

"You really think he's gonna give you the Cook? Easy as that?"

"Yes," said Dean, both proud and stern.

"And during that time?"

"Safety measures for all of you. Allison and her family, you, Reg and Dorothy. They are gonna be busy elsewhere though, I'm telling ya. I can't disclose our plan, but they will be reeling. They'll have no time to go on the offense."

"Really? Well, that's convenient for you guys then, isn't it?" Tom snapped. "You're putting us all in danger, don't try and sugar-coat it. How in the hell did this get rubber stamped?"

"This is the Cook, Tom. Moby Dick. You're really surprised?"

Tom's eased up. It wasn't really Dean's fault, aside from not giving him the advance information like a friend should.

"A whole two days notice. Seems professional. I guess we all just adjust on the fly," said Tom.

Tom downed his drink and Denise was there to fill it back up.

"What's this about, really? How'd you catch wind on this?" Dean asked.

"Went to see Hank Collins."

"Why?"

"I'm back on the case."

"What case?"

"Dee's"

There it was. He didn't need that pitied look from Dean. Usually they could go about their business without any emotional strings attached. Just facts. Just work.

"She's not dead."

"Tom, you've been drinking-"

"Oh, cut that shit. I'm fine."

"You don't look fine."

Tom ignored his last comment as he admired his whiskey glass. Denise only brought out the fine glassware for Tom, or so he thought anyway.

"Kidnapping without a word after doesn't fit. Something would have come up by now," said Dean.

Dean should have known better than to question him, after all he was a big reason Dean was where he was with the force. He had been there for him the whole way through, not that he felt like he was doing him any favors just to be friendly, but he saw the talent there. Dean had a nose for crime scenes.

"No one had a bigger reason for revenge. No greater enemy out there. How can you be so dismissive?"

"Because they would have wanted something in return. They are always making deals. That's how they operate. And if it ends in death, it's gruesome, with theatrics. They put on a show, they get away with it. Or one of their low level shit-stains gets nicked."

"Certain circumstances though. Things can change."

He shook his head. Tom was agitated. *Not drunk enough yet.* He took two more sips of his expensive scotch.

"Think you might slow your pace?" said Dean.

"I need updated files on their outside activity and Abe Collins's halfway location." It came out as an order.

"Tom-"

"You owe me."

Dean's face reddened.

"I appreciate everything you have done for me. You helped me up the ladder and opened doors for me. I can't thank you enough for that, man, but you're a PI. You aren't a detective for IPD anymore." Tom could only taste bitter, despite the smoky richness of his drink.

"You're welcome. Will you please do this for me, Dean?" False begging tone. Hopefully he'd buy it.

"I'm sorry, brother. About everything that happened, but-"

"I don't need to hear another apology about what happened. I need you to be a friend and say, yes, Tom, of course I'll do that."

Dean leaned forward. "Let's say I give you this information. What are you gonna end up doing? 'Cause that's on me then."

"I'm gonna do what I have to do until I get her." Tom was well aware of the edge in his voice.

Dean adjusted nervously in his chair, choosing his words wisely. "Exactly. I can't be implicated with that. Frankly, I can't trust your judgment right now."

Tom leaned in and grabbed Dean's arm, squeezing hard. "I had to go to my little girl's funeral. Someday she's gonna be at mine. You're going to help me because I need you to. You're worried about your career? I gave you your career."

His hand didn't leave Dean's arm, squeezing his thick triceps muscle. Their eyes were locked.

"Is this you threatening me?"

"I'll await your call."

Dean got up from his chair and stared down Tom for a moment. Dean was no pushover. It was a look of intimidation, of authority and power, but more honestly, it was a look of sympathy. "You're moving in a circle, Tom. Your shoes are on the wrong feet and it's gonna get you burned. Keep digging and you know what will happen."

"My shoes fit just fine. Broken in."

"You know I'm just looking out for you. Reg. He's just looking out for you. We want the best for you."

"Then help me with this. You two girls sure like to complicate things."

The soul patch under his lip twisted up. "There's no more *this*. Only now. And a future that won't happen for you. You're-"

"Yes, I'm trapped in a circle. You're worse than my shrink."

He didn't blink. "I pray your girl has found peace. She was a wonderful kid. And if she's still alive, I hope she's happy. I hope she's got a roof, food in her belly, and a bed to sleep in, but Tom...she's out of your reach. Just let it be." Dean's eyes were glassed with tears.

"You have the luxury of pretending all that. I live in the reality of knowing the suffering she's had to endure. The torture. Because she's my flesh. I'm sorry, Dean, but you don't know a damn thing about it, so you can take your prayers and send 'em elsewhere. I need a favor. Not your prayers. Do this one thing for me and you'll never deal with me again."

"Yeah. Sure thing, Tom. Because that's what I want."

Tom pretended to admire his glass this time. Dean turned and left, closing the door softly. Tom pointed at his glass and Denise topped him up.

"Hun, you fancy a water with your whiskey?"

"Sure." Why fight her on it?

She poured him a glass and slid it over. "Judging by the look on your face, I'm not getting lucky tonight."

"Not tonight I'm afraid. I'd like to, but sometimes the heart falls a little sour."

"Poetry ain't as sweet coming from you, my dear. Best stick with your investigations."

"Oh, I am."

Strings of sympathy adjusted Denise's face. He looked down at his drink, ready to drown in it.

"You're a good man."

"There comes a time when that stops being true."

Denise leaned over the counter. The bar light illuminated her whiskers at the perfect angle and Tom's quick smirk disappeared in an instant as she spoke.

LOSS OF THE DECADE

"Life's not fair. It's harsh and it's cold. Everyone's always yakking about how people can change. I think it's important to realize that who you were *can't* be erased. I would venture you've been a good man since you were knee-high and shitting your pants, and you still are today; a good man that is." She waved her hand to the side and continued. "I don't know the details of what's going on with you right now and I don't wanna know. Just keep doing what you're supposed to be doing. Find peace in that. We can only tackle what's in front of us."

Her gaze faded into the floor and suddenly she stomped at something. "Shit," she muttered, "they're gettin' bigger."

Tom sipped his whiskey, then from his glass of water.

Denise changed conversational position, "You putting in a shift, babe?"

"Nah. Better get some sleep."

"I think that's a fine idea."

Tom picked himself off his barstool.

"Your fine ass is welcome in my bar any time. But someday you gotta make an honest woman out of me."

"Soon enough. I just gotta figure a few things out here."

She smiled warmly, threw a rag over her shoulder, and waved goodbye.

Tom left the bar with a buzz, feeling better about himself for a brief moment. She always found a way to make him feel like everything was all right. But as he left the bar and looked up at a full moon, he was reminded that nothing was all right. His world was nothing short of fucked. Every night to him was a full moon night, his world filled with craziness.

• • •

The next day, Tom met Dean on a park bench. He provided him with all of Abe Collins files and most importantly his current location. Dean was stepping way out on a ledge with this, knowing Tom was in a desperate state of mind, perhaps willing to do just about anything to find his daughter. There was only one thing that worried Tom even more than Collins men having his daughter. What if she was passed along to someone even more dangerous?

• • •

Tom stood in the case room looking at a photo of Abe Collins, his fat stocky neck hiding any outline of a chin.

"Been at it all night?" Reg stood around the corner. He was always around the corner as of late.

"Hey," Tom said quietly.

"It had been years since you spent any time in this room and now you live in it."

Tom didn't break his focus.

"What are you working on?" Reg questioned.

"I've had a tail. Possibly more than one. For years."

"What are you talking about?"

"Abe Collins is involved, I know it."

Reg frowned at Tom's response.

"Tom-"

Tom interjected, "I don't have time to do this dance, already did it once."

"This guy is locked up."

"He's getting out." Tom couldn't stand the silence and concerned eyes. "Either help me on this or get out of my way."

"Says who?"

"Dean."

Reg leaned up against the wall and exhaled. "Well, I imagine they'll assign guardian angels to us."

"Guess so." Tom was busy, wrapped up in a tangled web of tried theories. His mind couldn't stop.

"I thought we were done with this?" Reg frowned.

"Done with this?" The heat rose in Tom's face.

"We can't do this again."

"There's no we. Focus your talents elsewhere."

"Think of the time you'd put into this. The pain you endured. You were doing so well, I thought. What happened?"

"Oh, Reg. I don't get to do well."

"You think looking into the same guys is playing the odds right? 'Cause I don't."

Tom stopped what he was doing, planted his feet and twisted, throwing his coffee mug against the wall, shattering it into pieces. Reg didn't flinch. "Collins has her somewhere. He's waiting for a moment when he needs something from me. Something big. And it's coming."

"And that something wouldn't have come along until what? Ten years later? Come on, kid. What something, exactly?"

"Reg, open your eyes! He's getting out! It had to happen with one of them out of prison."

Reg took a beat and played with the wrinkled skin over his knuckle. "You lost you're child. Such an unbearable thing. And I feel that I'm losing mine…I won't take you back into that damn place. I won't".

"And you won't."

Tom's memory of St. Vincent Mental Hospital was still crystal clear. His first day had been terrifying. He'd sworn he would never step foot in there again. The troubled minds around him, trapped in their own confused worlds.

Reg got in one last word, watching Tom fade out into his work. "When will it end?"

Chapter 17

Fading

SANTIAGO'S ONLY SUPPLEMENTATION were pellets that may as well have been puppy food. She had been served the pellets on two different occasions as punishment, but it hadn't lasted long. During that time, he had assured her that they held all nutritional components the human body required. Every time she ate, there was a risk of throwing them back up. She had no energy.

Santiago hadn't seen any sunlight in that time and the wounds on her face from his attacks were not healing all that well. The cut over her eye had formed crusted puss over the edges and the scab on her nose was oozing. She needed strength to execute her plan. She needed real food.

The man entered her room through the steel door. He had stitches in his forehead and a shaved spot on his head with more stitches in place. He approached and sat down on the edge of the bed. She looked through the open door to find that the phone was no longer there, next to the couch.

"I'm not going to lie to you. What you did hurt me. I thought you cared about me." He looked into his palms. His voice cracked. "Don't you love me?"

Feeling a crushing weight on her chest, she said, "Yes."

"Then, why?"

"I wanted to be outside. That's all."

He glanced outside the door where the phone used to be, then back to her.

"I know this isn't what you had planned. Being a house wife. But I just wanted you to be happy. I thought you were happy."

Santiago closed her eyes, unable to prevent a tear from falling down her cheek. "I am. I need you to take me places, though."

"Someday. I need to trust you again. I need time."

She couldn't hold it in anymore. The fatigue of playing his games finally broke her. "Please let me go." She expected an angry response.

Instead, he rose to his feet with a deadened look in his eyes and left the room, closing the door firmly behind him. The door always made the same groaning sound when it closed. She had heard it one too many times. She began to sob and the more she cried, the higher the volume was until finally, she buried her face in her pillow and screamed. It was a scream that didn't want to end, her vocal chords stretching.

Santiago lifted her head from the pillow, slid off the bed and stepped around to the other side where the loose coil was. Her legs were thin and wobbly. Her head ached and she often felt woozy, possibly concussed from his attack. She pulled the metallic piece back out and slid her finger down it until it reached a fused point, joining the other coils it had broken free from. The material was hard enough to do some serious damage, but also had enough flexibility to be bent and tied off. The fused center that each four corners would run to was not overly thick, which was why one piece and maybe others had broken free from wear and tear. Her new finding was uplifting, but she had to keep herself down. It was not healthy for her to get her hopes up.

Chapter 18

Collins II

HOT WATER RUSHED DOWN Tom's body as he soaped his chest hair and arm-pits. He watched the soapy water swirl down the drain, waiting for clarity. He used to shower twice a day for that specific reason. A break away from it, hit the reboot button, let his randomly wandering mind find something new, waiting for a light bulb to shine.

He had felt like a madman chasing ghosts, a loose strategy at best, simply poking and prodding at his past failures. With most of his past kidnapping cases, each piece of information he collected would narrow his options, until he was left with only one. But now he was a scrambled mess, a shadow of what he used to be. He ran his finger over the old bullet wound on his leg and it lit up like a target. Then, the knife wound across his leg, running his fingers gently up through the rough terrain of his chest hair to his shoulder, where Collins's knife had sunk. It tingled from his touch. It all still had life, the memories fresh, the pain still lingering.

• • •

LOSS OF THE DECADE

Tom took one more glance at his map to make sure he was in the right neighborhood in Indianapolis. He had checked his rear view for a tail, but there was nothing. A neighborhood lookout would be a potential threat. The street was lined with old cookie cutter houses, some ready to topple over. He neared the address of Abe Collins feeling anxious. The street was filled with rusted-out cars, and also some expensive luxury cars and SUVs, nothing in between it seemed. His palms were sweating and he felt chilled. As much as Tom wanted answers, it terrified him that he might get answers he didn't want to hear.

Abe's halfway house was a glorified shack. It appeared that the lights were off, but he couldn't tell if he was home or not. Tom's heart was thudding uncontrollably against the walls of his chest, while his hand gripped around his truck door handle. Before he opened it, he spotted Abe moving down the sidewalk with a bag of McDonald's in his hand, a drink in the other. He entered his house and Tom quickly followed.

Tom searched for any bystanders, but the streets were quiet.

He strolled across the street and stepped lightly up to the door. He turned the doorknob and it gave way.

Tom burst through the door with his gun raised, ready to use as a last resort in case Collins drew on him. Right away he was exposed in the open space, Abe Collins sitting at the kitchen table with a mouthful of burger. He looked at Tom with little surprise as he took another big bite of the Big Mac, orange Mac sauce sticking to the hair on his chin. He then reached into his brown bag and pulled out some fries, ramming them into an already full mouth.

Tom approached cautiously. Abe's gun sat there on the table, almost out of arm's reach, but he paid it no attention. Again, back to the bag he pulled out a box of chicken McNuggets, completing his spread. He didn't focus on one item of food, instead attacking the line of options with a bite from each, chasing the food down with his soft drink. Finally, he looked up at Tom, emitting no emotion. He grunted with satisfaction, then extended the drink to Tom. "It's a chocolate milkshake. You want?"

"No. I'm okay."

He held up his finger and popped in the last of his Mac and chewed it down with an exhale of relief, like he had been so horribly starved in prison. It didn't show. In fact, it appeared he got his fair share of starch just like his old man. Finally, the chewing stopped. "Why are you here?" His voice was playful.

He paid no attention to Tom's gun as it shook against the side of his leg.

"I'm here to ask questions, that is all."

"Nugget?" He extended his offering with some sweet and sour sauce in the other hand.

"I'm not hungry."

"Suit yourself. I'll eat 'em later."

"What do you want with me? Why have you been tailing me?"

"What we all want. Your toe nails pulled out. For starters."

"Why'd you try and kidnap my wife in '78?"

"I've told you. That wasn't me, player."

"You're lying."

He took another sip of his milkshake, making a slurping noise as he had reached the bottom. "Let's say that was my doing, you know, for your own peace of mind. It would have a been a three-pronged approach. Let us out of that barbaric place you call a prison, take the heat off and let us disappear, playtime with the wifey, exchange wifey for Tommy. Scalp Tommy. Nah, maybe we would have used you for your various skills and connections. Whose to say? Was that more than three prongs?" He sipped from his empty drink. "That was when you had any sort of value. You're washed up now. Used and abused. No pull with PD, we both know that."

"Your father assures me you had nothing to do with the kidnapping of my daughter. Is that true?"

He wiped his hands on a napkin with a shit-eating grin on his face. "You're no longer relevant, Bennett. And I'd say you got about sixty seconds before your ass gets hauled out of here and cut into pieces."

Tom looked over his shoulder toward the door.

Abe crumbled up a wrapper and took another sip from his shake. "Fifty-two."

Tom jolted forward, snagging his gun off the table. Abe never even made a move at it. He just sat back relaxed, popping golden fries into his fat head.

Tom pulled a roll of duct tape from his jacket and moved around the backside of Abe. He complied and put his hands behind his back so Tom could very easily tie him to the back of his chair. He rushed to the front door and locked it, before moving down the hall to his left, checking every room along the way. One by one, they were all clear. He made his way back to Abe, who had a stupid grin on his face. "What two bit losers you got watching the house? You just got out, you're gonna risk it all trying to kill me here?"

"Losers? You'd like 'em. And no, I'm not doing anything here. They might kill you somewhere else though. That's their call. About twenty seconds now." He laughed, his face was so arrogant. "Heard you went to see Daddy-o. How's he doing?"

Tom punched him in the face with his gun and he just smiled. "Shit!" he laughed.

"Just tell me where she is and you'll never see me again."

"Or...I'll just never see you again after my boys put you in the dirt."

Tom hit him again and he laughed. "Ten years in prison, brother. You should have come more prepared. No tool kit?"

The front door exploded off its hinges. Two men entered behind with guns pointed directly at his chest. Tom turned back to Abe, his face bloodied. He then proceeded to rip Tom's whole world apart. "I know where she is."

Tom was lost in his menacing smile, the hate in his eyes, when suddenly he was tasered in his ribs, bringing him to his knees.

His voice moved in and out of shrieking to grunts, all of his muscles completely seized as his teeth clamped into one another, the pain echoing throughout his body. *I am being electrocuted.* He collapsed to the floor and they finally ceased the electrical current as he pretended to be out cold, drooling face first on the floor. "Untie me and take him to our spot," said Abe.

Tom was dragged to his feet by one of the young goons. From limp to attack mode, he struck the goon in the throat with a precise shot, and grabbed hold of his gun, but he fought back, holding his grip tight. The other goon who was helping untie Abe had drawn his gun, when Tom (still in a deadlock) fired, hitting the other in the chest.

They continued to wrestle over the weapon, Tom's body still contracting from the Taser. He lifted up his foot and struck the man in the knee, causing him to pull down on the trigger, sending another bullet out. The goon got back up to his feet and threw Tom up onto the kitchen table, gaining position on him, tilting the gun closer to his head.

Tom sneaked his finger back over top of the goon's and he pressed down four times, as quickly as possibly. The gun-shots were deafening, leaving him not a trace of hearing, the entire room silent as Tom twisted his wrist and jerked the gun out of his hand and pushed him away. The goon bent over to pick the gun up while Tom snatched Abe's gun off the kitchen table. Tom fired first, hitting him square in the chest.

Tom looked down at two bodies, then quickly turned to face Collins, but he was gone.

He wiped down the guns he handled along with the kitchen table. He grabbed his own pistol and recalled the action. *Did I shoot my gun?* He knelt to check for bullet casings when he came to the realization that he indeed hadn't used it. Only the thugs.

As he stood, he saw movement in the other corner of the room. It was Abe laying on the floor. He gasped for breath, blood sputtering out of his mouth, gagging and choking sounds lessening with each attempt at breathing. His eyes faded out. "No! No! Where is she? Just tell me where she is!"

He was lying to you. It's okay. It was all lies. Get up, Tom. Get up! Tom had heard Abe mention taking him to 'their spot'. Tom searched all three of them for any clues that may guide him to the destination Abe had planned. Nothing but cash and IDs that were likely fake.

Tom hovered over Abe's bloodied body, completely shaken. He walked through the back exit of the home, rather slowly, legs doused in liquid lead, trying to hold back the ball of nausea that was shifting up toward his throat. He walked through the backyard and out into the alley. He stopped. He puked.

Tom got back into his truck and opened his glove box to get at his whiskey.

He drove outside of Indy into some familiar country on his way back to Rocanville. What just transpired had not yet become a reality for him. The way Abe had smiled when he said it. He knew where she was. He had her taken for a reason, and using Tom was part of that plan. Who would he go to for answers now? Their gang had been disassembled.

He put the mickey of booze back to his lips, and his phone rang. Tom answered but said nothing, playing the waiting game. They didn't speak for about ten seconds until... "You've been busy," a man's voice stated coldly.

"Who's this?" Tom was surprised not to hear his daughter's voice.

"Murder. It looks good on you."

Just as Tom's pulse had finally settled, it was jolted to life again. He was a puppet, strings being pulled.

"Who the hell is this?"

"The answer to your questions."

"Whoever this is, you don't want me in your world right now. I promise you that."

"Mr. Bennett. How could you be in my world? You'd have to find me."

"Who is this?"

"Karmic retribution."

"Cut the shit. What do you want?"

"There is a time and a place. And that is to be determined."

Tom cleared his throat. "Where is she?" A question he was growing tired of asking.

"I'll be keeping an eye on things. You have a good night." The man hung up before Tom could continue his line of questions.

Tom hit the gas and sped down the highway.

Chapter 19

Movie Time

ANNA SAT AT HER DESK finalizing some notes on her last patient session. Her stomach growled angrily at her, telling her she was a fool for starting her diet. She'd had a flat stomach her whole life, but as of late she had developed what she called a roo pouch and she couldn't let it slide any further. She squeezed her pen with frustration and opened a drawer, pulling out a granola bar. It was organic. No sugars, no artificial flavors. No good.

Before she could swallow the first chalky mouthful, Tom had cruised past reception and barged into her office. He looked absolutely dreadful, almost hysterical, despite his best efforts to mask it.

"Are you okay?"

He was formulating choice words. Tom leaned over the back of the chair, pretending to examine her office as he always does. His eyes darted back and forth, then focused back on her window behind her. She knew he had forced himself into a decision of some sort. Tom's hamster wheel continued to churn and she waited patiently.

"I, uh. If I tell you this, you promise to keep this off record?"

"I'm not a reporter. You're my patient."

"I need you to be my friend right now."

She was shocked to hear something so vulnerable right off the bat. "Your hallucinations are bad again?"

"No." He was terribly agitated.

"Are they the same?"

"This isn't about me seeing Dee."

"So there's nothing else you're questioning the validity of?"

"No…" he said unconvincingly at first. "No. That's not it."

"What do you see?"

"I-I've been getting phone calls from people. I know how that sounds, just let me…"

She waited patiently. "Take your time."

"A man called me today. He knows things. I think he has Dee."

"Okay, why do you think he has Deanna? What did he say?"

"Commenting on where I was. I think he was following me. He, uh, also said that I wasn't capable of finding people."

Anna adjusted her glasses, feeling the pressure of the pivotal moment. She and Tom had reached a small but important breakthrough only a few days ago and now he had relapsed to a point that reminded her very much of when he was admitted to St. Vincent. She had to tread lightly. He needed to come to his own conclusions.

"Do you think that comment was connected to Deanna?"

"Yeah, it was personal."

Tom liked direct lines of questioning. "You tried the number back?"

"From a pay phone. In state."

"Okay, how do you know that?"

"I traced the call. A different call. From earlier."

"Where were you when you got the call?"

"In my truck."

"Okay. Let's start over. Give me a full picture here. Why were you in your truck? Where were you going? What happened precisely before you were driving? How did you trace a call from your vehicle?"

Tom paused for a moment. "I was in Indy. Just collecting information on a new case, more of a domestic family-type issue, nothing crazy." His voice had changed pitches, slightly too high, then low. *Lies.* "I was heading back when I got the call. They informed me that they had eyes on me, commenting on my location. He was disturbed. The phone call was feeding his ego. It's connected, I know it." *Truth. In his mind.*

"And the traced call?" Anna asked.

"That was a different time. Still to my cell originally though."

Anna furrowed her brow, trying to decipher which information was the best to use. "So he had already called you once before?"

"No, well, several times, but it wasn't him. It was the calls from Deanna, with the static. I know how this sounds Anna. Trust me."

"I'm not implying you don't. When is the last time you've had a good meal? A full night's rest?"

"I'm not some loony, Doc."

"I know. Food though?"

"I don't know."

"Your face is so pale. You continue to lose weight. You look so tired. I'm not saying you haven't received any calls, but I'm sure you know what the mind is capable of when severely deprived of sleep. How's the drinking coming?"

He looked angry, but she continued anyway. "You should stop in at a clinic."

"Been there. Once was enough."

"You saw a doctor?"

She was losing him.

"I don't wanna get into that. You're my doctor right now."

She couldn't push much harder. "I think you need time away from work. Clear your head. Even just a couple days of real meals and sleep. I've seen you slip before and we can't have this again."

"They aren't hallucinations. Not these."

"Regardless, you need rest and food."

"This man knows something."

"I'm not gonna try and talk you out of anything. Just, be careful okay?"

"How can I be sure?" Tom asked.

Anna wrote a prescription and handed it to Tom. "Cut back on the booze. Sleep."

"What about memory recall?"

"What about it? We've exercised your mind over and over again. All we can hope is that it comes with time. Rest and recovery will help." There were no tricks when dealing with trauma, only time and good habits.

"And if this is real?" Tom asked, leaning forward listening intently for a response.

"Then do your job. The right way, sober and rested."

"I can feel it, Anna. I just don't know who."

Anna nodded in understanding, trying not to let her disbelief show through a look of condescension. She wanted to believe him, but her belief in functionality of the mind was greater. The case of Jessica Hill had most likely triggered a relapse. One that Tom would have great difficulty escaping.

"Please remember you still have a support group. Don't forget it."

Tom got up from his chair and walked toward the office door. She was terribly worried. "Tom." She wished she could help him. "I'll see you soon, okay?"

Tom nodded and left. Anna tossed the granola bar in the trash.

• • •

Reg had not seen Tom in over twenty-four hours.

He had been sitting in his car on the street, outside of their basement office for about an hour now. He was ready to head inside when he spotted Tom pull up into the driveway. Reg's eyes wandered off of Tom and down the street where a truck pulled to the side of the road and killed the engine. It was too far away to get a look at who was driving, but there were two people in the truck, neither of which got out. They simply sat there, waiting.

Reg waited another five minutes, without taking his eyes off the truck. It bugged him that they hadn't gotten out yet. After another minute, Reg got out of the truck and started walking down the sidewalk toward them. As he grew nearer, the truck fired back up and pulled back out onto the street. They drove on by.

• • •

Tom had just opened up the Collins files that Dean supplied him with, when his office phone rang. He took a second to prepare himself. "Bennett here."

It was Dean on the other end. "Will you please tell me what the hell you did?"

"What are you talking about?"

"Shit, Tom. Why'd you do it?".

"Dean calm down. Do what?" He pictured the blood sputtering from Abe's mouth.

"Abe Collins is dead. Along with two others."

"Well, it wasn't me," replied Tom, trying his best to sound hurt by his accusations.

"You expect me to believe that? Right after I give you his location!"

"I'm telling you it wasn't me, Dean."

"You realize my ass is on the line for this?"

"Don't you think he may have had other enemies out there? Perhaps one he had just rolled over on to gain his freedom?"

"There were no prints found. And I'm guessing the bullet won't match your registered piece, will it?"

"No, it won't. Because I didn't do what you think I did. Pretty easy to avoid prints. How about you give me the benefit of the doubt?"

"It doesn't even matter!"

"What do you mean?"

"It's my job to give this information to my department. You are gonna be the number one suspect. Innocent or not."

"You can't run this. Not yet. I need time."

There was a pause on the line, then, "You're far gone. Aren't you?"

"Don't say anything about the information. It'll all be burned by morning."

"Christ, Tom. If anything leads to you I'm not stopping it."

"Understood." A notion suddenly swept through Tom, something he should have questioned earlier but had been too consumed by shock. *What if he not only knew where she was, but had specific orders for the captor. What if he gave instructions to kill her if they received no word from him?*

"I can't make any promises, Tom. It might not be long."

"I just need a little more time."

"Tom. Please tell me you didn't."

"I gotta go, Dean. It'll all be over soon. One way or another." He couldn't waste time explaining himself.

"Tom-" He hung up. Tom heard the clang of his mailbox closing. By the time he got to his door, he heard a car drive away out front. He opened the door and reached into his mailbox, pulling out a parcel. It was unmarked. He took it into the Deanna case room and opened it to find a tape. It was labeled, "Crazy ex-cop."

He slid it into his camcorder and hit play. Tom watched a video of himself walking into Abe's house. The footage was coming from across the street, down the block a ways. He fast-forward the video closer to the end when, *BANG*, a gunshot went off, followed by several others. Then clear footage of him of walking to his truck around the block. It zoomed in on his face, clear enough to see the panic in his eyes. He was completely screwed. Whoever filmed it had other copies ready to send out if they didn't get whatever it is they wanted.

Reg entered the office and Tom put the camcorder in his bottom desk drawer.

"Reg. What're you doing here so late?"

"Where the hell have you been?"

He had to make a decision on which way he wanted to take this.

"I'm sorry. I've been figuring some things out. I-"

Reg interrupted. "I just wanted to let you know, you can rely on me to help you, and I won't get in your way. I'm here to help you out. Always."

He'd be putting him in a tough spot by continuing to keep in contact with Reg. "No. It's okay."

"What's okay?"

"I'm not. I can't do that anymore. You're right, these old suspects are a waste of time. Collins. The Harrison's. They're not it. There's just not enough there."

Reg looked relieved to hear those words, still concealing it with a beard stroke. "It don't mean we stop looking."

"I know. I don't know." Tom was convincing in selling his defeat. "All I know is I need ten hours of sleep."

Tom could see a weight lift off of Reg's shoulders. "Go, now. No alarm."

He slapped Reg on the shoulder as he walked by. "Goodnight."

"Goodnight, kid."

• • •

Tom collapsed onto his bed, feeling the sleeping pills take over. Tomorrow would be a long day. He would have to pack up and leave first thing. With IPD right around the corner, Tom would have to conduct his investigation on the run. He needed a new lead linked to Abe Collins, unless his secret admirer decided to shed a little light. The sunlight would come too early, so he closed his eyes, took two deep breaths, and hoped to fade into oblivion. He did not.

PART III

Chapter 20

Ella, Where Art Thou?

THE OCEAN WATER RUSHED up her legs and the breeze lifted her hair. The humidity was drinkable, her skin enjoyably sticky with sweat. The beach was nearly empty, only a young man sitting on a towel in the red sand, looking out at the sun as it lowered toward the water in the distance. She walked the shoreline, feeling the water cover her feet every time the tide pushed in. She marveled at each footstep made in the sand, until she was in line with the young man. He was older than she, maybe twenty? He had light peach fuzz above his lip and a darker shade on his chin. He was handsome and mysterious. He didn't say a word, didn't pay any attention to her at first. She initiated, walking over, butterflies in her stomach, but she was now comfortable in her own skin. His smile drew her in closer. "Hello," he said first.

"Hello."

Had she seen him somewhere before? "May I?"

"Please." He held out his hand offering her a place in the sand next to him as he didn't offer up a portion of his small towel. Instead, he rotated to lay on his side, facing her.

The sun was almost gone, the sky amber. She looked back to him. "Where am I?" She felt light. Free.

He laughed and shook his head. "Can't be sure."

He was peculiar looking the more she examined his face, but still uniquely attractive. She liked finding rarities on a man's face. His forehead was larger than average, and his nose skinny, but his jawline was square and strong, his smile almost elegant like a beautiful woman would smile. He had a presence that made her want to know more.

"Why are you here alone?" she asked.

"Oh…I can't answer that." Not implying secrecy, just a fact.

"Why not?"

"I just go where my feet take me. Sometimes there are people with me, sometimes it's just me." He smiled. "I do enjoy the sunset."

She rolled on her side to face him, her elbow sinking in the soft, warm sand. "I like the red sand."

He nodded in agreement.

"Do you live here?"

"For now. Do you?"

She tilted her head in confusion. "I think so."

• • •

His dark hair blew back in the wind as they drove down a dirt road, not another vehicle in sight. The night had fallen on them along with the stars. The wind, his strangely handsome face, the stars, the sound of gravel flying, it all made her heart rest unconcerned. His jeep rattled over the bumps, its shocks rigid and uncomfortable, yet she had never been more comfortable in her entire life. His right hand extended a little further, resting on her shoulder. His touch made her feel like she was flying, the top down enhancing that feeling. She was unsure whether it was a lifetime friendship in creation or if they'd be lovers, spending their days carefree. Both thoughts were exhilarating, the latter more so.

She didn't know if they were at her place or his, but it didn't matter. It was small, and she could hear teenagers laughing and drinking down below. A hostel perhaps? They sat on the balcony, the railing made of old stone. She could smell the roast of his coffee. She had herbal tea with lemon. They looked out over a small strip mall and a swimming pool. Past that was another beach, the sand color more neutral white, but pretty nonetheless.

"How's your tea?"

"Perfection."

"It's a good word. Perfection." The way his lips curved around the word. She could have stayed there forever.

"Can we stay here a while?"

"We can stay. Doesn't much matter to me where we are."

She rose to her feet and leaned out over the balcony. There was a group of rebellious youths on the beach, their drunken conversations loud, their laughter louder. Two were detached from the rest, kissing passionately. Before she could turn back to her friend, his arm was already around her. She felt his breath by her cheek. He had graciously popped in a piece of gum to mask the coffee. She wouldn't have cared. She turned her cheek, grazing against his, and their lips touched. Oh, the feeling.

• • •

Ella awoke in bed. In her trailer. She couldn't get back. Even if she fell asleep again, which was unlikely, she couldn't get back there. Her cries were trapped in her throat but she choked them down like sardines. Her clock read 2:06 a.m.

When she and Simon arrived in Indianapolis a year ago, she was not in a good place. The move came at a time when she had an actual friend. He reminded her of the man in her dream, but they looked different. There was no attraction in that case. He was her only friend, a dear friend at that. And then they left. She had never felt loss quite like that. Once they were settled in Indy, she had been told of a place not much more than a stone's throw away from Mum's Bakery, their specialty there, not the classic glazed donut. Rather, heroin. However, Ella was not so bold, not so destroyed that she'd give in to a drug like that, but weak enough she was in need of some weed, something she was familiar with already. A few blocks over from Mum's, with a neighborhood far from perfect but less dangerous, comprising community college kids and old folks retiring on a budget, was where she was told to go for a score. She made the long walk to get her marijuana. With her pot came a sample of Oxy.

When she returned to the trailer, she was as quiet as a church mouse, Simon still asleep in his room; she heard his light snore. Ella brushed her teeth. After she scrubbed the top row a second time, she spat and rinsed. She wiped the corners of her mouth and looked back at her reflection. Something was different. She no longer hated the construct of her face, now merely indifferent about it.

Ella had lived a life on the run for too long, so long that she felt she had become the stretch of highway between towns. She would never experience the comfort of normal. As long as she was living with Simon, she would always be like that highway, continuously stuck, life ever fleeting above her at the same time.

He had agreed to activate their final job which originally gave her a great deal of relief. But after that lonely night several days ago, when she came to him in tears and he made his promise for execution, he had been stalling. He was *always* stalling.

Ella couldn't wait for life to happen any longer, or else it never would. Whether the plan was executed or not, she would be forever stuck with Simon, living on the outskirts of a life she wanted but never touched. It was up to her to make her life something different and she had come to the conclusion that it would have to be done alone.

She finished up in the bathroom and stepped out into the hall, conducted a double check to make sure he was still asleep, and grabbed her packed bag off of her bed. She put her headphones in and listened to a soft ballad and began humming to the song as she walked away from the trailer.

• • •

Ella walked down that lonely highway 41 with her thumb out, hood up, headphones in. Walking down that road, she felt the tingling sensation of freedom. It was within her reach.

The road was not overly busy that day, several cars passing her in an hour. She was okay with walking. It was a nice mild temperature that day, and she had packed water and snacks that would last her for a lengthy trek. After another hour of walking, a semi with a van trailer, pulled to the side of the road, setting his four-way blinkers on. She had always wanted to ride in a big truck, but never had the chance. She wasn't much fazed by the reputation of truck drivers being rough around the edges. The man hopped down and came around to greet her and she liked him instantly. He didn't look her up and down to judge her Gothic exterior; he looked her directly in the eyes. "What the hell you doing out here?"

"I need a lift."

"I see that. Why?"

Ella looked down to the ground then back to him. He probably figured she was a drifter. Maybe she was.

"Just onto the next one?"

"Hopefully the right one," she answered.

She expected the next words out of his mouth to be "You're too young for this." or "What does your mother think of this?" and she was grateful that he didn't say it. Instead he said, "Hope you like dirty gas station sandwiches, cheap diner coffee, and trucker farts."

Ella laughed. "I love diners. Could do without the farts."

"Well. This rig runs north into Canada believe it or not. You'll have plenty of options for stops. But if your game plan doesn't involve shelter, I'd avoid the neighbors up there. Too cold."

"Well, if it's alright with you, I'll think about it."

"Fine by me. Danny's the name. You are?"

"Ella."

They shook hands. He had long slender fingers, a neatly groomed goatee, and wore a long sleeve plaid shirt that was tucked into his blue jeans. He was a very skinny man, but still looked like he had some wiry strength to him. Ella felt very comfortable around him, making the decision to leave easier than it was before.

Moving down the quiet highway at sixty miles per hour, Ella asked if she could roll the window down.

"Thought it was fresh like flowers in here?" he responded.

Ella grinned. "Just want to feel the wind."

"Get rolling then." He gestured toward the hand crank.

She rolled it down and the wind raged through her open hand. She closed her eyes and immediately let her mind drift to her music. She pictured herself on stage in a simple bar, half of her audience blended with a smoky haze, the other half listening intently. It didn't matter where she was; the thought of being on a stage made her feel nervously blissful. When she opened her eyes, she saw a picture of who she assumed was the driver's daughter. She looked part Latino, maybe ten years old.

"This is your daughter?"

His goatee shifted with his smile. "Little star."

"Where do you live?" A longing in Ella's eyes. *Live.*

"Unfortunately, I live in this thing for the most part. She's in Wisconsin with her mom. I've got a place about a half hour from them."

Ella nodded, not wanting to press on his marriage. He went there anyway, "Divorced. She's a good mother."

She paused, hesitant about asking a blunt and personal question. "And you are a good father?"

"When I'm there, yeah," he said with a sad look. "She's a damn good athlete already. Track and softball. I told her, don't you ever let anyone tell you otherwise, you can play a sport for a living if you want it bad enough. Better to give it a try than do this shit straight out of tenth grade. Plus she could get one of those fancy scholarships, get a degree. Let Dad park this hunk of shit once in a while."

"That sounds like a nice plan."

"Just life. So you don't have a destination?"

Ella shook her head no.

"Well, that's okay. If you could be anywhere, where would that be?"

Ella thought of that beach, the eccentric red sand but a step away. She could smell the ocean, hear the waves crashing softly on shore. "I don't know…how would I know?"

Danny double clutched, shifting gears. "You don't."

She was intrigued by his response, feeling an urge to converse like she never had before; other than with Franklin from the diner. "Aren't I about to decide?"

"Are you?"

She watched him shift gears again, eyes still on the road. "Home is where the heart is," he said with a corny smirk, "You hear that one?" She nodded and Danny continued. "Correction. Home is where life takes you. There's no predestined location for one of us to find because that climate, that culture, that restaurant, makes us feel good. Nah, it's just a place that we wind up. We make things happen, things happen to us-a constant push and pull. We call places home because of the people in our lives. That's all. My home is wherever I'm with my little star. Yup, she's my home. Not that shit box apartment I live in two towns over. This truck here is more of a home than that place."

Danny faded into silence and then laughed. "This is the punishment you get for hitchhiking. Dangerous is right. Hear some washed out trucker try and answer life's greatest questions... Maybe they aren't so great."

"I like hearing you talk."

He laughed softly through his nose. "Maybe I'll stick with this whole hitchhiker business. Only polite young women such as yourself though. I deal with enough crude men in my line of work. Makes me less of a gentleman being around that crap." His words could have been seen as creepy, but they weren't at all. He was a good man.

He finally took his eyes off the road to look at Ella. "You look tired. There's a bed in the back. Sleep if you like."

"I wouldn't be much of a passenger if I did that."

"I spend most of my time alone. Besides, I'm sick of your company anyway," he said with a friendly grin.

"I like being up front."

"Suit yourself."

Ella rested her head against the window using her sweater as a pillow.

• • •

Ella was woken by the truck coming to a stop in a hotel parking lot. Danny noticed her right away. "Milwaukee."

"How long was I out?"

"Quite a while. You ready to take over?"

Ella was worried he was serious. "I'm kidding. I'll get you set up with a room and I'll take the truck here."

She wasn't surprised by his generous offer. "I can pay for my own room, thanks though."

"No. You save your money for your new home."

"You save yours for your daughter."

"She's just fine. Her grandfather, her mother's father, he's about to croak any second now. It's time for that miserable old fart, believe you me. He's got a big old life insurance policy. My girl will be just fine."

Ella found herself at a loss. "Why are you being so kind to me?"

He looked sorry for her in a respectful way if such a thing were possible. "What if you were my daughter walking down the side of the highway?" He took the keys out of the ignition and looked back at her. "I hope you get to where you need to be. I have a feeling there are a few people in your life that feel the same. Now, don't be too appreciative. I'm getting you the cheapest room."

His kindness was bright. She thanked him for the room and he told her that he wanted her ready to hit the road by six in the morning if she still wanted to keep going.

Ella sat on the edge of her bed looking at her duffel bag. She opened it up and spread out her drugs on the bed. She played with the bag of white Oxy pills, opened it up and dropped one pill into her hand. She dumped another pill into her hand. Then another. Then the whole bag. She rose to her feet, walked to the bathroom, lifted the toilet lid and dropped them. Flush. Ella walked back to the bed, rolled a joint, and lit up. She liked the smell, not so much the burn hitting her lungs. She coughed a little as she exhaled. By the time she was halfway through her joint, she was in a comfortable place, mind working smoothly. She opened her window to let some of the smoke out, the cool night breeze refreshing her as she rested her head on a pillow.

Ella didn't sleep. She thought of Simon. She recalled everything he had done for her, the way he looked at her when she was upset. He must have been going crazy with her gone from the trailer. She knew he deserved better than her walking out of his life without a good-bye. She thought about Danny's daughter and what it would do to him if she were to leave him he would no longer have purpose; his heart would be broken. It wasn't fair to blame everything on Simon. At the very least, she owed him a discussion.

She left her room at 2:00 a.m and thankfully the diner next to the hotel was open 24/7. She went inside and stood in the entrance taking in the surroundings, comparing it to her favorite spot back in Indy. It was just as out-dated as her spot, but it was dirtier, probably from more foot traffic and lack of dedication from the man or woman running it. She took a seat near the window by the entrance and a grumpy old bird staggered over with a pot of coffee. She eye-balled Ella in disgust. "Coffee?" she muttered.

"Do you have tea?"

The wrinkly old woman gave her a sour look without a response and staggered back behind the counter, proceeding to fill a cup with boiling water. She came back with the water and a tea bag without removing it from its package, no spoon. Ella sure wasn't about to ask. "Thanks."

The old lady let out a grunt and went back behind the counter to serve other customers with the same countryside manners.

Ella wished she had brought a book, but she didn't want to go back to her room to get one. Instead, she removed the tea bag and grabbed a straw from a container to press it down with.

Giving it some time to release, she thought of the nice man from the diner at home, Franklin. The word "home" rang like a bell in her mind and it drew a smile to her face. Wisdom came from all kinds of sources, and Danny had shown her that.

"Excuse me, miss?" Ella voiced rather loudly and assertively.

"What you want?" the old bag snarled.

"I'd like a slice of pie, please."

The old girl squinted bitterly, her wrinkled face squishing together. In an instant, she straightened up. "Coming right up."

The pie looked old and tasted old. As she choked down the first bite, the pay phone outside caught her eye. She became entranced by it, a deep obsession looming. She rose to her feet and exited the diner into the brisk night.

She stared at the pay phone for a while, slid her change in, and dialed.

Simon sounded more than panicked; he was distraught. "Please tell me it's you."

"It's me. I'm sorry."

"Are you okay?"

"I'm fine. Really."

"Where on earth are you?"

"Milwaukee."

"How'd you get there?!"

"I caught a ride."

There was a pause on the line and Ella sensed that he was crying though she could not hear it. Finally, he mustered up a hurtful, "Why are you there?"

Ella thought of everything she wanted to say to him, how she had been feeling all these years, what she needed, how he was holding her back, what had to change, but it all came to a crashing halt. Did she truly know what she needed? Her desires were merely fantasy.

"Can you come pick me up?"

"I've been praying for the last six hours hoping you'd call and ask that."

"I didn't think you prayed anymore."

"For you I do."

Ella wiped her wet nose. "I can try and meet you half-way."

"Stay put. I don't want you out on the road again. Give me the address."

Chapter 21

St. Vincent

TOM LOOKED RESTED, sober, and dressed with purpose. He straightened his tie in the mirror and grabbed his suit jacket off the bed. He had packed lightly, despite knowing he would be living the future on the road until he solved his daughter's case or the authorities had caught up with him.

He couldn't go back to see Collins in prison. If Hank didn't know yet that Tom had killed his son, it was possible that the video from the anonymous source would be sent to him on the inside. Before IPD were to make a move, surely Collins would have him hunted down.

He needed to further study the new files on Abe (from Dean) to find a lead, no matter how thin, and he couldn't do that from home. She was in state, so he'd have to remain in Indiana as well, his path of mobility still uncertain. One thing he had to do first though, was see his dear friend at St. Vincent Mental Hospital in Indianapolis. He was the only reason Tom was able to survive in that place, and perhaps the only reason he was able to get out and function enough to do his job.

It would be a final goodbye, one that he *had* to make. He missed him.

Tom climbed into his truck, opened the glove compartment, and took out his bottle of whiskey for a quick nip to reduce some of his shakes. As he drove through the neighborhood, he noticed a Ford truck tailing him in the distance, far enough back that he believed it was legitimate.

The route to St. Vincent had been inscribed in his mind. After forty-two minutes of highway time to Indy, the truck was no longer visible. Instead of taking the usual path to the hospital, Tom played around with a randomized, indirect route. He came to a four-way stop and looked into his rear view mirror, expecting the same truck to pull up behind. He waited, his detective sensors going off as he anticipated their arrival. But instead, a car pulled in behind him and he continued to wait, causing some confusion at the four-way stop. The car behind him honked and he continued on through.

• • •

The entrance of St. Vincent was not at all what Tom had expected. Renovations had happened since his release. It was very modern and sleek, with various private rooms on the main floor that had see-through glass for walls, most likely so they could keep an eye on patients. Instead of various browns and beiges, all of the walls were luminous with yellows, blues, and whites. There was a certain zest for life in St. Vincent replacing the aura of impending doom when Tom had been there.

He walked up a winding staircase leading to the second floor, a sign for reception pointing him that way. He arrived at a front desk to find a stout young woman with a beaming smile so wide it seemed comically forced. "Hi." Her chipper, high pitch stung Tom's ears.

"Hello, I…" Tom trailed off as soon as he glanced into the reading room straight ahead. He had disliked his time in that room every day, despite the comfort his friend had provided. In the outside world, Tom needed his private time, and in this world, he was desperate for it, for he feared that he would catch the crazy like a bad flu.

"Sorry." He broke out of his trance, "I'm looking to speak with Pat Ferris if he's available. I'm an old friend."

Her chubby cheeks flattened out as her smile faded and she examined Tom's appearance. "I'm so sorry. He passed."

Of course he passed. "When?"

"A couple years ago, I'm afraid. Would you like to speak with Dr. Levine?" Levine was the same Doc that had been there during Tom's stay. She was a very kind woman, one of select words. They got along just fine, the second key piece in keeping him sane in an insane place.

"Sure."

The woman smiled sympathetically and scurried away down the hall.

As he waited, his eyes wandered back to the reading area, and his usual table in the corner. His mind, uncontrolled, went back to his first day there.

Loss of the Decade

• • •

Tom looked down at his white uniform in denial as he tip-toed into the common area. Most of the other patients were pre-occupied with their own crazed thoughts and games, but he still sensed they were analyzing his every move. One side of the room appeared to be a lot more calm than the other side. Sitting in the corner was a man that didn't look to belong at all. He watched the babbling, shouting, laughing patients and shook his head. He was bald on top, wearing a button up short sleeve shirt, sitting upright in his chair with pristine posture, brow furrowed as he analyzed the rest of the flock.

Tom approached and he looked at him with nervous assessment.

"You wanna play?" he asked, nodding to the chess board on the table, waiting for a coo-coo response.

"Sure. It's been quite a while though. Maybe when I was a kid was the last time."

He lightened up. "It'll all come back to you." The man seemed normal to Tom. They were both relieved.

"So, what have you been up to today?" Tom disliked small talk but given his particular setting he was just grateful to find someone lucid.

"Oh, not too much really. Was hoping to go out to the water. Maybe do a little snorkeling, but Mary, my wife, is held up in our room. Caught a bug I guess."

Here we go. "Your wife is here too?" Tom asked, skeptically.

"Oh, of course. She always drags me places. I suppose I end up enjoying it most of the time."

After the initial shock, Tom envied the man. He wished that he thought his life was one big forced tropical holiday. After another glance around the room, Tom was ready to latch on to old Pat.

"Right," Tom finally replied.

The man moved one of his pawns with a smirk, like he knew something Tom didn't. "You got a timeshare here or is this your first visit?" he asked Tom.

"First time. Short trip."

"That's too bad. You'll have to make the most of it then."

Tom nodded politely and was then startled by a woman screaming at one of the guards. "I told you I'm not gonna do you! What is wrong with you? Didn't get a look the first time when you were watching me in the shower?" The woman spat at the guard. She then lifted up her gown revealing an old weathered body, breasts sagging. "Put your dick back in your pants," she hissed. The outburst caused Tom to re-analyze the room, setting his sights on patients rocking back and forth, mumbling to themselves in various voices, and some just staring into space. He looked back into the eyes of his new friend. Poor Pat was lost in his own mind.

• • •

Footsteps down the hall alerted Tom, breaking his daydream. He glanced at the same deep yellow lighting leading into the reading room. It was suffocating. He couldn't face being in that building for a second longer, let alone have a discussion with Dr. Levine.

Tom sneaked back down the staircase before the receptionist returned. Instead of leaving out the front entrance, he exited through the back so that he could walk by the garden where he had spent many hours in the summer. His greatest joy of that place was being outside tending to his tomatoes, carrots, potatoes, raspberries, etc. He made sure the chef at St. Vincent used his fresh produce and actually took pride in providing for everyone, even though he was terrified of the company he was feeding. Nostalgia canceled the eeriness that had been lingering inside the building. The cool autumn air hitting his lungs reminded him that he was a free man, but perhaps not for long.

He continued walking down a small trail and then cut across a basket-ball court that was often being used by high schoolers when he was a patient. He could hear his knee creak with each step like loose floorboards. Once he found Deanna, he'd probably get surgery.

Tom faked shooting a basket. When he turned, he spotted the same Ford he had seen earlier, parked across the street with two gentlemen inside looking toward St. Vincent. Tom patted down his side, relieved to discover he had remembered his gun. This was an opportunity for answers. He took in a deep breath, exhaled, and began to move.

Tom looped around them and approached from the rear, using a bush line to separate him from the sidewalk that their truck was parked along. With each step he took, he felt closer to Deanna. Tom peered through the shrubs and could see the same truck with two men inside. Lynard Skynard was playing. Tom gathered himself and with one burst, jumped the shrubs and slid into the back seat of their truck gun raised. "Why are you following me?" For a moment Tom worried that they weren't following him, and he was just some crazy stranger pointing a gun at innocent civilians.

In the driver's seat was a husky man who seemed immune to fear. He looked in the rear view mirror with annoyance on his face. The skinny man in the passenger seat, however, was not so cool and collected.

"You don't really wanna do this," the husky man assured Tom.

"Yes, I do." He had almost grown accustomed to his cowardly panic attacks. But now, not so.

"Just put the gun down and you won't get hurt."

"Start driving before this guy's brain is on the dash." Tom pointed his gun at the back of the skinny man's head. He had long straggly blond hair and a slender face.

"You wouldn't do that."

"No?" Tom tested. He looked the husky man in the eyes through the mirror. "Drive." He threw it in drive and they proceeded down the road at dawdling speed.

"What's the point of all this, gentlemen?" He didn't get a response. Good, he thought. "Who do you work for?"

The men exchanged a subtle look. "Where we going?" the husky man asked.

"Where you might feel inclined to answer some of my questions."

Tom glanced around at his whereabouts. He remembered there was an old abandoned warehouse a few blocks away. He had made some minor drug busts there years ago, but it became a place where he would go to drink in silence after a job was finished. Tom guided them there and they put the truck in park, a weighted suspense hanging in the air of the stuffy truck.

The skinny man spoke. "Man. I think it's in your best interest to just let us go on our way and you go yours." He seemed oddly genuine.

"No, that would be your best interest."

The husky man looked out the window at the old warehouse and chuckled, his voice deep and powerful. "You serious?"

"Yes."

Both men got out of the truck as instructed. Tom could see that they each had guns on their hips. He grabbed the skinny man's gun and slid it into his waistline while taking a few steps back from the two men.

"What now, genius?" said the husky man.

Snow began to fall, wet flakes disappearing on his skin. It was early for snow. Scenarios played over in his mind. *Torture? Threats? The big one isn't taking me seriously. The skinny guy is my ticket. I don't know a damn thing about him though… God dammit, I have nothing on these guys.* He had a feeling of deja vu, this path having existed in countless time lines, inevitable results pending. Tom aimed and fired. He hit the skinny man in the knee cap sending him to the ground. He screamed in disbelief.

This was different than the scrambled showdown at Abe's. He was ferocious. Tom turned to the husky man. "Your gun. Toss it."

The husky man was stubborn so Tom blasted another round into the skinny man's other knee cap, then aimed back at the husky man. "Give him your damn gun!" yelled the skinny man.

A second stare down commenced between Tom and the husky man. There was a competitiveness between the two of them, circumstances aside. Finally he smiled and tossed his gun over toward Tom's feet. "Help him up. Take him into the warehouse."

He obeyed and Tom followed them in. There was no going back now.

The building was almost emptied out. There were a couple areas with high tables for shop-related projects and a conveyor belt leading up to the second floor. Pigeons scurried away from them when they walked in. The skinny man leaned up against the conveyor belt while the other stood confidently, still slightly amused by what was occurring, despite his partner's agony. The dark and drab setting made Tom feel alive, spit and vinegar mixing to form an irrevocable dudgeon.

"It's pretty simple. I just need to know who sent you to keep tabs on me. That's it. Then you can go."

The husky man countered, "Otherwise what? You'll kill us? You're a cop."

"I'm no cop. Not anymore."

"No difference, you ain't no killer."

The skinny man squirmed with each comment his partner made, clearly taking Tom seriously, what with the holes in his knees.

"Should we test that theory? I think you picked a good day for it."

"I don't rat."

"What about your friend?" The skinny man was bent over the conveyor cursing from the blinding pain.

"You hear him saying anything?"

"Why you following me, huh? Your boss wants me for something, is that it? Cause I'm right here. He can't do it himself?" Tom's voice rumbled the already shaking tin box they stood in. "He's had plenty of opportunities, for years. Why not take his shot? What does he want? Connections with IPD for business? Is it drugs? Money? What?!" The pigeons all flew out from the building through a large hole in the ceiling.

"Is it Collins?" asked Tom.

The husky man laughed. "You realize we have nothing to do with the operation, right?"

"Just surveillance then?"

Silence.

"Does he have my daughter? Do you know who has her?"

"No idea what you're talking about. Sorry, boss. All I know is you're fucked one way or another."

"You're just not hearing me," Tom said through ground teeth.

"We free to go then?" His arrogance wouldn't leave, a strong confidence on display, assuming he'd leave untouched somehow.

"Who you working for?"

He shook his head and looked over at his friend, blood dripping down each pant legs. "What are you after anyway?"

"The man you're working for, whether it's Collins or someone working with Collins, they took my daughter."

"I don't know anything about no Collins."

He's lying.

"Look at you. If this guy actually has your girl, that's a good thing. You're a few screws loose. You don't exactly look like daddy material to me."

Tom let it slide for the moment. "Tell me his name."

"You've lost it man. You probably killed your kid."

Tom, in a not so begging tone, replied, "Please. I'm begging you."

"I ain't telling you shit. And if you're referring to who I think you are, I'm keeping that little piece for myself. She's real tight. 'Course I'll wait till she's eighteen, I'm not a monster."

Tom fired a bullet through the husky man's forehead. He was dead before he hit the concrete. There was no peace to be made with his actions, no rationalization of the kill. It was what it was.

He approached the skinny man, knelt down, and slid the end of his gun in the man's mouth. "This is important. Nod yes if you are able to help me." He nodded, wide-eyed in horror. Tom pulled the gun out.

"Jesus, I'm a carpenter."

"Who sent you?"

"Simon. Simon Brooks."

Nothing registered. Tom had never once heard the name Simon Brooks. The reveal was earth shattering, not in the way he had expected. "I don't even know a Simon Brooks."

"I'm sorry!"

"Simon Brooks… What…" He thought back to his case files, the name certainly didn't stick.

"Please just let me go."

"He's your employer. You must know something about him."

"I swear! Nothing!"

Tom pressed his gun against the man's wounded knee. "Okay!" His eyes moved back and forth as he searched for something that might be useful to Tom. "I know where he lives. I know the address. I can give that to you."

"What else?"

"Uh, uh. I don't know, man! He-he's real private. Quiet guy. Likes to keep to himself," he stammered.

"What does he look like?"

"Average height. Short dark hair. I dunno! He's average build. Wears glasses. Maybe on the smaller side but kinda intimidating. Real intense dude."

"Ever hear the name Collins?"

"Nah, no I swear, man."

"You wouldn't lie, hey?"

"Swear to you. You have my word."

"Connor Harrison. How about that one?"

"Honestly. No. God damn, my knees! It hurts!"

"I didn't hit any major arteries. You'll survive," Tom said. "Tell me about your orders."

"We were just supposed to drive into Rocanville and keep watch on random days. He would just call us. He'd ask for reports on your activities and then ask weird questions. Like if you were drinking and shit and if you looked stressed, drunk, shit like that. Then we got the call into that place in Indy. Where you shot those guys. How'd you get out of there alive?"

It looked to be something separate from his daughter. Blackmail of some sort in the making, waiting to leverage some of his contacts with the IPD maybe. It was entirely possible that this Brooks was in on something with Collins. Sure as hell picked the wrong guy for money, if that was the play. His bridge with the IPD was undoubtedly burned at this point too, Dean soon to be nipping at his heels. It was possible that he decided to go with his own approach after witnesses Collins go down.

"Why keep eyes on me? Did he say why?"

"I don't know."

"When did you start?"

"I dunno. Like a year ago, maybe. But not much off the start. Just lots recently. Like the last week. That's it, I swear."

When the phone calls from Deanna started. "There were no special orders he gave you? Search your brain so I don't have to touch your knees."

"He told us to make sure to contact him if you got too close to his part of town."

"He's in Indy?"

He nodded and sighed in pain.

"Your friend. He mentioned a girl. This Simon has a daughter?"

"Don't know if she's his kid for sure. But yeah, he had a young girl living with him in his trailer."

"How old?"

"Didn't get a good look at her. Could be anywhere from fifteen to twenty I'd say."

"What'd she looked like?"

"Real punk-like how some of the weird kids do it. Dark make-up, dark hair. Tall. Very tall."

None of this was helpful, not yet anyway.

"You gonna let me go man? I don't care if you tell him I ratted." His eyes lifted. "It's not just us neither. I know he's been watching you. Yeah, yeah! I followed him into Rocanville the one time. Had a different job in town anyway, I do some carpentry work here and there, and anyway, I noticed his truck in town so I followed him. He spent the whole day watching you, I'm sure of it."

"What else?"

"I dunno what else." He glanced over at his partners body and cringed. "Mark. My God, Mark... He figured whatever Simon had planned had to do with a big score. Said he had friends in Indy who spotted him at these high stakes poker games all the time. Guy usually cleaned up, but he had some big losses. Came unglued, owed a lot of money."

"So you were fine doing your little spy job, knowing you'd rob him after he robbed me?"

The skinny man adjusted his balance and spit on the floor. "Yeah. I just didn't know if it was cash. But we figured. Why not stick around and see how it played out, you know?"

Tom tapped him in the chest with his gun. "You're gonna talk to him."

"I'm not pulling any tricks for you-"

Tom pressed the gun against his knee. "Okay, okay! What do I tell him?"

"The truth. What all happened here. Ask him what he wants. Tell him... It doesn't matter anymore. Have him call me tonight. I'll hear out his demands. You give me that address just in case. If I don't hear from him by sunrise I'm coming after him. Video released or not."

He couldn't just come breaking down Simon's door without knowing more. Especially on the off chance that he had Deanna.

Tom leaned in closer, one last glare of intimidation. "Where is he?"

• • •

It was a risk, but he had to head back to Rocanville. The first thing Tom did when he got home was check the records that Dean had supplied him with from the Holy Angels congregation. His heart raced as he moved from "A" to "B" but there was no Brooks. Tom spent the next three hours looking through old case files, every single damn one he could get his hands on, only to find nothing on a Simon Brooks. Not mentioned once on a single file. His eyes were going buggy on him as he had started to double check, making sure he hadn't missed anything. He was connected to one of his suspects, he had to be. Question was—which one?

Tom checked his email to find a new message from Dean. It was information, or lack there of, on Paulette Graves, the mother to Jerry Lehman's daughter. Paulette had no record. She lived in California and worked at her father's accounting firm. A flight to California wasn't really in the cards at the moment.

Tom grabbed his coat and left for cigarettes.

Chapter 22

Fuel the Fire

SANTIAGO WORKED RELENTLESSLY on her new weapon, spending the past three days pulling bed-springs. Her bony fingers ached from the tedious process. Ripping coils free from the fused center took repetitive force and some were more stubborn than others. She wore a pair of mittens that were left in the closet, but the wire still to bruised her fingers. She had separated three coils and needed to break another three in order to have enough length. Fatigue played a factor. The food pellets were not enough and her water intake had been so little.

To distract her mind from the thirst and give her hands a break, she would still segment her days with reading breaks. She read a youth novel about a little boy that was being bullied at school, and an idea took shape. To trick his mom that he was sick he would hold his lamp against his forehead, separated by a thin bed sheet. When she came into his room to feel his head, he was obviously running a "fever" and needed to stay home to rest. Santiago would do the same. She would wear the thick parka-that was left in her closet-and mittens to hide her injured hands, and she would heat her forehead intermittently, hopefully timing the man's daily visits.

The pellets were a far cry from the soup that her captor would make from scratch with a creamy broth. They were dusty and stale with an odd artificial meat taste that was rather foul. It probably wasn't the worst thing one could consume, but the smell and dryness of it made her stomach turn. She would plug her nose and fill her mouth up with a handful. If she could get enough in and chew rapidly without tasting as she chomped, she could get it all down.

Her whole body hurt. The light in the center of her body was slowly dimming, approaching darkness. The end of it all. *If I die, will I get to leave this room?*

• • •

Her captor entered and she was laying on the floor, pretending to be passed out. She was covered head to toe in the winter apparel he had stowed away in the closet. The man gasped and rushed to her side. He shook her gently trying to wake her up, but she wouldn't dare open her eyes.

In sync with her desperate thoughts, his hand slid across her forehead, "No, no." He held his ear to her mouth and could hear that she was still breathing steadily. Like every move was an orchestrated play, he spoke into her ear, "Can you hear me? Please wake up, please." She hadn't heard this level of panic from him her whole life. He started tapping her cheek lightly with his hand, trying to get her to wake up.

She opened her eyes very slowly, his face coming into focus. She made sure her voice sounded weak-it *was* weak. "Are you okay?" His eyes welled up with tears.

"Cold."

"Are you thirsty?" he asked.

She nodded weakly and put her hand on his.

He stepped outside the door and came back with glass of water and a four-liter jug, what she hoped was for refills. "Can you sit up?"

She whimpered, and could see it was working.

"Here, let me help you," he continued. He helped her sit up against the foot of the bed and held the water to her lips. She didn't take the glass in her own hands and she didn't drink too fast as she needed to sell how weak she really was. She coughed up the water and exhaled like it would be her last breath. He brushed the side of her hair as she took a second try at the water. She wanted to rip it out of his hands and chug it so badly, but she held off, granting him the satisfaction of nursing her back to health. She drank the cup down slowly and he filled another glass which she drank quicker than the last.

Santiago closed her eyes like she was going to fade out again. "Hey, hey," he urged gently. She opened her eyes on cue to hear what he had to say. "You need to eat something. I know you've been having a tough time with your appetite, but I need you to try." She wanted to scream in his face. "Okay, I'll try," she replied.

"Lay down on the bed. I will go get you something."

He helped her to the bed and left, locking the steel door behind him. She looked up at the ceiling, refusing to cry.

He came back down with a pot of soup and a bowl for her. The smell of chicken broth made her mouth water. Her stomach was gurgling in anticipation of receiving her fuel. He fed her slowly, blowing on each spoonful of broth. She ate, acting timid, even though she wanted to drink down the entire bowl like a starving dog. She hated how he blew on each spoonful before he fed it to her. The loving look in his eyes disgusted her. She had grown beyond tired of his twisted personality and contradiction between punishment and affection.

As they started the second bowl, he paused, looking at her ratty hair and ghostly face. "I love you and I'm sorry."

"I love you too." Now the soup tasted like vinegar.

He smiled and stroked her messy hair. "You'll be up and running in no time."

Ready to receive her second bowl of soup, she said, "Yes, thanks to you."

He allowed her to have a third bowl of soup. She felt power flowing through her. She squeezed her right hand into a fist, embracing the pain of her bruised hand.

He removed the wooden block from her window, the sunlight bursting through, burning her eyes. The warmth hugged her.

"You're all that matters. Someday soon you'll see that."

"I already do," she said.

"My love. Soon."

He grabbed the empty bowl from her along with the pot, "I'll check on you first thing in the morning before work. Like usual, okay?"

"You're leaving the window?" she blurted out.

"Some sunshine for my sunshine." She felt thankful despite everything. It was so terribly wrong, but she couldn't help it.

Before he exited, he said, "Rest well, my sweetness. Drink the rest of the water slowly, not all at once." He nodded toward the jug that was half gone.

Santiago walked to her closet to admire her dresses. She felt more like a woman when she wore them. *Should I take them with me when I go?*

Chapter 23

Reginald

REG LEANED UP AGAINST the front of Tom's house, cigarette in hand. He had kept away from them as Tom had the past five years or so, but after smelling it on Tom, he caved. He had been outside for two hours, gone through five smokes, no longer enjoying them. His mouth was filled with cotton and his head was light and drifting. Reg watched a Ford truck pull to the side of the street in the distance. Tom had done something bad enough to draw attention in again.

Two teenagers ran out of their house and jumped into the truck and it took off. Deanna would have been about the same age as those two kids.

But she was gone, most likely dead, and he hated thinking it but knew it to be true. If she was alive, she was no longer herself, not the daughter he'd expect, or at least *want* to expect. He had witnessed a couple cases of the missing person returning home after ten, fifteen years. It was never good. Stockholm syndrome came in various unique forms, preventing the victim from making a return that would be deemed normal. There was no normal. It wore on the parents almost as much as when the child had been gone. A new hell.

An old beater car pulled up to the side of the curb at the far end of the street. Reg had eyes on it. Neither of them exited the car, same as last time with the truck.

Lights sparked his attention. A truck, coming his way. It was pulling directly in front of the house and Reg grabbed his pistol and dove for the line of shrubs to his left, separating from the driveway. Expecting a drive-by spray of bullets, Reg was ready to pull the trigger. But there was no sound of gunfire. No attack. He glanced at the driveway to see that it was Tom's truck that had pulled in.

Tom sprung out of his truck, gun raised at Reg on the ground. "What's going on? Who's out there?"

Reg exhaled the embarrassment and struggled to his feet. "You are." They both holstered their guns. Reg walked toward the basement office. "We need to talk. Now."

Back in the office, Reg thought of a way to tip-toe in, instead he dove head first. "What'd you do, Tom?"

Taken aback Tom replied, "What do you mean?"

"You *do* have a tail. You weren't kidding."

"You're sure?"

Reg wasn't positive, but he had that gut feeling that was often right. "I'm sure."

"Collins and I had a less than a friendly conversation."

"You went and saw Collins? Christ, Tom."

"You and Dorothy should leave town for a little while. It's just a precaution."

"Yeah, right."

"Reg, I'm really sorry."

"You're sure it's Collins? You make a deal with someone?"

"Reg-"

"I won't be a part of this."

"I don't want you to be."

They shared a glance, trying to figure out what one another was thinking. Reg opened his mouth to speak, stopped, then started again. "Tell me one thing. Your investigation…you haven't crossed any lines?"

"Crossed any lines?"

"You gonna make me say it?"

"Say what, Reg?"

"Use that gun of yours without another pointing your way."

Tom scoffed at the accusation.

"That doesn't go away. Killing an unarmed man," Reg said.

Tom glanced past Reg into the old case room. Reg knew his friend and partner all too well. He had a way of separating the obsessed and paranoid from the real. "What have you done? You can tell me."

Tom looked down at his palms and scrubbed his hands together, as if to wash away the metaphoric blood.

"Abe Collins?"

Tom didn't deny it, he simply responded with, "I found her."

After all the hits along the way, he had finally lost all control of reality. He belonged in that facility. Reg had dragged him out and immersed him in the same world that put him in that place to begin with.

"Did you hear me?" Tom pleaded.

"I didn't realize you were in this tough. We should get you some help."

"Are you listening to me? I know who has her."

"Why didn't you talk to me? There's nothing I can do for you now. You get that?"

"You think I'm crazy."

"What the hell am I supposed to do now?" Reg knew what he had to do. He had to turn Tom in before he got himself killed. He could potentially be putting himself, Dorothy, Allison and her boys all in danger with his actions. He should take Dorothy away from this town and live the rest of their days together somewhere else, just the two of them.

"I should take you in."

"Reg! You're not listening to me. Simon Brooks! His name is Simon Brooks. He sent men after me and I got them to talk. He's been my tail. I just have to find out how he's connected to all this. He knows where Deanna is. Simon Brooks. We have a name."

He was spinning ridiculous fiction, creating elaborate delusions. "Okay, okay. Everything is okay. Take a seat, let's have a cup of shit roast and we'll just relax. Get our bearings straight here."

"No!"

"There's no Simon! Not a real person, Tom. Only in your mind is he real. I'm sorry kid, but it's the truth."

"He has the answers we need. I'm getting her back."

Reg shook his head, eyes closed, hating himself for what he had done to Tom. "This ain't good."

Tom sat in his roller chair. Reg leaned up against the desk.

Tom spoke calmly. "Yes, it was possible that she was dead all this time. But the information at hand didn't tell me that. It didn't correlate with the statistics of kidnappings. She wasn't a statistic because I'm no ordinary subject, you know that. I'm a detective with enemies. This wasn't some spontaneous move. There had to be a motive so grand that there was no chance of a murder without a show, without pageantry. So I kept searching. I could feel her crying out for her mother and me every single night for ten years. And now, she can't remember our faces. She hasn't the faintest clue who she is. Can you imagine that?" Tom tried to gather himself. "I wonder how long it took her to stop thinking about us?"

Reg understood his pain, still shared it even. "So many lives sat over in the corner there, collecting dust. We've put aside so many cases looking for her. And I'm not saying that was wrong, but I don't know what to believe. All I know is that every time I'm in this god forsaken hole, I'm reminded of the others. They've got parents too. Just like you." Reg regretted calling their office a hole. "I'm sorry. I'm just worn out."

"IPD has more resources than we do anyway."

"No. They didn't have you."

"You're really throwing this in my face?"

"No. I'm just-I don't know what I am. Just a tired old man."

Reg wanted to believe him, but it had been too many years of this for Tom to be at all objective. "Who's been following you?"

"Simon's men," said Tom. "Come here."

Reg followed him over to Deanna's case room. He showed Reg the tape from Simon Brooks including video footage of Tom breaking into Abe Collins's house, -filmed by Simon's hired men-the gun shots firing off before Tom returned back to his truck.

Reg couldn't believe his eyes. Maybe he wasn't making any of it up. Maybe it was all true.

"What are you gonna do?" asked Reg.

"He has tonight to call. If he doesn't, I'm heading straight for him. Or out on a permanent road trip."

"Odds are Hank Collins knows. You're unprotected if you don't take yourself in."

Tom nodded. "PD will close in on me soon. Dean knows. I don't have much time."

Reg sighed. "Why'd you do it? Kill Collins."

Tom got up from his chair and looked around at his office. "It wasn't my intention. Of course that doesn't matter now. I gotta pack."

Reg wanted to stop him, but there was nothing he could say or do.

Chapter 24

The Final Stand

THE STEEL DOOR GROANED as the lever was pulled. Santiago sat on the edge of her bed wearing his favorite flowered dress. After back-to-back days of soup and sandwiches, she felt like an entirely different person.

Underneath the mattress was her completed weapon. The brass was strong enough, it had to be. The challenge had been tying off the metal springs tight enough so that they wouldn't give way when she used it. The sunlight continued to shine through. When she wasn't working on her weapon, she stood by the window and meditated, feeling the warm light sink into her skin and flow throughout her body.

The door creaked open. He seemed to be happier with each day. She rose to her feet, eying him up bashfully as she glanced back to the floor. She stepped in closer, feeling the heat rise in her chest as she gazed into his eyes hoping they'd search hers. They did. She smiled and caressed his arm. "Thanks for taking care of me. I'm sorry I scared you like that." She placed her hands on each shoulder then dropped her head to his chest.

His voice vibrated from his chest. "I'm just glad you're okay." She nuzzled into the nape of his neck, her breath directed on his skin. She could feel goosebumps spread on his arm. She started to sway back and forth with him lagging behind, not understanding at first that he was supposed to dance with her. After about thirty seconds of awkward dancing, he laughed softly.

She pulled back to get another look at his eyes. "Sorry. I've never danced before. I've heard you play music outside before and well…I just wanted to try. I feel silly. I'm no good at it."

He was pleased but still cautious. "You should have asked. Mind you, a lady shouldn't have to. The fault is all my own." He took more lead this time, moving her more swiftly around the room. "I care about you a great deal."

Another longing gaze followed as he continued to guide her around the small room. "I've always known that," she replied. She had made sure her make up was applied perfectly to his liking. Her eye lashes were long and curled, helping her pull off the classical type of pretty that he preferred.

"I'd like you to take me outside somewhere."

He stopped swaying. "Where?"

"Anywhere."

He shook his head, searching for an answer. "I'm not sure. Not yet."

"What can I do to make it up to you?" she asked.

His affectionate eyes transformed into a different beast; the man that abused for control. "It's out of your control. Time is the only thing that can help. And if you don't see that by now, then we may have a problem."

Her heart sank as she feared losing the moment. She couldn't wait though, not anymore. "I've been thinking about it a lot lately. I think I know why I've done what I've done-acted out." She had his attention. "I was scared. I'm terrified that you won't be able to show me a life together. A life where we can trust each other, and love each other, outside of here. You're scared I'll leave you. I can see it on your face all the time. Well, I won't. I'll be by your side, out where the world is, feeling the sun burn my skin, hearing the wind roll through the trees. I want to smell flowers and feel soil run through my fingertips. I want to run until I'm out of breath. And I need you to be there with me. Time won't change anything, time will continue to hurt me. Do you understand?"

His face was perplexed.

He took a step away and stared out the small window, the sun now hiding behind clouds. She slowly removed the straps of her dress and it fell to the floor. "I know somewhere in your mind, you know this isn't a life for me down here."

He stepped in closer, and then turned back to face the window. "The time might be right actually. I've got a meeting booked with a travel agent for next week. She tells me we could get a good deal to Playa Del Carmen. Paris is too expensive, I'm afraid." He turned back to her. "Our Europe trip will have to wait until I can take more than two weeks off. I'm so sorry, I know you've had your heart set on it."

She placed her hand on his chest to interrupt his delusional thoughts, then wrapped her arms around him and kissed him softly. She hugged him and backed up to the bed and lay down, submitting to what she hoped would be a gentle reaction. For the first time in a while, it was.

They made love and she tried to enjoy it like it was the last time, fantasizing about being outside again, far, far away from that place. She whispered in his ear, "Turn over."

"Why?"

"I know what you like. Let me look after you."

He turned over on his stomach. As she slid her hand up his leg, her other hand reached underneath the side of the bed. Her left hand caressed his backside and in one smooth motion she shifted, grabbed hold of her weapon and reached around his throat. She squeezed with all her might, the wire digging into his skin, his veins bulging in his neck. She strangled him with all her might. Her hands turned red, along with the red that dripped slowly from his neck. His back arched and he made a horrific gagging sound as he tried to get out of his vulnerable position.

Santiago leaned her weight back as hard as she could, while pressing his head forward with her foot. With one last, final ditch effort, he moved his head and her foot slipped. As he tried to pull away, her foot met the back of his head again with force, smacking it into the head-board. She kept pulling on the wire for what she thought was another minute but was probably only ten seconds, until finally becoming aware that his body was limp, no longer fighting her. When she released him, all she saw was red. The entire room, red. She sat frozen for a moment and then rushed out the door toward the phone. But the phone was no longer there in the basement. She'd have to go upstairs and then, outside.

• • •

Simon sat on the edge of his bed looking at his two packed suitcases on the floor. They were an ugly pea soup green, previously owned by his father. His father died when he was younger, but Simon hadn't felt the loss. They weren't close. He wasn't around enough for them to be close.

Simon hadn't gotten along with his mother either, but there had been more of an unspoken loyalty between the two of them. She was a devout Christian and he was a devout pool hall brat, a drunk in the makings. He rejected God's love and it put a strain on his relationship with his mother. It hurt her deeply. When she passed away, he went further down the rabbit hole, throwing himself into alcohol, high-stakes poker, and pool hustling. The wins came often, until one night, a few years later, he started losing, and he kept losing, until there was nothing left.

There was a knock at his trailer door.

He cracked it open cautiously to find the same skinny man, Teddy. He was clearly in pain, holding himself up with crutches, and had an urgent look on his narrow face.

"What happened?"

"What happened?! That guy is crazy, that's what happened. I didn't sign up for this shit."

"Where is Mark?"

"He's dead, Simon. He's dead."

Simon looked back into the trailer to make sure Ella didn't hear. "Be quiet."

"This guy shot my knees out and shot Mark in the head. My cut should be half. Look at me."

"I'm assuming he has our location."

"There was nothing I could do."

Simon tried to show sympathy with an awkward shoulder pat, but it was not sincere at all. He was never good at showing affection through physical contact.

"Yeah, I'm fine, thanks. He wants me to tell you to call him. Says he's ready to hear your demands."

Simon looked past Teddy at the row of other trailers, most of them still lit up. It was a heavy drinking community, but everyone recycled. Seemed there was a different elementary school collecting bottles at least once a month which was good. The folks around there were older drunks so they kept quiet and to themselves and they often handed over cash to the kids if they didn't have bottles left. It wasn't that bad of a place.

Simon motioned to close the door on Teddy.

"Whoa, whoa, hold on now. What about our deal?"

"It's not safe."

"You think?"

Simon stared awkwardly at Teddy.

"So what?" Teddy asked.

"I'm sorry."

"Why are you telling me you're sorry?"

"Because we need to disappear."

"You're kidding right?"

"Stay there." Simon went inside to fetch some cash from his bag. He handed over one thousand dollars in hundred-dollar bills. He could afford to be generous with the next score coming up.

"This isn't enough."

"You failed. You're lucky to get this. Use it for rehabilitation."

"You can't do this to me man."

"Please leave."

"I'm gonna-"

"You're gonna what? I'll kill you right now. Who's gonna care? Who-Who's gonna come looking? Huh?"

Simon pulled back the reins after his outburst. "I suggest you keep your distance from Bennett. And from me."

Teddy left slowly, limping horribly with his crutches toward his truck. His right crutch got caught in a hole and he tumbled forward awkwardly to the ground.

The sight of Teddy tangled in his crutches on the ground, made him feel something he hadn't been in touch with for quite some time. Compassion. Simon rushed out to stop Teddy from leaving. He helped him up to his feet. "Tell him we left. Permanently."

"No."

"I need you to do this."

"Do it yourself."

"Please." His tune had changed. Simon had felt it pulling him that direction more and more each day. He thought of Ella and how fragile she really was. She almost walked out of his life forever. Nothing was worth the risk. He could see that now. Not money. A new life wasn't created with cash and he had forgotten that. *How could I have been so blind?*

"He knows where you are. You get that?"

"He won't find us," said Simon.

"I'm no intellect or anything, but I'm telling you, after the time I just spent with that man? You're wrong. He's gonna find you. He won't stop. He just won't. And it's gonna end with you dead. He will find you eventually and he will kill you."

Simon reached back into his pocket and pulled out another stack of cash. "I've got another job here coming up. Half of that as well." A white lie.

After a moment of consideration, he accepted the cash and turned the ignition.

"Tell him we were gone when you got here. Emptied out."

"And when he shoots my third knee for information?"

"Did I say where we are going?" Simon continued, attempting to provide some level of comfort, "He has no reason to kill you."

"You really take his daughter?"

"Of course not. This is just business."

• • •

Simon watched her sleep with her headphones in. He removed them gently without waking her and placed another blanket on top of her for extra warmth. As he watched her sleep, he thought about how difficult it was going to be to tell her they were changing plans and heading down the road. What would they do with their new life? As long as she was happy, he didn't care.

He went back out to the living room and sat at his tiny desk in the corner. He pressed play on his camcorder and watched the video of Tom entering Abe Collins halfway house.

Chapter 25

The Bridge

TOM COULDN'T SIT STILL, awaiting a call from the man named Simon Brooks. Reg called Dean for any information in the database on Mr. Brooks. They spoke about Tom and Abe Collins, keeping the conversation confidential. Tom had *some* time, but not much according to Dean. He had pressed pause for Tom, withholding information until IPD had made a determination on the murder scene. He'd been hopeful that they were going to rule it as a quarrel between gang members, but it just wasn't the way it fell. As they began to build a suspect list, he had come forward informing them on the information he had leaked to Tom, in order to ensure his safety. Of course he did what he could to try and convince them that Tom had nothing to do with the shoot out, but they were still looking into him heavily for the murders. Dean would inform Reg before they were about to arrest Tom. They hadn't suspended Dean outright, but were going to deal with discipline matters after the case was closed. At least Tom would have a head start. But there was nothing on file according to Dean in regards to Simon Brooks. No birth records accounted for even. Probably an alias.

Loss of the Decade

Tom lay on his back staring up at that same ceiling fan, the anxiety eating at him. He hated waiting. Tom popped up and moved downstairs to his office. He took another peek at the list of names from the church's congregation. *Jerry Lehman...Harrison's. Connected both through the loss of their children and Tom's inability to find them. Did this Simon really have Deanna or was it something else entirely? Was it possible he was linked to Lehman or the Harrison's? Or was it a power play with Collins?*

The memory of Jerry's suicide was still freshly painted in Tom's mind.

Lehman's plummet from the bridge off road 218 was more than far enough when colliding with rocks. He had gone head first, no timid attempt at suicide. The body had moved downstream only about fifty yards before it was caught up on another set of boulders. Tom had taken a quick glance at his face, before the white sheet was pulled back over. There was not much left of it, the bone structure shattered, his eyes closed up; it looked like everything was blended together like Play-Dough. Tom had failed to deliver, and even as a man of great faith, Jerry took his own life.

*Took his own life...*A minister. A man of God took his own life. With his only desire to be with his daughter, he committed suicide. Tom was now on his feet pacing in his basement office. Tom wasn't exactly a spiritual man. Like anyone, he sure hoped there was an afterlife instead of nothingness. The details of creation, however, were not something he had given much thought to. He had not read the Bible, but it dawned on him now, in his basement of misery, how strict to the rules of the Bible Jerry would have been, especially based on the ways in which Minister Doherty spoke of him. Tom's exposure to the laws of Christianity was very limited, however, he had heard both sides of the story regarding suicide. It was a gray area that was heavily frowned upon in any Christian church. Given who Jerry was, it was doubtful he would have taken such a risk, ignoring the possible afterlife repercussions. If suicide was considered murder in Jerry's eyes, it was difficult to believe he'd risk eternity with his daughter.

An eternity of damnation. Perhaps the spiritual punishment wasn't that extreme, perhaps he could still seek forgiveness, but maybe not in the mind and heart of Lehman. Tom couldn't believe his own idiocy. In all his searching, all his suspects over the years, the answer lay with not the living, but the dead. Though the crime scene showed no evidence of it, Jerry Lehman could have been murdered. He had missed something at the scene. Overcome with somber guilt, he missed something. He remembered that day. It was hazy. His crushed face…

"I tried to tell him not to use you. Now he's dead." Leanne's words. Who would do that to the man? And why? After his daughter was taken from him, no less.

His clock read 3:30 a.m, still no call. Tom walked to the water cooler and poured a glass when his phone rang. The voice sounded familiar right away.

"Bennett here."

"Yeah, it's Teddy. The guy you shot."

"Why am I talking to you Teddy?"

"Because my employer-ex employer has told me to pass along a message. He is taking the day to arrange his affairs. He will contact you in twenty-four hours."

"That's not good enough."

"I'm just the messenger."

"For his sake I hope he doesn't sleep."

"Ah, come on. You think I gave you his actual address? He would of had my head." Tom had no response. "Twenty-four hours." He hung up.

• • •

Tom took the same sad stretch of highway to Indy. The road was quiet as he drove into the depths of nighttime, the sound of his muffler rumbling as he stepped on the gas. He watched his speedometer climb to ninety mph and he settled there, his Chevy roaring. He checked his rear view mirror, something he hadn't apparently been doing enough of over the years. But there was no tail. Just him, all alone.

The gravel down 218 was loose, his tires slipping a couple times along the way making his heart dance. *Wouldn't that be something? Kick the bucket hitting the ditch.*

He arrived at the old bridge. He stepped out and walked onto the platform, hearing the water babbling down below. Crickets chirped and critters rustled around in the bushes nearby. He hadn't been there since he got the call in for Lehman's body. He walked over to the ledge where it was presumed he took the plunge. The guard-rail consisted of cement blocks, built into the foundation of the bridge along each side, about thigh high. Jerry would have stepped onto the ledge, collected his final thoughts of his daughter, and jumped.

They couldn't make a specific set of tire tracks, as there had been too many over the summer. No sudden spinning out of the tires showing an urgent flee or approach. No identifiable boot prints on the ledge. No blood, hair, prints, gun casings, fragments of clothing up top or on the body, nothing. It was a clean suicide. Tom took a step back and looked across the bridge to the other side, where the gravel road continued. It was pitch black there, trees hovering above the road on both sides. He walked over to the dark, a perfect place to hide, to take a shot. But there were no shots fired.

He turned back around noticing a small worn footpath underneath the overpass. He shone his flashlight down it, following with slow steps. There was a walking path underneath, a place to stand, a place to wait. He stepped back around and walked halfway up the slope, his eye line level with the overpass, where Jerry once stood. He had been waiting for someone. An arranged meeting. Who though?

"He was there for us when the authorities had failed us." Leanne's words had indicated faith at the time, but maybe they were more literal. Tom leaned his head up against the stone siding of the bridge. Connor and Leanne Harrison could have been helping Jerry with his search. If he was murdered, and Connor and Leanne were involved with the ongoing search, maybe they knew more than they led on.

"Just stop. Stop looking. Trust me." Leanne had said after sobbing violently in his arms. She had spoken of alibis, financial records, phone call records, anything

he needed. She had sounded so exhausted. It was a bluff that wasn't really a bluff. She was done with it. Either he believed her and backed off, or he pursued. Maybe she just didn't care anymore. Lehman and the Harrison's had to be intertwined. If Lehman was murdered, was it possible the Harrison's were protecting someone?

Tom's body shuddered as he breathed in the cool air. He stepped back from his truck and imagined it. A man of the night greeting him face-to-face, or sneaking in stealthily from behind. One hard push, the cement guard taking him out just above the knees.

• • •

Tom drove into Indy. His clock read 3:50 a.m. There was so much more that Leanne Harrison wasn't telling him. He shouldn't have let it slide. He never should have. He had let alcohol and emotion control him. Regardless, she had information that he had to extract, one way or another. What was he going to do? Just confront her? Break in? The cops were already after him for murder. He was screwed one way or another, time working against him.

Chapter 26

Tell The Truth

THERE WAS A SECURITY DETAIL three houses down from Leanne's. Tom couldn't wait for daylight. IPD's pending investigation was looming, and he figured there wouldn't be much of an advance warning, just a swarm of boys in blue. He noticed a vehicle parked out on the street, not far from Leanne's house. Was it the same security guard staked out that he had seen last time? It didn't matter, he'd have to try and gain access from the back side of the house through their yard.

He continued through the intersection instead of turning into their street. He took the next parallel street, not noticing any spot-cars with eyes. Driveways had luxury cars parked, but there were none on the street except for a souped up Chevy with a lift kit, chromed to the nines. Probably not security. He drove by and got a look at the back yard that sloped down toward the house. They had a walk-out basement. No Rottweiler that he could see. The fence was closed off, but he'd just jump it with elegant, knee-crippling grace. The alarm system was going to make things interesting.

Tom rolled to a stop one block over and exited the truck with his pistol holstered at his side. It was ludicrous, but he was out of options and time. He sneaked between houses and into the back alley like a cat burglar in the night. He approached the wooden fence, a nice redwood. He got his hands over the top and in one quick pull he was at the top, his fall down to the ground was quiet, but he felt a strong twinge in his bad knee. The street was quiet, the lights were out, and he crept low, moving down toward their basement door, following the path between flowers on each side of him.

He tried the handle and it was of course locked. If he smashed the window he'd trip the alarm immediately, but if he picked the lock, he'd have time to disable the security system, which he wasn't certain would work. Every brand differed and he had no idea what he was walking into. Instead he'd better opt to cut the power. Lights were still out in the house so it shouldn't wake anyone. He walked around to the side of the house and located the power box. He turned everything off then located the power line that ran along tightly to the base of the house. He used wire cutters that he had along with his lock-pick set.

Tom fumbled with the lock pick for about three minutes, the sweat running down his back. Finally he felt a click and cracked the door open. He was in. He checked the security monitor to find that it was out, black screen. It was possible that the house would get a call within a few minutes due to the power outage, but there was no time to worry about that. He had to work quickly, find anything that linked the Harrison's to Lehman, even Collins for that matter. The basement was a good place to start. If there were secrets buried they'd be down here, or in their bedroom upstairs, which would mean SOL for Tom. He flashed his light around the entire basement to get a full visual. To his immediate left was a spare bedroom, next to it the bathroom, then the cold storage or furnace/laundry room.

He moved into the spare room, the bed was made perfectly, tucked in tightly in all corners. He opened the closet to find nothing but extra blankets. Then he moved to the dresser. The top drawer was empty. So was the second, third, then the fourth. In the bottom drawer, Tom discovered picture after picture of their son, Jared. They probably didn't want all of them up around the house, reminding them day after day of what they lost. Tom understood that, having taken down most of Dee's himself. It was like re-opening a wound, having all the reminders of her around the house.

He flipped through all of the photos until he reached the bottom, seeing a picture of Jared with Minister Lehman. He was wearing blue jeans and an old t-shirt instead of his heavenly robes. Tom reached back into the bottom drawer, and underneath some empty manila folders, he found a frame. He pulled out the framed picture to find Connor and Lehman together, Jerry holding a small-mouth bass, Connor's arm around him. No doubt, Leanne took the picture. They were friends.

"Don't move."

Tom dropped his flashlight to the floor. It rolled over, pointing at the feet of Leanne. "I've got a gun. And if I even feel you move an inch I'll shoot."

He could evade her. Drop down. She'd either miss high or freeze, and he'd take her out at the knees, disarm her. He could take control, tie her up with duct tape and leave her unhurt, look for more evidence, maybe question her with an assertive edge. "Leanne. It's Tom Bennett." His voice was calm.

"Don't move."

"I won't. Grab the flashlight at your feet. You're safe I promise."

"I should shoot you." Her voice was scared and dangerously edgy.

"Maybe. But you won't do that. Just stay calm. I am armed, but I'm gonna put my gun on the floor, okay?"

"Don't move!"

Finally he saw her kneel down and pick up the flashlight, shining it in his eyes on her way back up.

"My gun is on my hip here."

She moved the light down off his eyes to his midsection.

"I'm not here to hurt you."

"You broke into my home!"

"Do you want me to remove the gun?"

"Just...stay there. Don't move."

"Okay."

She backed up to an end table next to a leather couch. She picked up a portable phone off of the receiver, and Tom could here the first dial tone.

"Don't call the cops."

"Too late for that."

She hit another button, presumably a one after the nine she had already pressed.

He had to get straight to the point or he'd lose everything with that phone call to the cops. "I know you were friends with Jerry."

He didn't hear another dial, and she didn't speak.

"Did he tell you he was meeting someone? The night he was killed?"

She didn't answer and she didn't dial.

"It wasn't a suicide and you know that," he said.

Her voice broke the silence. It was flat, confident. "He did commit suicide." She sounded sure of it.

"Leanne...who was he supposed to meet that night?"

Silence.

"Someone who worked for Collins? Or was it you?"

"He wasn't meeting anyone. It was just where he chose to do it."

"Because of his daughter?"

"They'd tour the country-side. Once a week usually if they could. She liked a spot close by."

"Why'd you lie to me earlier? About not having a relationship with Jerry."

Again she was silent.

"Please, Leanne...can we talk outside? In the light."

"You broke into our home. I should call the cops."

"Don't do that. Leanne, listen to me. I'm already going away to prison. It's a matter of days, hours even. I'm already getting the justice that you want for me. You have my word. I just need the truth from you."

"There are no truths. Just one big nightmare."

Her gun was shaking much less now that they were conversing.

"Even if you don't think you're keeping something of importance from me, anything you know could be a tipping point right now. I'm close, Leanne."

He could hear a sharp inhale. "Where was this persistence for my son?"

He wanted to tell her about all of the difficulties that came with the job, about the odds being stacked against him, to tell her the emotional distress of finding children either dead or so damaged that they'd never be the same. "Just a few minutes of your time. I need you."

"I needed you." Her words ached.

She sighed. "Go. Out the back, the way you broke in."

She followed him outside.

Tom didn't know what to believe. It was all there, just waiting to be put together. For once, he knew with certainty that he was looking in the right place. The answer didn't lay elsewhere.

There was a patio set with a magnetized light attached to the pole underneath the umbrella she popped open. She set the flashlight down on the table, then added the second light. They sat across from one another, both with tired blood-shot eyes.

"Why are you in my house?"

"The past week has been chaos and I'm just trying to get my bearings straight. I've been pulled in two different directions and then I got thinking about Jerry's suicide, and something felt wrong about it all." Tom had to play another angle first to see what sort of reaction he'd receive from her. "I'm sorry, it was a mistake. I've been making many of those it seems. However, I have reason to suspect that the head of a major drug syndicate, one we stripped apart over ten years ago, is responsible for taking my daughter as a form of revenge, or possibly something more. I would need more time though. Time to disappear, track members of their organization. It could take years potentially. And that would be as a free man without anyone pursuing me." He wasn't ready to accuse her of anything just yet. "Do you know the name Collins?"

She turned her face to the side. "Yeah. From the news, I remember vaguely. What brought you to this conclusion?" she asked.

"I worked with the DEA to bring down their operation. The leader's son, Abe Collins, is being released, gave up a bigger fish."

Her face remained neutral, but it seemed forcedly so. "Well, sounds like an obvious fit to me. What else you got on him?"

"For starters, he told me they had her."

"Really?"

"His father said otherwise."

"And who do you believe?"

"The father. It was a jab from the son. They had me cornered not long ago and it appeared I was done for. He had to get his shot in before they killed me, or else he never would have gotten the satisfaction. That's because they didn't have her. If they did, he wouldn't have said anything. He would have showed me her face, tortured me."

"How can you be so sure?"

Tom took his focus off the conversation for a second to survey the backyard and surrounding neighbors. He heard a man coughing on his deck across the alley.

"I'm not sure about anything anymore, Leanne. Truth is I'm not a good detective anymore, and maybe I wasn't back then either. I was sloppy, and now I can't function. My instincts are gone."

"Your sudden humbleness doesn't change anything."

"I know." Tom used a lull in dialog to read Leanne's face and body language. She fell back in her chair in a relaxed position, her eyes flicking away then back to him. "Not to make any excuses, I don't deserve any, but… I've made too many enemies, Leanne. I was looking in the wrong places. There were too many options out there for me to look into a man that was already dead."

It took a second for it to sink in. Her body tensed up, but she caught herself, pulling her hands back off the table and resting them in her lap. "Jerry?" Her face shifted. "You think Jerry was involved?" The notion seemed overly ridiculous to her.

Tom removed the clip from his gun that he'd rested on the table. "Jerry… Jim Doherty said he was a strict minister. By the book, so to speak. A very literal believer. Old Testament guy."

"So?"

"You think he'd take his own life?"

"Haven't you thought of it? Killing yourself."

"Sure. Thinking is a far step away from doing," he said. "You were friends. For how long?"

"We met when he started at Angels. Be close to fifteen years now. Something like that."

"And?"

"Connor's an eccentric man. He was a churchgoer. Me, not so much. He and Jerry hit it off. We had stopped going almost altogether, then he took over as minister. We had marital problems, but he helped us."

"And the three of you became close?"

She paused. "He was Jared's godfather."

Tom was such a fool. How had he not came across both of them together during his investigations? On second thought, looking into their church wouldn't have made a whole lot of sense at the time. People have lots of friends. Leanne had probably been so disgusted when Tom took control of Jerry's daughter's investigation, that she kept herself away from it all.

"Why did you keep that from me?"

She raised her brow with a matter-of-fact look. "I didn't want to share anything with you. I was pissed."

"Or it made you look guilty."

"You're still on me?"

"Maybe you snapped. Your son, Jerry, his daughter. All gone." He almost hadn't finished the sentence. He sounded villainous with his delivery.

There was enough light from the lamp to show Leanne's red and bittered face. "You can go to hell."

"Who had reason to kill Jerry?"

Her phone rang. "Your security system," Tom said.

Leanne answered and told them everything was fine and that she'd get the power back up soon. They asked if she needed help sent to her house and she declined.

"Listen-" She looked to be in pain, her mind collecting past images, colliding with her current train of thought. Was she conjuring up a lie, or the bravery to speak a painful truth? "He was beloved by everyone. The church was everything to him. He had few connections outside of that. None that would make him a threat. Why would someone murder him a year after his daughter went missing. He had crawled into a dark hole already." Her voice was strained, the tendons in her neck flexing as she fought off her tears. "We tried to help each other. Hold onto hope. But he couldn't hold on anymore."

"His Godson. Then his daughter." Tom was more sincere the second time around.

"A man can only take so much. That includes those of faith," she said. "Maybe he was even more vulnerable because of it."

Tom deflated in his chair. "You had said you told Jerry not to hire me. Why did he?"

"He said he couldn't explain it. That he just felt it. It was God's will." She straightened up and looked him square in the eyes. "I lied to you about our relationship with Jerry because I was mad at you. I didn't want to help you. Maybe our children are out there. But I don't even like thinking about that anymore. What's been done to them?!" Her voice cracked and her eyes glazed. It appeared she slipped into a daze to escape her nightmare of a reality.

"I don't know," said Tom. Every single time he met with this woman, he had troubles seeing it. There was no evil driving her, no manipulation, no menacing force. She had lied though. There was something she was holding onto still.

"There's nothing in our church. Nothing that stands for suspicion. If you wanted to look into it you'd have to do research on like three hundred people. Question them. Follow them. I just don't think so. You'd need months, right?"

It was still possible, but she was right. He had zero time. He'd have to hear what Brooks had to say from a position of utter weakness. "You haven't heard the name Simon Brooks?"

"No. Sorry."

Tom exhaled. The simpler solution was one that Tom just didn't want to be true. *Abe Collins had my girl kidnapped. Jerry Lehman took his own life. And this woman has been through the same hell and back that I have.*

What was he going to do, torture her? "Thanks for not shooting me," said Tom.

"Can you wait here? I have something I need to give you."

She scurried off before he could answer.

Leanne came back with an envelope and handed it over. It was marked Bennett. "I wrote this for you after you stopped by last time. I was so angry. I've been so angry for so long...and the more I wrote, the better I felt."

Tears spilled over the cusp of her eye lids. "I'm really sorry about your girl."

"I'm sorry about-I'm sorry too."

She wiped her eyes. "Go home. Read it. It will help me move on, more than you know. Maybe it will help you too."

"Okay."

"Promise me you'll read it?"

"I promise. Has Connor left yet?"

She wiped snot from her nose and nodded. "It just didn't work."

"I understand. Where did he go?"

She sniffled, her nose now glowing red. "Florida. Just for starters. He's supposed to let me know when he moves on. Talked about Ireland next," she said. "I'm glad you didn't approach him. Thanks for that, I guess. He's not as strong as I am. I worry about him. I don't know what kind of trouble you're in, but as I said before, I'm ready to cooperate, truly this time. Though I'd rather not, for your sake. It's no world to live in. The allure of hope is cruel. It takes a piece of you each day."

"Maybe it was an allure. I just don't know if that's true anymore."

She bit her bottom lip gently, her head nodding yes and no simultaneously. "I hope you get things straightened out with the cops." She blew out her next breath emphatically, making a *whoosh* sound. "Read that letter when you get home. Or wherever it is you're going."

"Okay, I will."

"I'll pray for you."

Tom left and got into his truck and didn't know where to go. He wanted to go to a bar. He wanted to go see Reg, but it was a risk.

About forty-five minutes later, he found himself driving a few miles out of Indy, down a random dirt road. The sun was coming up and the birds were starting to chirp.

His cell phone rang, and he prepared himself for his long awaited conversation with Simon Brooks. But it was Reg. "Where are you? Did you find anything?" He sounded panicked.

"No, we're in the dark. All that's left to do is wait for that call and keep vigilant."

"Where'd you go?"

"It doesn't matter. My theories dried up."

"Listen…I got word from IPD, then Dean."

Here it was. His arrest down the pipeline. They were moving in on him.

"Leanne Harrison is dead. Gun shot to the head."

Everything slowed down.

"It looked like suicide, but they found the power line cut outside."

There were no words. None.

"Tom? Were you there?"

He could hear the uncertainty in Reg's voice. He didn't trust Tom's sanity. Not even close.

"I was there, but I did *not* kill her. She was fine when I left. I'm on my way to the office. Do I have time?"

A long pause followed. "I haven't noticed anyone around your place waiting to make an arrest. Dean said by afternoon, once they had this other scene all dealt with. I imagine they're gonna find your prints over there?"

"Yes. I'll see you in a half hour." Tom hung up.

He was just with her. How could that be?

Tom turned his head to the letter from Leanne, sitting on the passenger seat, waiting to be read.

Chapter 27

The Letter

HE OPENED THE ENVELOPE and removed the letter.

The corners folded around his shaking fingers as he peeled it open and flattened out the creases. He turned his interior lights on and sitting in his old Chevy, in the middle of nowhere, he read:

Dated, Sept 05/1985. Five years ago. *Not* a couple days ago.

It was supposed to be temporary. Maybe a year, no more. And now, the grips of time have me filled with dreadful torment. My son is gone, and I've come to know he won't be coming back to me. I blamed you. I guess I still do in part. Maybe it was justified at the time, but that doesn't matter anymore. What matters is what happened September 28th, 1979. Before I explain, please understand that I was broken more than a human being should ever be broken. I don't expect your forgiveness nor do I don't want it. I just want you to know the truth. I've written this letter hoping that I wouldn't have to send it out to you, for its delivery means either my probable incarceration or death.

It didn't seem possible. My boy. Then Jerry's girl. We wondered if they were linked or if it was just sick, disturbing randomness. But there was certainly one connection between the two, and that was you. We were both so angry. The way his daughter's case was handled by you is now neither here nor there. He came to me with his plan exactly two days after the break-in at your home, involving a criminal organization, as we were informed by our own private eye. You see, we had been watching you. For months we had surveillance on you, our reasoning somewhat clouded, but we hoped to catch you in the act of doing something wrong. Any sort of evidence against you, to bring us some form of justice. Stripping you of your PI license would have been a good start. But what was discovered one night was rather profound. The attempted kidnapping of your wife and child. You weren't living in a safe world. Your wife and daughter were in grave danger and I couldn't stand to see another child hurt because of you. Our PI didn't have much information on these criminals, but he knew that they were very dangerous people. I understand it doesn't make it right, but it sure helps. We felt, at the time, that we had to protect your daughter.

Jerry's plan began with the bridge where he faked his death. Our business had many connections, one of which had access in the IPD's forensics. That part was simple. We also facilitated him with fake identifications for himself and for your daughter Deanna. I will not share the names of our contacts as it is now beside the point. Jerry waited for the right moment, drugged you, and left you in a field, the same way he had once felt helpless in a field. And he took her. His intent, though fueled by anger, was supported by the circumstances. Your daughter wasn't safe. Not under your roof, not sharing your last name. He was to keep her for a short span of time, we had agreed on under a year. During that time you would experience the true pain that we had both felt when losing our own. You would also experience failure to find her. Failing to be a father. When the time was right, the anonymous negotiation would be simple. Sell your PI firm, retire from it, never practice it again, and move far away from this place. Your daughter would then be returned to her mother.

This was the plan. Simon and Ella Brooks would escape. She would be returned to her mother and he would flee. As I mentioned, we believed in the safety of your daughter, but make no mistake, this was also an act of revenge. You were to pay for your actions. You were meant to feel exactly what we had felt. It all seemed more clear back then.

Then, Jerry broke contact. As soon as we heard that your daughter had indeed gone missing, we were unable to reach him. Not once did he try to contact us again. That was it.

And by now, I'm sure you understand what the passage of time can do to a person. Not only is my Jared gone-that never gets any easier-but I've assisted a man in taking your baby from not only you but your wife, who had nothing to do with this. I didn't want this. Not like this. I regretted the decision after day one and the guilt has become unfathomable. My husband and I can't look each other in the eyes, let alone our own reflections in the mirror. I can't help you find him and your daughter. Just know that he'd never hurt her and she will be alive, unscathed by the abuse that so many kidnapped children endure.

Leanne.

Sept. 30th, 1989
I can't believe the harshness of my words to you, knowing everything I know. There was no other way for me to act, I guess. I couldn't face you with the truth. I wasn't ready for your visit.

The page was now spotted with droplets of tears. Tom set the letter back down on the passenger seat.

She was alive and he was receiving a call in only hours.

Collins had nothing to do with her kidnapping. It had been their attempted kidnapping of Allison that urged both the Harrison's and Jerry to make their move. Abe Collins never knew a thing about his girl. He had been simply tormenting Tom for sport.

The tail that Hank Collins had referred to was Harrison's PI. The other one, that started roughly a year ago, was of course Jerry Lehman's hired men.

The drive home was one of muddled shock. He couldn't stop picturing Deanna's face.

PART IV

Chapter 28

Heavenly Father

SIMON BROOKS-JERRY LEHMAN-sat in the front pew of the small United Church that he worked at. He had been there since their arrival to Indy a year ago.

The church was empty. He walked into the back and down an office hallway. He approached the minister's chambers and poked his head in. Finally, the minister lifted his head from his readings and addressed Jerry. "Simon, what can I do for you?"

"Oh, nothing. I best be getting home now."

"Of course. You finished the washrooms? I'm sorry, I know how particular I can be."

"It's no problem. Yes, they are done. Floors too."

"Thank-you, Simon. We'd be lost without you."

"Is there anything else I can do before I leave?"

"Have a good night. Oh and bring that girl of yours one of these Sundays. It would be nice to see her here."

Jerry must have shown discordance with the Minister's suggestion. He picked up on this rather quickly, "When she's ready of course."

"Yes, I will do my best."

"Goodnight, Simon."

The minister returned to his reading material. Jerry exited and moved into a different room. It was a small office that had only been used for storage purposes. It was old and it smelled of musty carpet. There were boxes stowed away in an unorganized fashion, the clutter reminding Jerry of how he and Ella hadn't been able to settle down in one place. He knelt down beside a small safe and put in the combination. He cracked it open to find a large sum of cash exposed. Collections were typically counted and distributed to various charities weekly; however, they had stalk piled a larger amount for a couple larger upcoming initiatives.

Jerry placed the cash in his backpack. He counted it roughly. It was enough to get them settled into a new place. When he rose to his feet he noticed the collection plate on a table filled with cash. He pulled off his old ecclesiastical ring and dropped it in the plate on top of the money. Jerry walked back out into the hall and exited out the back of the church.

• • •

Ella-Deanna-sat on the edge of her bed listening to soft jazz on her stereo. Her room was almost completely bare. Nothing was posted up on the white walls, only some clothing scattered on the floor and her backpacks heaped. There was a knock at her door followed by a ten-second pause until she finally rolled her eyes and turned down the music. "Come in."

Jerry entered and looked down at her packed suitcases and the remaining clothing strewn across the floor. He took a seat at the edge of her bed and looked at Deanna sheepishly. She took a quiet, deep breath in, prepping herself for an uncomfortable conversation. Many of them were.

"I see you are almost packed."

"Yeah."

"We need to have a discussion."

She saw something different this time. He looked incredibly sorry about something.

"What's wrong?"

Jerry shifted nervously on the bed, trying to formulate words. Horrific news was on the tip of his tongue.

"I was only ever thinking about myself. I've been selfish, and you deserve much better than that."

"Simon, you-"

He interjected graciously, "I care about you and you only, but that doesn't mean I haven't been putting my own desires first. What's best for you *should* be what is best for me. I-I-think we need to look at this differently."

"What are you saying?" She could feel where he was going. After everything, he was bailing.

"Everything we've ever needed has been there for us. We've done our part. We should move on. Start our lives the right way. No more hustling, no more theft, no more moving around."

Deanna felt like she was going to be sick. They had to follow through with the plan. Money was a byproduct, but that son of a bitch had to pay. She needed to look him in the eye while they emptied his pockets. She had to see his surprised face.

"How can you sit there and tell me this?"

"It's not safe either, Ella. He's become so dangerous."

"I don't want to be here anymore. Can't you see that?"

"We won't be. We are leaving. I just don't want us doing this anymore."

"If not now, when?"

"Never," he murmured.

"Is this because I ran away? Because that's not why I left. I'm ready for this."

"We don't have to do this."

"Are you afraid he'll take me away from you?"

He shook his head. "I just want you to be safe. We don't need this."

"How could you do this to me?"

"This was a mistake. One we should remove ourselves from."

"This is the plan, this has always been the plan! And now he's too dangerous? I'm dangerous!" shouted Deanna.

"I know you're upset-"

"No, you don't! You don't know. You don't know what my life is like. You don't know how I feel sick everyday, Simon." Her toes were curled, body tense. Jerry's eyes shifted back and forth as he looked down at the bed.

"Where are we gonna go without the money?" she asked, waiting for a quick answer. "Well what?!"

"I don't know! I don't know!" he yelled.

Jerry glanced out her tiny window.

"What have you always told me all these years?" she asked calmly.

He came to a stop and faced her. She continued, "Remember. I know it hurts but you need to remember."

He caved, looking her in the eyes, his face now steady. "And what do you remember?"

The memories of her real father were fuzzy, his image entirely forgotten. What she was able to recall was incredibly faint, like a dream she had only once, a long time ago. But it was still there. Being locked up in a small dark room. Her mouth so dry. She was so thirsty. She begged to hear footsteps up to her door. Footsteps that were both terrifying and hopeful.

She remembered Simon. The faded imprint in her mind of him taking her from a dirty truck. She remembered being frightened in the moment, but it soon went away. He showed her the first church she ever remembered. The colorful artwork of the windowpanes were gorgeous. She remembered feeling safe.

Deanna had been neglected, abused, and he saved her from it all. As stuck as she felt now, he had given her a chance at life to begin with. And now, with their plan in place, she needed him to come through for her one more time.

"I remember enough," she said to Jerry.

She could see he didn't want to, but he spoke words she needed to hear. "Well, let's finish it then. Put it all behind us."

"What will we do after?"

"A new beginning that we can build upon. A true start with a proper home. Maybe you'll find something in music."

The thought chilled her. Finally, she could live.

•••

The digital clock on his nightstand read 5:50 a.m. Tom looked down at his packed bags and then up at his big cell phone. He had waited but received no phone call from Jerry. The anticipation of seeing his daughter again was an unnerving torture, one that was new even to him. Those phone calls from Dee must have been equally painfully for her. He shook at the thought of her holding the phone to one side of her head, a gun pressed on the other side. That wouldn't have been the case though. Jerry would have been more subtle with his threats. Tom recalled from his previous conversation with the skinny man, Teddy, in the warehouse. He had seen her before. Described her. She was kept in plain sight, making it possible that she trusted Jerry.

The door-bell rang and Tom sprung to his feet. He hadn't noticed anyone approach through his window. *Please don't be IPD.* Looking back out his bedroom window first, he noticed a car covered in rust out on the street that wasn't there before.

He approached his front door slowly, hand on his pistol at his side. He looked through the peep hole to find Teddy hovering over a set of crutches. Tom swung the door open.

"What the hell are you doing here?"

"You're not gonna let a cripple inside? It's brisk out."

He winced as he entered Tom's home, taking in his surroundings.

"Nice place you got here." He forced out nervously, trying to seem casual.

"Why are you here?"

He grimaced again when trying to adjust his crutches. "It's tough when both legs have been shot."

Tom left the room and came back with his bags, dropping them on the floor loudly. "I don't have time for this."

Teddy exhaled and spoke calmly.

"Simon sent me. He's decided against making any negotiations with you. He wants to leave with the girl, start a new life he said."

He felt like he was falling, like the words weren't real. Tom refused to believe the news. He had come so close, just to have the rug pulled out from underneath. *It's just another part of his game.*

Teddy continued with compassion in his voice, "They ain't coming back. I wouldn't guess as much anyway. They'll be out of state at the very least, maybe out of country, but they didn't say. I don't know for sure."

Tom's ears perked up. "The girl was still with him?"

"Yeah."

"Was she okay?"

"I don't know. I think so man."

"You had seen her though?"

"Yeah. She's okay. Seemed just fine the times I saw her."

At least he knew who he was chasing now. He could go on his quest, tear down walls, and scratch and claw his way to her. But that would be easier said than done. Jerry had proved himself resourceful. He would eliminate any trail, generate new identities, and leave him once and for all. Tom was running on fumes at this point, and IPD breathing down his neck would most likely prevent him from getting very far. He kept rejecting the feeling as he stood there in shock, but it just felt…over.

Teddy could see the mixed emotion contorting Tom's lost face. "I'm sorry man."

Tom shook his head. *Another ploy.* He raised his gun. "Where are they? And don't tell me you don't know."

"Tom, is it?" His tone was comforting, staring down the barrel of Tom's gun. "Think about it. I didn't have to come here. Simon is gone. And that's the truth. I don't know the details of this war and I don't have a hand in it. And I hate to come here and tell you this, but I felt you deserved to know as soon as possible."

"Why?"

"Because I believe you."

Tom lowered his gun, the color in his face flushed away. Teddy had a confused look on his face, perhaps dismayed by Tom's lack of gumption.

"I mean I thought you'd figure this much. You're a PI right? You got your guy. You just gotta track him, or whatever. I can show you where he was staying and maybe you'll find some clues or something."

Tom felt like he was suspended in mid-air, floating aimlessly. He could feel his drive and his will to save her drifting out into space.

"They probably already have new identities," Tom mumbled to himself. He had the letter as proof, but IPD would deal with his own crimes first. With Tom's medical history, they could argue that he coerced

Leanne to write that letter. They'd prove he was unstable. "They'll be coming soon."

A silence followed. Tom looked down at his packed bags.

"You wanna shoot me?"

"You're sure she was okay? Where was she being held? How did you see her?"

"I only saw her a few times, but yeah. In that trailer. It seemed he took care of her. I think I saw her walk to school once. She always had headphones in her ears when I saw her."

The calls couldn't have been coming from her. If she was free to go to school and move around in public, why hadn't she used any of these opportunities to escape? Unless he was holding something over her... It must have been someone else. Or were there any calls at all? Maybe I've lost it. She is being fed, clothed, has a roof over her head, and an education...

Tom moved past Teddy, picked up his bags, and walked through the door, leaving him behind.

"What are you gonna do?!" he yelled.

Tom climbed into his truck and took off with a specific destination in mind.

Tom sped down the highway and turned off west down a gravel road. He stopped at his spot. He'd been there many times before.

He stared out into a familiar corn field, parked on the side of the road. He could still remember the horrible feeling when he woke up in that field, without his daughter by his side.

Everything had changed from an hour ago. A new thought pattern took over his brain, infecting his entire mind like a virus. It weighed on him, unforgiving. His gun was overwhelmingly appealing as the thought of Jerry Lehman's reaction played out like projection slides.

• • •

May, 1978. Ella Lehman's search party.

The smell of spring was in full effect. The leaves crunched beneath Tom's feet as he jogged toward a search party through the trees. They were twenty miles out of town, somewhere between Indy and Rocanville, west of the highway among the grid roads. It was dry, dust lingering in the air congesting Tom's sinuses. The search party was spread vast, but Tom was able to find Jerry Lehman leading the charge. The cool air awakened Tom from an all-night shift. He felt badly about what he had to do.

As Tom ran toward Jerry, he wanted to turn back around and phone him in the evening instead. This was not Tom's style, however, and it never would be. He needed to tell him face to face. Jerry continued calling out, "Ella! Ella!" The shouts were still hopeful.

"Detective."

"Hey, Jerry. How's everything going?" Tom regretted his poor attempt at small talk. Obviously things weren't going well.

Jerry ignored and continued to call out for his daughter. "Listen, Jerry. Can we talk?"

He twisted in shock, looking ready to tackle Tom, his eyes frantic.

Loss of the Decade

Tom had been working on the case for a month. Jerry's daughter Ella was only five years old. She was always one to wander but never too far, Jerry had mentioned on several occasions. Jerry was working overtime in his church, where Ella would often join him after daycare if she didn't have school that day. She enjoyed the church and loved spending time there with her dad.

Jerry had been in his chambers, going over his sermon for the next morning and that was when she left through the front doors. Jerry had given her some change earlier that day, so he assumed she had slipped out to get some candy from the convenience store down the street, but she never came back.

"It hasn't been near long enough." His voice was high, already pleading. His desperate eyes searched for understanding in Tom's, needing him, needing her.

"My hands are tied here, Jerry. I have other cases."

"Untie them. This is my daughter we're talking about." That look. Out of all the tragic facial responses to the end of their child's search, that one was the worst. The Cadillac of fear. His baby, gone.

"I understand, but it's not just up to me." There was nothing he could say that would make things better. Droplets of rain scattered the bald trees, lowering the floating dust back to the soil. Rain slid down Jerry's betrayed face, mixing into a cocktail of tears.

"What does that mean? You're your own boss. You do what you want. So help me."

"I am. But there are other cases. And I still work in partnership with the police department. They're backlogged. There are a lot of other worried folks out there too." All facial expressions vanished from his face. "I know this is difficult to hear. I'm sorry."

"You can't do this to me. Please don't. I-I need you to help me. Please, I'm begging you."

"It's been three weeks and there are other kids out there that need our help."

"She's my girl. I'll keep helping you. We're close, I know it."

"We already used resources out here in the country. I'm sorry, but I told you this was not the primary place to be looking."

"She likes it out here! I told you that! We spent countless days out here. We...we picnicked!"

"I'm sorry." Tom had to be firm. He had to be strong.

"I'm telling you we just need a little more time. She's fine still. We just need time."

The calls from other searchers continued, Ella's name echoing.

Tom shook his head sadly, rejecting Jerry's request.

"How could you do this to her?"

"I'm sorry, Jerry. At this stage we have to move on."

"No, no, no." Jerry grabbed hold of Tom's arm and squeezed tightly.

It was difficult for all of his clients to grasp. When desperation is at play, there was rarely an understanding. Tom's contracts always had a time limit, usually being a month. Feeling the pressure of the clock while he worked was a lot for him to stomach. With IPD bringing him over half of his business, it was in his best interest to keep them happy. That aside, it just made sense. The statistics for a missing person returning home plummet after one week. After three or four, the chances become almost inexistent in most cases. It was a sad truth.

Tom pulled away from Jerry with an apologetic stare, before turning and walking back through the trees.

He reached an opening and walked through it into an open field.

Jerry's voice no longer carried her name.

Chapter 29

The Arrangement

TOM'S GUN SAT IN HIS LAP. He rolled open the window and leaned his head back against the headrest. Pumpkins and dusted wheat residue hung in the air, mixing with ash. A crop must have been burning in the distance, the smoke not visible. More flashes of Deanna hit him like a title wave. She wasn't going to be the same. He'd be foreign to her, just a face you see on a train or a bus, then gone. She'd have no desire to escape her world, unless Jerry had instilled a great deal of fear within her. Based on his heavenly background, Tom doubted this. Leanne said as much in her preemptive suicide note.

He looked down at his pistol. The ending to his existence, one that was no longer necessary moving forward. As he raised the gun to his temple, he didn't think of his daughter, rather Reg and Allison. It would bring them pain, but they would understand, and that understanding would result in a quicker recovery. Time had always been cruel to him, but in this situation he was hopeful that time would be generous to them. They deserved at least that. Bob Seager's "Like A Rock" played on the radio.

His hand held steady pressure, the tip of his pistol pressed against his head. He closed his eyes to hold onto an image of her, but she disappeared. Tom squeezed the trigger slowly, trying to clear his mind of any selfish leftover desires for living. The phone rang and he pulled his finger off the trigger. He exhaled loudly, and inhaled sharply. He had been holding his breath for quite some time.

Tom grabbed his cell phone and answered without saying anything.

"You know, I've envisioned having a conversation with you for years now and I'm not sure what to say."

In one fell swoop, his fatherly instincts kicked in. "If you touched her-"

"I would never hurt a child. Ever," Jerry said.

"Why are you doing this?"

"I shouldn't have to lay it out for you, should I?"

"There was nothing I could do. I-"

"No, no. That's a lie…you gave up. It was your job and you just quit."

"We had a contract. We did what we could. For every broken parent, there are five more in line waiting for us. You know this, Jerry."

"Don't call me that," he snapped. "You're a drunk. A drunk that accepts no responsibly for his actions."

"So what then? You take a little girl away from her family? Traumatize her?"

"I am her family. She received more care than she was ever going to get from you."

"Where is she?"

Jerry ignored Tom's question and continued on with his frustrations. "I didn't ask for much. One detective. One search party. But no, not enough evidence, don't have the resources to continue. You killed her."

Jerry's hatred hit him through the phone. Tom understood the blindness, the loss, the chaos of it all.

"What do you want from me?"

"What do I want? I wanted your miserable life to continue until the day you died. So that the rest of your days were filled with regret, guilt, and uncertainty. I wanted you to feel how I felt the day you gave up on my girl, the day I had to bury an empty coffin. I wanted you to feel like that for the rest of your drunken life."

"Is that why you moved back to Indianapolis? To be close to me. To get your pleasure from my pain, is that it?"

Jerry remained quiet.

"What if someone from your past saw you? Pretty big risk considering you're dead."

"Nobody from my past was gonna find me. Not where we were."

"What's with the home video?"

"Insurance."

"If you had really been doing your job, you'd know that footage doesn't change a thing. I'm locked in for those murders regardless."

"I suspect there are some people in IPD that would still go out of their way to vouch for you. The tape helps. You'll play by my rules."

"Maybe you've already sent it in to IPD?"

"That would get in the way of my plans. Think you could keep the authorities off you for a couple days?"

"I'll manage."

Tom slid his gun over to the passenger seat. "I didn't do this to you, Jerry. Someone else did. And now you've become that someone else. You've accomplished your goals. At the very least she deserves to know the truth."

"I won't fall victim to your twisted words. You are treachery in the flesh. Your negligence was cold. I could feel it coming off your skin. You think I'd forget such a cold look? She's gone because of you."

"What's the plan here, Jerry?"

"Yes, well. Your finances for your daughter. I'm guessing $500,000.00 is in the scope of possible."

"Really? Money after all this time?"

"We do what we must."

"I can't come up with that in cash this instant."

"No, I'm sure there are others that would help you for the time being. Don't try anything, Bennett. You don't want to see where I can be pushed."

"Eye for an eye. Is that the idea?"

"For starters."

"And what about God? Think he's a big fan of what you've done?" Tom asked, his voice reverberating.

"God. He called in sick the day you took my girl's case. I don't know if he ever came back."

"How'd you pull this off?" He knew but wanted to hear his answer.

"You're not the only one with friends. Although you're running thin in that department by now."

Tom's next breath muffled the phone much like the calls he had been receiving. "Leanne is dead, Jerry.

She killed herself last night." Silence followed on the other end. "Sorry. Simon I mean."

"You're lying."

"She couldn't deal with what she had done anymore. What *you* had done. Would you like me to fax you the letter she wrote for me?"

Silence again.

"Let me speak to my daughter." Saying the words, hearing them as reality, made his heart stall.

"She's not here with me now. Tomorrow, seven p.m. Grid road 751 off Highway nine. Take it west, you'll pass two farm yards, continue on until you drive down a steep hill. Pull in at the second bluff of trees. Please don't bring anyone else. I don't want to kill her. She's important to me."

Implying that Deanna belonged to him pissed Tom off. The threat pissed him off even more. The gun in Tom's hand would no longer fire upon himself as it seemed that Jerry would now be a more suited recipient.

"Fine. I'll get the money. She better be there."

Jerry was the first to hang up.

Tom could drain his 401K and sell all of his PI assets to another outfit he knew in Chicago. He'd still be a ways short and would need sizable contributions from Reg and Allison.

• • •

Reg emptied out his savings, giving Tom roughly $125,000. He was aiding an alleged murderer and still handed the money over without any hesitation.

Loss of the Decade

Allison was full of concerned questions. He told her that when his drinking had reached it's worse, he acquired a rather lofty gambling debt. He never gambled before in his life. Tom told her he'd sell his practice and start over to pay her back and she told him he was *not* allowed to do that. He desperately wanted to fill her in on what was going on, but it would've torn her apart. Instead, he would execute and deliver.

Between Reg, Allison, and himself, he was able to come up with $460,000. It would have to do. If the exchange wasn't made or she wasn't brought to him, Tom was prepared for a shoot out.

Tom met Reg on the side of the road outside Rocanville. He loaded up the cash in his truck and then faced Reg awkwardly, unsure what to say.

Reg spoke first. "You sure you don't need backup?"

"No. I can't afford any risks. I need to do this alone."

"What if she ain't there?"

"Then I'll kill him."

"Then what?"

"She'll be there."

Tom searched for heartfelt words but couldn't find the bravery to say them out loud. It was always more difficult in the moment, easier to just not.

"You take care of yourself," Reg said to Tom, his old eyes tired and wispy. Reg stroked his beard and got one last look at Tom before turning and entering his own truck.

Tom leaned up against the side of his truck and looked out at the setting sun over the bare wheat field.

The flat land in every direction made him feel more lonely than usual.

• • •

Jerry sat in the kitchen of a restaurant at a fold out table, a plate of spaghetti placed in front of him. A bald man entered and set down two passports and two IDs next to his dish of pasta. Jerry took a bite of his pasta and reached into his briefcase, pulling out a stack of cash for the man. Despite the man's illegal operations, he had enjoyed his company from multiple conversations at church, where Jerry had worked as a custodian and usher when he was called upon. Plus, who was he to judge a man based on his moral compass? Jerry had crossed that immoral threshold long ago.

The bald man hovered over Jerry, waiting for a comment. He dug in for another bite of pasta.

"You gonna check 'em out?"

"I know they're good. Your eyes are better than mine," said Jerry.

"So, where to then?"

Jerry hesitated, his eye catching a calendar hung up on the wall. The theme was tropical destinations; it appeared to be places along the Caribbean maybe. The smooth sands and crystal clear ocean water was not particularly what he wanted, then again he didn't really know what he wanted.

"Our own paradise maybe."

"What, like Florida?"

"Yeah, maybe Florida."

"Guess I won't be seeing you at church no more then."

Loss of the Decade

"Guess not."

Eyes still glued to the calendar, Jerry voiced a direct and personal question seamlessly. "Have you always been a religious man?"

"Yeah, of course. My mother wouldn't have it any other way."

"Your faith has always been strong?" Jerry tilted his head, interested in the man's philosophy to come. After a pause of contemplation. "No?"

"No, sir, God is great in his almighty power and everything, but I think that a lot of the time he leaves it to us. You have faith in others first, then you can have faith in Him again. Or something like that."

Trust in others was a language Jerry no longer spoke. It had become foreign to him long ago. He could sense where the conversation would travel, and he had no interest in it. Jerry was a man of tangible realism, and had no time for spiritual falsities. The charade of Christianity had crumbled like ancient stone, evaporated to dust.

He set a hundred dollar bill next to his plate of half eaten spaghetti. "Thanks for the meal."

"Yeah, of course. Good luck in Florida."

Jerry exited out the back with his new identities. The pressure of completing the job was beginning to stir in his stomach.

• • •

Tom sat on the edge of an old springy mattress in his motel room looking down at his gun. He pointed it at the door as if someone were about to enter. Tom turned and faced the mirror, pointing the gun at his reflection.

The man staring back at him was exhausted, white-faced, and slimmer. His once monstrous frame had endured muscle loss. The tip of his pistol began vibrating back and forth as the thought of seeing his daughter made him succumb to unbearable nerves.

He needed a drink now more than ever, but was fighting like hell to prevent himself from walking over to the hotel bar and getting hammered. It wasn't Allison, nor was it his health that kept him fighting. It was that he didn't want to disappoint his daughter. Even though she didn't know a thing about him, he wanted to be as acceptable as possible, without a scent of liquor on his breath. Once they were re-united, he needed to impress her.

Sitting there in his crummy hotel room, he knew two things for certain. One, the next hour and a half sitting in that room would feel like an eternity; and two, he required his best motor skills and mental clarity when meeting with Simon and Deanna. He couldn't do that if he was a shaky mess. The only way he'd be on his game was if he'd have a couple drinks. *A couple. That's it.* Tom rose to his feet too quickly, and the nausea took over. He sprinted to the bathroom and expelled everything he had stored away. After a water splash to the face, and a sampler of mouthwash, he left for the bar.

It was nearly empty, except for a couple under-agers playing pool in the far corner. Tom chose a stool at the end of the bar and ordered a whiskey neat. The bartender was a young man, incredibly tall, narrow shoulders, with big Dumbo ears flared outward. Tom stared at his glass of whiskey, the way one might look at a fish in a tank. The barkeep picked up on his resistance and grinned.

"Slide it on back and I'll pour you a soda."

Tom fingered the glass gently, protecting it from the bartender. He spoke up again, "I'll let ya think on it."

Tom tapped his finger nails on the bar top surface, feeling a dizziness play with his eyesight. The bartender slid a stick of gum beside the double of whiskey. "Whether you take it down or not, this feeling will continue to happen. May as well put it in your calendar."

Tom grit his teeth, took a breath, and drank the shot down. He unwrapped the foil from the spearmint stick and started chewing. "I'm meeting with someone." Tom was shocked by the words he blurted out to the barkeep.

"Oh yeah? Hot date?"

Tom grumbled at the thought of going on a date. "Seeing the kid. It's been a while."

"Oh yeah, I hear ya. Got one myself," he said, wiping a condensation ring of the counter. "Kids forgive you know? A hell of a lot quicker than we do. Just make sure your definition of 'a while' is like a week max." He looked up at Tom, waiting for a reply. "From now on," he added.

Tom nodded and tapped on his drink for a refill. The bartender hesitated, looking Tom in the eyes with an honest understanding. After a second thought, Tom tipped the glass over, open end down on the bar top. "How you gonna pay for your kid's college if you keep turning away all the alcoholics?"

The barkeep released a light chuckle and grabbed Tom's glass, filling it up for himself. He took a sip, "Maybe I'm a day-trader guru. Conquering the stock market by day, selling to under-agers by night."

"Seems plausible."

"Thankfully his mother's family comes from money. I'm the cliché degenerate ex-husband that was never good enough for their girl and they're happy she came to her senses. I must say I pull it off just right." He held up both arms, acknowledging the classy motel bar he stood in.

"Think I gotta disagree with you there. After five minutes I like you. And I don't like people."

"Jeez, you're not coming on to me are you? You seem like a good guy and all but…"

"Shut it. You're driving me to drink."

"You're cut off."

Tom glanced to his left to find the youngsters had left and were replaced by a young woman. Her dark hair was messy and she had pointed facial features that made her look like a bird. She looked tough. Tom watched as she took a seat in the far corner, then she put her hand to her face and snorted; the bartender also noticed the bump of cocaine she had consumed.

Tom had seen the type too often in his line of work. He couldn't stand to be around it.

His entire body ached. He was so tired.

Tom slapped his hand on the counter. "I'd love to stay and chat about nothing important, but I'm on a time-line."

"Good luck."

"To you as well."

Tom reached into his jacket pocket and pulled out five, hundred-dollar bills. He set them on the counter and walked away.

• • •

Their office had been completely emptied, excluding one small desk in the corner. Reg sat in a fold-out chair in the middle of the room. It all felt like one big resounding mistake in gloomy hindsight. A dark hole, remnants of their past selves trapped in it. They had done plenty of good together as partners, but it no longer seemed like enough. It had ruined Tom, and Reg wasn't quite sure what exactly it had done to him. Hard to place.

The dark open space made him feel very alone, that much he knew. Escaping the suffocation, he thought of his wife Dorothy. She'd be waiting for him in the living room, raunchy "romantic" novel in hand, blanket draped around her shoulders. Through all their years together, she refused to go to bed without Reg joining her. There were a lot of late nights when he'd finally get home and she would be zonked out on the couch. Her loyalty was forever binding, and he owed her back some time. Time that he had been longing for ever since Deanna had disappeared.

He was hopeful that Dean could get him out of the mess he found himself in, but there were no guarantees in a situation such as this, if there ever was one. The best he could do now was go home to his wife, kiss her, and follow her up the steps to their bedroom.

Reg put on his favorite fedora and walked to the door. As he turned the doorknob there was a knock. He opened up to find two detectives. He didn't recognize them. Without any resistance or attempts to act dumbfounded, he followed the two men to their black sedan. *Good luck, kid.*

Chapter 30

Motel 6

TIRES ROLLED OVER LOOSE ROCKS on pavement. Tom rose to his feet and walked to his hotel room door, but stopped abruptly, hearing footsteps approach. He looked through the peep-hole to find two men with pistols in their hands.

Tom rushed to the bathroom and squeezed through the small window. He darted around the far side of the building and peered around the corner to find that the men were gone, probably inside his room. He made a break for it and sprinted toward his truck, back turned to the hotel. Gun shots rang out quicker than he had expected as they missed him, smacking against the tailgate of his truck. He climbed in, fired up the ignition, and peeled out. More shots tore through his truck as the two men ran toward him. Glass shattered. He felt a sharp burn in his shoulder as he drove away, but was easily distracted from it, deeply immersed in the action. Looking in his rear view mirror he could see the two men get back into their car, their engine growled, and they surged ahead in hot pursuit.

He took the exit onto the highway that would lead him to his meeting. They continued after him down the road, reaching bumper-to-bumper. Tom hammered on the brakes and they rear-ended him with a massive thud. His hitch supplied a lot more damage than the front of their car had to his truck. They swung around to the left and the man's partner held his gun out the window, firing twice. The glass shattered on the second shot.

It was arduous to comprehend that his destined moment to meet face-to-face with his daughter was being compromised by these nobodies.

Tom fired back and missed as they had touched the brakes when he fired. He could see the thrill in the eyes of both men as they pursued him. Both parties weren't walking away from this. In the midst of all the gun fire and colliding metal, Tom kept looking at the clock in his truck. He was barely going to be on time, excluding all the madness.

Like an inverted shot out of a cannon, Tom hammered on the brakes and turned right sharply, leading them down an old summer grid road that clearly hadn't been used by many, grass filling in on the sides. The car made a slow turn to backtrack, losing some distance, separating them from Tom. He punched the gas for five seconds, lengthening the gap between the two of them before hammering on the brakes, spinning his truck sideways across the narrow road. As his truck was coming to a stop, he leaped out, barrel rolled, and popped up to his feet and began firing his gun, emptying most of his clip into the front windshield of their car. In the throws of chaos, Tom could see a splatter of blood hit the glass and he continued to squeeze the trigger. Milliseconds were seconds. Feeling like a soldier at war, undeterred by fear, Tom was daring the driver to run him over. About to be struck by the front of the car, he jumped to his right, the driver's side headlight clipping his foot. *Crack.* He could feel his ankle bone pop, shrill and intense, then warm as his shoulder hit the grassy edge of the road. They crashed hard into the side of his truck, nearly knocking it over on its side.

Tom hobbled over to his truck and grabbed a fresh clip, his broken ankle shooting lightning fire into his leg. He staggered over to the car cautiously, gun raised. His mind was bogged down with a weighted fog. He could see that the passenger was dead, his head covered in blood. Tom stepped around the car and approached the driver side from the rear. He opened the door to find the driver, his face covered in blood. He was still breathing. With each labored breath, his lips vibrated together, red spit flying. "Who are you?" Tom asked.

He coughed.

"Collins sent you?" Tom asked.

There was no intellect within the man's eyes. He tried to laugh, but instead grimaced. "Fuck you."

Tom raised his gun and put a bullet in his head. The coppery smell of blood was overwhelming.

He climbed back into his truck, the pain of three injuries hitting his brain at once. His knee hurt from the jarring landing out of his truck. His broken ankle shot pain up his leg, and even more so, the sting in his shoulder, which continued to intensify with each second gone by. He touched near the wound and grimaced. The bullet wound was the least of his problems now, he was going to be late, and he didn't want to take his chances with Jerry's patience. Just like that, they could be gone with the wind.

• • •

Deanna sat in the passenger seat with her ear buds in as she listened to classical music, trumpets exemplifying morbid loss. A crucifix draped around the rear view mirror was dancing left and right. The hate in her heart was turning to fear, but she tried her best to prevent it from crossing over. She would look that man in the eyes and in the moment, she would know what to say. And he would listen.

She was quite young when Jerry first spoke to her about her real father. That he was still alive, wanting her back. Then Jerry introduced the plan. The plan to take him for everything he had. The calls were her own idea, created by chance. The first time she had used the pay phone by her favorite diner, she discovered it was hardly functional, a terrible muffling sound consistent with each attempted call. As time moved forward from that point, she wanted it to happen increasingly more.

"Are you okay?" Jerry asked. Deanna pressed pause on her cassette player.

"I'm fine."

"You're sure?"

"Just ready."

Chapter 31

The Exchange

THEY WAITED. DEANNA SAT SILENTLY, gazing out her window. Jerry didn't know what to say and was now wishing they had been the second party to arrive. His gut was telling him to drive away; Deanna wasn't ready for such a traumatic encounter. He hadn't even given any thought as to how he would react to Bennett's presence, having been only concerned for Deanna. No words were going to do their grim meeting justice. What does one say? He supposed he had covered it all on the phone.

Jerry was ashamed of his life's pattern. He had been a troubled teen with no concern for faith, unable to recognize his mother's love for him. Then he was a man of God, a true believer, then a destroyed and pitiful man, then a degenerate yet again, an enemy of God. Over the last few days, it had become clear to Jerry that there was no reason he had to be one or the other. He could ignore God and his existence, the same way he had been ignored. And he would be a good man moving forward. The father she deserved. It had to be as such.

Jerry peered over his shoulder through the bluff of trees. Still no sign of Bennett.

• • •

Tom followed the directions down the grid roads, his truck making various new clunking noises from the damage it had sustained. The sweat on his brow had pooled together and was now streaming down his face. His body was hot and cold, and the pain in his knees had doubled since the incident, on par with the bullet lodged in his shoulder. His throbbing ankle was a close second. He neared a bush line ahead in the distance where an old truck, similar to his own, was already parked. They were there waiting for him.

He pulled up close, but not too close. An anxiety attack begged to surface but he buried it. Deep, slow breaths. If he squinted, he could see the back of his daughter's head in the truck, waiting, looking forward. *That's her head right there. That's her.*

Tom wiggled his way out of the truck in a great deal of pain and grabbed both bags of cash from the back. He walked halfway to their truck and stared out at the open field. Despite his past horrors in a similar field, he felt a sense of peace from this one. He spotted a deer in the distance that also spotted him. Its head snapped up as they locked eyes for a staring contest. Its ears flickered, but it didn't run, instead it walked slowly, constantly looking back to Tom. The sound of a door opening alerted him, bringing him back to a reality that didn't feel as such. Jerry was the first to get out. He faced Tom, but made no eye contact, waiting for Deanna to come around and join him.

Both of their eyes were tired, an outline of gray around puffy purple shades. Tom was surprised by her long black hair, having always remembered her golden curly locks. She neared with her head down, concealing her face. Finally, as she stood next to Jerry, she lifted her head.

There was no question that this was his Deanna. It was shocking to see her grown-up face, but her eyes were still unmistakable. Her once chubby cheeks had flattened out, her face now slender and pale. She was thinner than he thought she'd be. Though her eyes were still the same sharp blue, he could only find misery, in place of what used to be. Jerry was the first to speak. "That's the man, Deanna."

He had waited for her for so long and all he wanted to do was hug her and take her home. He searched for words, lost in raw emotion, struggling to find any. "It's me."

"Bags." Jerry said.

Tom tossed them halfway. "Do you remember me?"

Her reaction was one of loathing. Jerry pointed his gun at her side and asked Tom to throw his gun over. Of course, he followed his rules, leaving himself completely exposed. *What has he done to her?*

"Dee, it's gonna be okay. You'll be all right."

Tom searched her face for anything good, but all he received from her was anger. He tossed the gun. "Deanna, look at me."

Jerry moved forward and collected the gun. Tom continued. "You're safe with me. You can come with me, okay?"

Her first words came in an angry burst, "Safe with you? Is that why you locked me in a room for days?

"Dee-"

"You're pathetic. I hope those phone calls messed you up."

Tom absorbed it. "Everything he's told you isn't true."

"Oh, I know the truth. It's always been clear."

"He's told you nothing but lies. I promise you nothing he's told you is true."

Deanna snatched the gun out of Jerry's hand and pointed it at Tom. "If it wasn't for Simon I would be dead. Because of you!"

"That's not true, Dee. That's not true." Maybe it was. He had lived in a dangerous world. Tom's mind searched for better responses, for clear explanations that would contradict what Jerry had washed her mind with.

Deanna was now crying angrily. "You're a disgrace. A drunk. How could you do that? To your own daughter!" Her hand was shaking the gun all over, her skinny wrist hardly keeping it held up.

"I never hurt you. That's not possible. Never, Deanna."

"I'm sorry, Ella. I'm sorry you had to go through this. But you'll you be stronger," said Jerry.

Tom's blood boiled. He had manipulated her, possibly beyond repair.

"You shut your mouth," Tom snapped.

"You see? The violence sitting under the surface." It was as though this was an educational seminar to Jerry and he was enjoying every second of it. When he glanced at her, his face softened.

"None of it's true, Dee. Let me prove it to you."

"Don't call me that! That's not my name!" Her gun was still raised.

"Yes, it is. Please tell me you remember our time together. You must remember something. Think."

"I remember it all too well."

"Look at me. There is nothing else in my life but you. You're it. There's nothing else. Never has been. Just you."

He could see a shred of belief creep in and she tried to reject the infectiousness of it, jabbing her gun at him. "Don't."

Jerry chimed in again, "This man is incapable of love."

"Jerry I'm sorry about what happened. I am. But you gotta see what's right here. I'm sorry I couldn't save your girl. I live with that every day, but it's the job. I failed you and I'm sorry for that. But what you've done here…she needs to know."

"What's he talking about?" she asked Jerry, still looking into Tom's desperate eyes.

"One of his twisted games. Don't believe a word he says."

"Let me tell you about *'Simon'*."

"It's not gonna work. You're a liar."

"This man took you. This is his sick way of getting back at me. It's his insane revenge plot."

He could feel himself winning some trust over, her brow clenched tight. "What's he talking about?" she asked Jerry.

"I'm talking about the day I took a case. A case to find his missing daughter. I failed him and he took you from me."

"You're a cop?"

"That's right. Do you remember?"

Deanna's eyes wandered and her gun lowered to her side. Jerry's rage was burning his face red.

With a commanding edge, he spoke. "Ella. We've prepared for this. You know his strategy. How he works. Stay inside yourself. Understand what's true."

"What was her name then? His daughter?" she asked, her black hair fluttering in a strong gust that came and went.

Tom could see that Jerry was now hanging in the balance. He gently removed the gun from Deanna's hand.

"Ella." Tom announced.

Jerry flinched.

As Deanna grappled with the new information, Jerry aimed and fired. The bullet hit Tom square in the stomach, dropping him down to one knee. The burning feeling that he had once felt on the job years ago had been duplicated. He didn't even have to look. It had entered through the same spot, his old scar now split wide, burned through by hot lead. He felt the coldness surge through his body, followed by a calming effect, like Ecstasy.

Tom reached into his pocket for something she would remember, something that could save her. He lowered to one knee. Then he rose. Tom managed to take three wobbly steps closer to his girl. She was so beautiful. There was still empathy there, an understanding. She was trying.

Before he could reach her, before he could just touch her face, another shot rang out. The bullet pierced through Tom's heart, folding him straight down to his knees. He looked skyward at a flock of crows flying from a tree.

Oxygen was no longer accessible. Everything was restricted, heavy. He closed his eyes and pictured her face. Five-year-old Deanna stuffing her face with cotton candy...

Deanna stood there shaking, sobs trapped in her throat. Simon tried to console her but she pulled away. He started to collect the bags and load up the truck, leaving her untouched for a moment. Too much had just happened for her to process and all she was left with was her programmed instincts to trust Jerry. He touched her arm gently and spoke softly. "I should have prepared you better for this. This is why I wanted to leave. He's a master of manipulation. He would have said anything to get you back. Those stories he told you were lies, he's still the man you know."

After her first phone call with Tom, Ella had discovered that her name was actually Deanna. She had confronted Simon and he informed her that they had to have their names changed long ago, when he saved her from him. She saw a sincerity in his eyes that she had seen many times before. It was difficult to deny.

Still though, something felt wrong about it all. He was still keeping something from her.

"You didn't have a daughter named Ella?"

His eyes flicked quickly to Tom then back to her. "Of course not. We've done it. We can move on now."

How had Tom chosen Ella as a name?

She could see that Jerry was searching her mind with concern. "My hired man spoke with him, Ella. They spoke of many things that were new to him. He would have used your name to trick you. A sick back-story. That's the kind of man he is…was."

There was a bitterness that altered the outline of his lips. He had murdered someone. Right in front of her.

"Please, only call me Simon. Nothing has changed."

They drove down the dirt road in silence and as they approached the highway, she could feel him looking at her sympathetically. "I'm sorry, Ella."

"You killed him."

"No one will ever know."

"You weren't supposed to kill him." The image of him being shot through the chest as he walked toward her, flashed through her mind. The gunfire was so loud.

"He was dangerous. He wouldn't have let us move on. He wouldn't have stopped. We can both move on now. I think this needed to happen. He would have continued after us."

"You should have told me this was your plan." She was listening close, analyzing each response that Jerry gave.

"I wasn't sure it was the plan."

Deanna shook her head.

"This man had to pay for everything he had done to you. In the moment, I lost control."

"I don't know...not like that."

"Ella. This is best for you."

"No," she said loudly. "What exactly was he talking about? He seemed pretty certain of it all."

"Complete nonsense. You are my daughter." He looked desperate and hurt. "He is a sick man, willing to say anything. Even though he did those unspeakable things to you, you once belonged to him, he had developed an obsession. An obsession for all the wrong reasons. It's difficult to understand. Everything will be all right. Tomorrow is a new day for us."

Tears stung her eyes as she looked away out the window. This was not how she expected to feel after all this time. She should have been ready for her new journey, but now, she felt lost more than ever.

"We will feel better tomorrow after a good sleep," he assured her.

• • •

Deanna lay in her bed, unable to sleep. A feeling in the pit of her stomach grew stronger. Rain spattered on her bedroom window softly at first, but it quickly increased to a loud downpour. She thought of his body lying there in the field, left for the coyotes to chew at and share among the pack. He was still a monster in his past, she thought, but could he have been a changed man? He was still her real father, and as she stared at the ceiling fan, the rain was washing away a pool of his blood.

The raging storm surged on. Lightning and thunder played with one another back and forth. The sounds of the storm stirred an urgency inside her as she replayed the murder of her estranged biological father over and over again. Amid those replays, she kept coming back to his odd look as he attempted approaching her after the first gunshot. He was so determined to get to her. It was important.

She popped out of bed, put on her coat, and tiptoed out of the trailer with the truck keys in hand. As she drove off through the booming rainstorm, she could see Jerry standing in the entrance of the trailer, yelling at her to come back.

The visibility on the road was poor. The rain was coming down hard enough that she was forced to do about fifty mph. Deanna neared the turn off when suddenly, a deer stood directly in her path. Before she could even think of swerving, she made direct contact, smoking the doe. The front end of the old truck gave way, jolting her head forward. Luckily, she had her belt on, but the impact rattled her cage, the whiplash making her feel disoriented. She saw stars for a moment before regaining her grip on reality and the steering wheel.

She exited the truck. Off to the side of the road she could see a red streak of blood and the deer lying on its side, twitching, as it tried to crawl toward the ditch. It must have broken its neck, making contact with the truck at the not so perfect angle.

Deanna could see the dirt road up ahead and decided to continue on, given there was nothing she could do for the poor deer. She thought about putting it out of its misery with a crow bar, but she didn't have the stomach for it, not after everything she had been through on this messed up day. Another wretched act of violence could be the end of her. She turned the ignition, but it argued, groaned, and spat, until finally she couldn't get any reaction from the old beast. It was completely dead and she was stranded on the side of the road, one that wasn't exactly busy with traffic in the middle of the night.

The logical choice was to stay in the truck and wait for someone to come by, staying out of the cold rain. But logical didn't interest Deanna. So, she proceeded by foot, each step taking great effort as she marched against the wind and the piercing rain. She walked for an eternity until finally, she could see the bush line where her father lay.

All extremities were numb. Deanna arrived at his body. Puddles had formed all around him and the dark red had pooled with the rain-water. She hovered over his body. "You son of a bitch," she said out loud, her voice shaky. His skin was so white.

She positioned herself by Tom's head and grabbed hold under his armpits. She dragged him through the mud toward the bush line. She fell into the mud several times in attempts at pulling his weighted down body through the sticky clay-based mud. Straining her shoulders and lower back, she clawed her way to the bush, her arms and legs on fire with lactic acid. She lay his body underneath some trees, sheltering him from the rain. She sat on her ass in the mud to catch her breath when something metallic caught her eye. Wrapped around his finger was a silver necklace that was half covered in mud.

She remained seated on the ground as she grasped the necklace. It had a heart shape at the end of it and she discovered a clasp on the back side of it. She opened it slowly as the fog from her breath cut through the cold night. Inside was a tiny picture of a little blond girl with a younger version of Tom. They were smiling. They were happy. She recognized the girl. The rain had stopped so abruptly, almost like it was never there to begin with. She felt something strange. It flowed through her like water. Floodgates opened in her mind and she remembered. They were only fragments. Pieces of a past she had forgotten. Truths buried. But she remembered.

She placed the side of her face against his cold wet chest. The whole world could have heard her cries, in the now quiet, storm-free night.

• • •

Deanna was distraught, making her way back to the road. She was so damn cold. She had made it to the highway but had no strength left.

She let her mind go to the only happy place she could find which was her diner, drinking hot tea. The thought warmed her up for a moment and then she collapsed.

Chapter 32

Confession

REG SAT IN AN INTERROGATION ROOM across from a frustrated young detective who was getting nowhere with him. Palmer was his name. He was cocky, arrogant. He slid his tongue along his top row of teeth with a half smile before he asked each question that he surely thought was insightful, strategic, unearthing. He figured he was hot shit, but was mostly full of shit.

Palmer leaned over the steel table. "Listen, Reg, you better start giving me something here. You know they're freezing your pension as we speak? They will take it from you. Think about your wife."

"I'm always thinking about my wife."

"And what you should also be doing is telling us why you loaned him your entire savings."

"Like I said, he needed a loan for an investment unrelated to our business. I didn't ask."

"Just like that, you forked over the cash."

"It's called trust. I gather you've never been able to find it with a partner thus far in your career."

Palmer chuckled. "I was told you'd be difficult."

"Surprised there was anyone left here to tell you that."

"Listen, we got Dean Patterson in the other room, you know. We know he leaked confidential information to Bennett, information that led to Abe Collins's murder, among others."

It would most likely all unfold sooner rather than later, but he didn't want to be the one throwing Tom under the bus. In fact, his mind was not with the amateur questioning him; his mind was with his friend and partner, praying that he was still alive.

"We got a body in a warehouse in Indy, not far from St. Vincent mental hospital, which of course was where Bennett spent time recovering from not only a tragedy but severe alcoholism. I'm sure the Doc's file runs longer than him replacing water with bourbon. He murder this guy too?"

"No clue."

Another teeth cleaning with his tongue. "We know he killed Collins. Listen to me. Tom's not well. We just want to bring him in before he gets himself killed. These guys he's put down are undoubtedly scum. But your partner's chasing ghosts. We have here that he was admitted to the hospital in Rocanville only a few days ago. You know anything about that?"

"I honestly don't."

"Here's a theory-"

"Oh good."

His brief "good cop" routine dissipated and he put on his best bad cop face. It was marginal at best. "Your partner became obsessive again, lost himself back in his daughter's case and into the bottle. He found out Abe Collins didn't have the information he needed so he killed him. Two wannabe thugs, who work for both Abe and Hank Collins, were ordered to keep tabs on Tom after his little visit to state Penn and pursued him when he located Abe. Tom got the upper hand and killed them too. The body in the warehouse, well, we're still working on that, but I'm sensing more of the same. And where does that leave us? Oh, yeah. Your office had been gutted, damning evidence surely destroyed, and Tom's off with $250,000 cash from you and his ex-wife. I'm assuming he's dug up some even thinner suspects from the past." Palmer leaned back. "Bennett isn't running with that money. We know he's doing what he thinks he has to do. He'll be in state and that leaves you telling us where."

"You really are good."

"Did I get the gist of it?" He seemed pleased with himself. "Because I think I did, and it struck a nerve." He rested his hands on the table, palms down, sliding them back and forth. His nails were too perfectly groomed.

Reg blinked his eyes slowly. His lids felt weighted. "My nerves don't exist any more you insignificant pussy. Bennett is a good man."

"So how'd we get here then?"

"If you want information, you tell your boss to bring in his boss. I'll talk to him. They can call me anytime to arrange a meeting. Now, it's late and I'm tired. My wife is waiting for me."

"You're not going anywhere, not yet."

"What's your charge then?"

"Aiding and abetting a murderer."

"Okay slick. You run that when you get proof on Tom. Come get me when you got it all straightened out."

Reg stepped around the detective and knocked on the door. A guard opened up and Reg walked out with an ugly hitch in his step. He saw that the detective was greeted by another officer with urgent news. Reg stopped in his tracks and turned his head to try and eavesdrop. He heard the word "body" murmured by the other officer. Reg jolted around. "Where?"

Palmer wasn't having any of it, his chest puffed out, back arched. He may as well have pissed around the desk next to him, marking his territory. "You're a suspect. Just go home, we will talk soon."

"Body wasn't halfway between here and Rocanville was it? In a field about nine miles or so west off the highway?"

The look on their faces confirmed it. The other officer helped him to a chair and brought him a cup of water, which Detective Palmer did not overly appreciate.

"Start talking."

"Tom handled a case. The alias is Simon Brooks. Real name Jerry Lehman. Tom and I couldn't find his girl years back and had to move on to other cases. Tom was lead on that one and Lehman apparently wasn't able to let go. Turns out he faked his suicide. Must have cut a deal with someone in forensics. He kidnapped Tom's daughter. He's had her this whole time."

"That's bull shit. Quit wasting my time."

"They were to meet this evening at that very location where you have your body. It'll either be a match to a Jerry Lehman, or…" He couldn't finish the sentence.

The detective shared a look with the other officer and then back to Reg.

"Just do me a favor will you. Let me know as soon as you can."

Tom was tough, but Reg knew he would have been at the mercy of Lehman in that situation.

• • •

Deanna awoke in an unfamiliar bedroom. She was wrapped tightly in several blankets, feeling trapped. Her hair was wet and clumped with bits of dirt and gravel. Heat radiated off her forehead and her tongue and throat were dried out. She twisted to her left and found a tall glass of water on her nightstand. She gulped it back, spilling some down her front, the cool moisture refreshing against her hot skin.

Once she gained her wits, she unwrapped herself and noticed she had been stripped of her wet clothes and was dressed with fuzzy pink pajama bottoms and an old John Deere t-shirt. She looked at herself in the mirror for a moment and felt that she was looking back at an entirely different person. Her make-up had mostly washed away, some black smudging still around her eyes. She wiped away the rest of the residue. She stepped over to the window and could see nothing but flat farm-land and trees, a tire swing attached to one. Last night's memories were still fresh leading up to her collapse but everything that transpired after was a blank. Clearly the person that rescued her had good intentions, or at least she hoped.

Deanna heard voices come from the other room and it sounded as though a guest had arrived at the front door. Then she heard, "She's in the bedroom resting." She back peddled away from the door. Looking out the window again, she saw a cop car. She couldn't risk being taken back to Jerry, nor could she withstand being taken to social services. Worse yet, it dawned on her that she was an accomplice to murder. Murder of a man that loved her more than anything in the world. A man that never stopped looking for her.

Footsteps moved toward her bedroom, halting her tears and activating her feet. She made a move for the window.

Rookie detective Palmer opened the bedroom door to find an empty bed with messed covers.

Palmer sprinted for the door, just in time to see her jack the farmer's new truck and take off.

• • •

As she sped down the gravel road, Deanna had no clue what she was going to do next until a thought crossed her mind-the money. She didn't remember Jerry bringing it into the trailer. She hit the gas and sped toward the highway distancing herself from the cops. Instead of choosing Indy or Rocanville, she proceeded through the highway and continued to travel down some back country roads, attempting to be as unpredictable as possible. After a half hour of driving, she returned back to her truck which thankfully hadn't been towed away by the cops yet. She rummaged through the back seat and then folded the seats down exposing a cubby hole in the floor where the bags of cash were stashed.

Without a second thought, she could make a run for it, ditch the truck, and catch a flight with her new identity to a tropical destination. Freedom should have never tasted so sweet.

The only thing stopping her now was the lack of information about her life. Not only did she wonder about the details between Jerry and Tom, but she thought of her mother and what she was like. *Was she alive? Did she mourn her loss still? Was she beautiful? Was she kind? Did she still think of me?*

She had been told that her mother was not in her life. That she had left her when she was too young to remember. Another lie.

• • •

Santiago cowered in the corner of her 1950s room with a migraine thumping in her skull. Both of her eyes were swollen and her head had been shaved to a young boy's buzz cut. Instead of a pretty flowered dress she was wearing sweat pants and a gray shirt. She was even thinner than before and had cold sores around her mouth. A constant tickle in the back of her throat refused to leave as she coughed aggressively to push out the annoying sensation. She could feel her cough getting worse, spreading into her chest and lungs, the phlegm building up.

Her attempted escape ended tragically when the man had gained consciousness. She had been outside for no more than two minutes, when he caught up with her. The nearest house was about a five-minute walk away and she had wasted time debating between asking the neighbors for help or making a run for it into unknown territory. His flesh had been opened up on each side of his neck where her hands held the wire. It was an awful sight, but the wound had not been deep enough to kill him. When he got a hold of her…he had never been that ruthless before with his punishment. His hands fell hard on her face without mercy.

The beatings were spaced out over the course of forty-eight hours. The remaining time had been spent in her room with small traces of water and food pellets. The wooden block was installed over the window and she knew she would never see the light again. It appeared that the abuse had likely stopped, though she couldn't be sure. He had placed a mirror in her room, made of plastic instead of glass.

He no longer looked at her the same. She knew he didn't see her as a woman he loved. She was only a girl who was a traitor. The enemy.

During the beatings she had tried to provoke him enough to take her life, but he was too smart for that. He would not allow her to entice him over the line. Her face hurt so badly, especially when trying to consume the hard and crunchy pellets.

She curled up in a ball on her bed and tried to sleep. Her stomach growled.

Chapter 33

New Beginning

DEANNA ROCKED ON A SWING at the elementary school playground in Rocanville. She had recognized the park when she drove into town and was lured in by it. She looked down at the ID she had found in Tom's wallet. Tom Bennett, age forty-three, hazel eyes, state of Indiana, address 401 Millstreet, Rocanville Indiana. Area Code, 46073. She opened up his wallet and tucked it back in, exchanging it for a picture. It was her as a young girl, no older than four, her and her mother with Christmas tuques on.

Deanna stepped off the swing and pulled out a metallic flask from her jacket pocket. It had belonged to Tom. There was no special engraving on it. Just plain, sticky around the edges at the top.

She drove the farmer's Chevy passed Tom's address, yellow tape and black sedan's parked out front, men in suits coming in and out.

She continued on. Deanna drove down Main street and parked in front of Leonard's Tavern. She entered.

She showed Tom's ID and the picture of her and her mother to the barkeep, an older gentleman, and she asked him one simple question.

Loss of the Decade

• • •

Allison's bare feet stuck to the linoleum floor in her kitchen. She looked down at a bowl of Cheerios that were floating in an overdrawn amount of skim milk. It had been almost two days since she had spoken with IPD about the loan she gave to Tom.

The phone rang, startling Allison. She answered. "Allison, it's Reg." He sounded shook up. Too rattled for Reg.

"Is he all right?" She covered her quivering lip with her hand, as if someone was there watching her.

Reg's voice was broken down into sob-like segments. "I'm afraid not…I want-I wanted you to hear it from me."

"No. Don't tell me that, Reg. Don't tell me that."

The pause that followed was a devastating one, including whimpers and short spasmodic breaths. Reg pushed through. "He was onto something big. We will find out more soon. All I will say is, he was helping someone important and you'll know soon. You'd be proud of him."

"Like hell. I'm not proud of him getting himself killed. How can I be proud if he's gone? You tell me how." There were times she had blamed him and it ate at her.

"I'm sorry. Listen, I gotta go, but…I'll be in touch again soon with answers. I'm sorry, Allison."

"What about his body?" She was faint, leaning over the kitchen island.

"He's being transported to Rocanville soon. IPD is on it."

"I don't want him poked and prodded."

"I know, I'm sorry, Allison. It's a homicide investigation though. I'm sure you know how these go."

Allison took a deep breath and the doorbell rang. She stood there in the kitchen looking at her bowl of cheerios, her chest wanting to heave. "I have to go. I'll call you back."

Allison, outside her body, opened the fridge and put her bowl of Cheerios inside along with the phone. She had no idea what to do, until the doorbell sounded again.

Running her hand through her hair, she arrived at the door, ready to be greeted by IPD. Probably Dean, she thought. Instead, she looked down at a skinny young woman with messy black hair and pale face. She seemed quite troubled. "Hi." Allison started. She had forgotten that her face had been swamped with tears, and she wiped them away.

"Are you Allison?" the girl asked so quietly that Allison hardly heard. She looked young, maybe fourteen or so.

Allison wiped away more tears and sniffled. "I am. What can I do for you?"

She looked down at the ground unable to make eye contact with Allison.

"Are you all right?" Allison asked.

"Are you?" she replied.

"Yeah. No, no I'm not really." Her face contracted to combat the crying that wanted so badly to persist.

"Your husband is Tom Bennett?"

"Yeah."

She locked eyes with the girl and began to see who she was. Disregarding her frame and focusing on the shape of her mouth, ears, and the color of her eyes. Allison began to think the unthinkable.

"Oh my God."

Deanna's smile was pained. "Hi."

"Deanna?!" Allison hadn't said her name out loud in a very long time. It was so sweet, but also scary coming out.

She could only muster a nod with her eyes to the floor and Allison tackled her with a hug, bringing her in close. Allison continued to hold on for dear life. "How…where-how did you find me?" Her hair smelled of honey, and her shirt of citrus soap mixed with marijuana.

"Tom found me."

They continued to hug and cry. "He…He-"

"I know. It's okay, I know." Allison shushed her daughter and held her close, squeezing her skinny frame to make sure that she actually existed. Derek stepped into the entrance. He stopped in his tracks, witnessing the impossible.

• • •

The funeral was small, but many of the IPD were in attendance. The minister chose to speak on new beginnings, which was fitting for everyone. In Tom's work, he had created so many new beginnings for young lost souls, sacrificing pieces of himself along the way. In his search for Deanna, he had endured more than a personal should be capable of. He had traveled the extra distance, and when he thought he couldn't do it anymore, he dug deep and traveled even further. There was no light at the end of the tunnel, only a relentless search that he seemed destined to walk.

Allison wore a lovely yellow dress instead of black. She was so beautiful. Deanna was in awe of how pretty she was, and how she had come from her. But her mother didn't do so well during the funeral. Outside at the grave-site was worse. She couldn't stop crying.

Deanna's world had transformed. Her tropical destination and singing career were both desires that would have to wait for a little while. Right now, she had this whole new family that cared about her. Tom didn't bring her home just so she could leave, not just yet anyhow. She didn't want to.

Reg was already in the process of retiring. He and his wife were getting set to move to California. It was going to take a bit of time but he was going to be cleared of all charges, given the circumstances and the facts that were currently being discovered by IPD. He kept pinching Deanna's cheeks to make sure she was real. His smile made her feel like she had a home, but every now and then his stare would go blank. Deanna figured she must have reminded him too much of Tom.

As for Jerry, IPD informed Reg that they had a promising lead and that it wouldn't be long until they found him. Deanna hoped he would find peace and properly grieve the loss of his daughter. She had no room for hate, regret, or guilt, especially if it was from the past. She wanted nothing to do with the past.

As Tom's coffin lowered into the ground, there were no tears from Deanna. She felt strong and powerful, the world was hers and she wasn't going to let it control her.

Icy rain started to fall during the service. It was an overcast, dreary day and the power of the wind grew with each passage read. Everyone held their hats and adjusted their scarves to ensure their faces were covered from the strong, cold wind.

As the preacher man continued, she pulled out the picture of her and her dad at the fair and gazed at it with a longing for time-time spent with him. She thought of the faint memories she had with him and the stories her mother had told her and she couldn't help but laugh. Her smiling lips touched tears that had trickled down her cheeks. Turned out there were just a few tears after all.

• • •

That night, she finished supper quickly and drove over to Tom's vacant home for some privacy. She let herself in through the basement door and flicked on the light. She entered the case room where Tom had spent so many hours working to find her. She ran her fingers along the cork-board, feeling all the pin holes from tacks.

There was one small desk and one chair placed in the far corner. The rest of the basement was empty. She took a seat and opened up each drawer, until she got to the bottom one on the right side. It was filled with about twenty or so files. They were all missing boys and girls under the age of sixteen, and were all open cases that had been labeled as a transfer back over to the IPD.

She looked through each file meticulously, one by one, page by page, until she realized it was midnight and her mother was most likely on her way over, throwing a shit fit in the process. After examining each of the missing kids, she felt an overwhelming sense of duty and responsibility.

Deanna opened another small drawer and found a mickey of whiskey that had slid to the back. The plastic bottle was old and unopened. She threw it in the empty garbage can next to the desk.

Deanna re-opened one of the files for another look. Ella Lehman.

The End

Epilogue

Twelve years later. Summer.

DEANNA WORKED CLOSELY WITH IPD on some cases. She didn't mind it, but she also liked her freedom. "Kidnapped girl returned home after ten years starts own investigations firm," was a nice punch line that had drummed up some business for her right out of the gate. Getting clients hadn't been that big of a challenge.

Deanna had no problem with traveling outside of state for business if she was called upon. She enjoyed seeing new places as much as she enjoyed her new home in Indianapolis. It was tough to say what enjoying something actually meant. A sense of familiarity, comfort, security; those things, maybe. At some point in time, the line between joy and tribulation was muddled. It bled over from each side.

The case she was working on now was a special one. Ella Lehman, the girl she had replaced long ago. It hadn't been her first case. She was far from ready in the beginning. Not even close, actually. But with time and practice, she had begun to pick away at it, slowly building a platform worth looking into further. IPD had agreed to hand over all unsolved case files that had been worked by Tom. They were cold anyway, just sitting at headquarters, collecting dust, occupying space in their file room.

Tom had looked at every angle that first popped into her mind as well. But Deanna had found something small, easily passed over. It was a doctor visit. Tom's notes made mention of it, Jerry informing him that she had gone in for simple cold symptoms a few months earlier. Deanna followed up at the hospital listed, but the doctor on file was no longer there. Because Ella had long ago been pronounced deceased, Deanna was able to access her medical files through authorization of the IPD.

Ella had not been in for cold symptoms. The description included incidents of anxiety and emotional outbursts. It was unusual behavior considering the positive relationship with her father at the time. The notes went on: *Patient shows no signs of social distress. Ella is more than functional in conversation and responds clearly when asked upon with no signs of discomfort. She has friends in school and does well with her kindergarten teacher. Father, Jerry Lehman, says the episodes are often specific to her need to visit 'favorite spot in the country'. If they do not make their weekly visit, patient experiences symptoms relative to a panic attack. Other signs of OCD shown through her repetition of daily habits; food, hygiene, studies. Example, Ella lost favorite book that is supposed to be read every night at nine p.m sharp. Episodes involve: compounding panic, shallow breathing, feeling enclosed. Patient also sometimes experiences intense worry for friends and teacher, regarding their home lives. Study habits are far advanced for Kindergarten and are strictly followed; reason being worry, just as much as curiosity. She feels the need to be prepared as much as possible. Generalized Anxiety Disorder is suspected. Refer to child therapy. Doctor Feaster or Doctor Little recommended.*

This was signed by Doctor Jasper Salenger. It was possible that Jerry chose not to divulge the information to Tom, as he was embarrassed that he had somehow failed as a parent. Or maybe she had been doing much better once therapy had started? It shouldn't have made a difference in the case, in his mind. Ella's stress shouldn't have had anything to do with her kidnapping.

• • •

Santiago rode a lawn mower back and forth, forming neatly cut patterns. The smell of freshly cut grass always lifted her spirits. Up ahead, she spotted his white Cadillac pull into the driveway. He got out and waved.

She was eager to chat. Ordinarily he wouldn't make it home from work so early. She turned off the mower.

"Beautiful day for it, isn't it?" he asked as he removed his glasses. She loved the way he looked without them. She had heard of this procedure call laser eye surgery, but he wouldn't do it. She didn't blame him, it sounded awfully invasive.

"Amazing."

"Good day?" He rubbed her shoulder.

"Really good, actually. I had coffee with Tina again. I can't believe you've only spoke with them twice. That ought to change, don't you think?"

His lips contracted. "Honey. You know me. Neighbors should just be neighbors."

He was always so private. Santiago had been longing for more friendships, but he never wanted to leave the house unless it was for work. That was about to change though. They were going on a vacation to the Bahamas in December. She had it marked in her calendar. She hoped they would meet all kinds of fascinating people while they were there.

"Hey. I'm gonna make an early dinner. Any requests?"

"Whatever you like."

The man turned to leave and she spoke again. "No kiss?"

He gave her a peck on the lips and turned back around toward the house. Maybe she would go for a quick bike ride after pruning the hedges.

Santiago looked up at the sun and felt as though she had forgotten something important. The rays were beating down harder now, causing a pool of sweat to run down her back. The missing thought from her mind was nipping at her. It was sitting right there, on the tip of her brain, but she couldn't access it. Couldn't have been too important, she told herself.

She wiped her brow and realized how thirsty she was. She had made a jug of lemonade that morning. She would have a quick glass and then get back to work, leaving her enough time for a bike ride after.

• • •

Deanna drove an old worn-down Jeep TJ, like the one she had dreamed about all those years ago, just off the coast of St. Martin (she decided after a little research). She loved her old Jeep. She never saw the need in buying brand new things. Anything that would simply get the task completed was just fine by her. Help the bottom line, add more resources, help more people. Easy enough.

Just off the highway on the way to Brownsburg, Deanna drove through the country finding massive new properties separated every few miles or so. She pulled up into a long, winding driveway to find a brand new Caddy parked. The home wasn't as new as some of the others she had passed, but it was still fairly large, the yard around it having enough room for a legitimate game of football. The design of the house was nice. It had a deep blue stucco that complemented the dark brick around the garage doors and front entrance.

She got out of her truck and noticed a pretty blond woman cutting grass to her right. She immediately stopped and turned it off to greet her.

Deanna thought she was overly eager, but she seemed genuine. "What a lovely place you have," Deanna said formally but politely.

"Thanks! What's your name?" She radiated optimism.

"Deanna Bennett."

"It's nice to meet you! Would you like to come inside for some coffee or iced tea?" She was so enthused that Deanna hadn't even explained the nature of her visit. Nor did the woman give a name.

"Sure, that would be great."

Her beautiful smile made Deanna feel less nervous.

"Sorry your name is?" Deanna asked.

She took Deanna's hand excitedly. "Sam. Come on, follow me." Deanna followed her to the entrance. "You must be friends with Jasper, I'm assuming."

"Actually no. But I was hoping to talk to him about his work."

"Oh. Well, he has no problem talking about that," she said with a playful smirk.

When they entered, Sam made sure they both removed their shoes. Once inside the house, she realized why; the place was immaculate. "Please, have a seat at the table and I will get the coffee going." Deanna did as she was told and examined her surroundings. There were no photographs, not a single one, only artwork.

Deanna's eyes caught a mirror across the room and was shocked to see a man standing behind her like a creepy deer caught in the headlights. He saw that she jumped in her chair slightly, and quickly wore a crooked smile to greet her.

"Sorry if I startled you. I'm guessing you met my wife."

"That's okay. Yeah, she convinced me I needed a cup of coffee. I'm guessing she noticed the bags under my eyes."

"That's nonsense. I'm sorry, you are?"

"Deanna Bennett. I'm a private investigator."

His eye-brows raised in curiosity, an expected response. "Oh my. Well, I'm Doctor Salenger and it's nice to meet you. Please, is there anything I can help you with?"

"In all honesty Doctor Salenger-"

"Jasper is fine."

"I'm following up on the thinnest of leads on a case that was dismissed years ago. I'm like the clean-up crew of sorts. Putting a finishing stamp on old cases, some fairly cold. It's quite sad and morbid, but someone has to do it. Sorry, I'm rambling. But if you have time, can we chat over coffee?"

He nodded. "A fine idea, Deanna."

"How is your summer going?" she asked.

"Busy as always, I'm afraid."

"Still practicing medicine?"

"Sure am. You've done your research on me?"

"Just being thorough, nothing to worry about. You used to work at Fairbanks Medical Clinic in Indianapolis, right?"

"Sure did."

"Where are you at now?"

"Bethlehem Royal. A lot closer to home."

"Ah, that's nice."

"Yes, I despised the commute into the city during rush-hour."

"I hear ya." The silence between exchanges was tense. "Anyways, I don't want to take up too much of your time. I'm looking into a kidnapping that took place over twenty years ago."

"Okay…"

"Well she used to be one of your patients. Does the name Ella Lehman ring any bells by chance?"

"I'm sorry, no. Too many years, too many patients."

"Sorry to have invaded your privacy. Obviously she's been listed as deceased for some time now, so we took a look at her file. I hope you don't mind."

"None at all. Tell me about her. Maybe I'll be able to recall."

"OCD. Anxiety. Fairly intense for a five-year-old child. Very bright girl for her age."

Sam walked in with cups. She set them in front of both Deanna and Jasper. She disappeared into the kitchen again and came back with a pot. "How do you take your coffee?" she asked.

"Just black is fine. Thank-you."

Sam filled Deanna's cup. She turned to Jasper and filled his cup up. "And I know you wouldn't dare ruin your coffee with any sugar or cream."

"Never." The way he looked at her; he absolutely adored her.

She poured herself a glass of lemonade instead and joined them at the table.

A highly uncomfortable silence followed. Jasper sipped his coffee. "I apologize, Deanna. I've had other cases like that. It's been so terribly long. I'm an old man now," he said with a nervous chuckle.

Deanna reached into her pocket and pulled out a picture of little Ella. She slid the photograph over to Jasper. It was brief, but there was no denying his reaction. A glimmer of shame. "I'm so sorry. All the faces and names blend. That's so terrible though. I wish I could be of better help." His eyes flicked toward Sam then back to Deanna.

"Poor girl," said Sam.

"Don't worry about it, Jasper. As I said, long shot." Deanna glanced at the beautiful Ella Lehman, sipping her lemonade, totally oblivious to the truth. A traumatic event at such a young age was a powerful thing. Deanna knew first hand. Like wiping the slate clean and building upon it with deceitful lies. The power of suggestion and time. Plant a seed and watch it grow.

Even in her shabby yard-work clothing, Ella was stunning.

Deanna turned back to Jasper. "Enough about that depressing business. Why don't you tell me how you two met?"

Acknowledgements

My first thanks belongs to Chris Musselman. Without his encouragement, I may have never started.

Second, my parents. They are the first to read my work and always will be.

Third, everyone who read my early drafts and provided me with helpful insights. Any errors made are, of course, someone else's fault. I apologize on their behalf :)

My deepest thanks to my family and friends who have all shown tremendous support.

About the Author

Brandon Enns is a novelist and award-winning screenwriter. Brandon's stories are suspenseful thrillers, mysteries, and dramas, often featuring a gritty and damaged protagonist.

Novel or film, he simply enjoys a good story that allows him to escape, and feels inclined to tell a few of his own. When he isn't writing, he is likely playing or watching sports.

Brandon currently lives in Saskatoon, Saskatchewan.

Visit www.brandonenns.com for more information on Brandon and his upcoming novels.

Upcoming novels

The Night is Cold

Islanders

Copperhead Road

Twitter @brandon_enns
Instagram @ennsbrandon
facebook.com/BrandonEnnsNovels/

Made in the USA
Lexington, KY
25 June 2018